STEALING SMOKES

STEALING SMOKES

STEALING SMOKES

SOME SURPRISING SHORT STORIES

JOHN HANLON

Contents

STEALING SMOKES

I recognised his voice immediately; it hurled me back to a small seaside town in New Zealand and a time of Beatles songs, paisley shirts, and girls with hairstyles like helmets.

Dennis 'Dorky' Dixon. I hadn't heard from him in years and I'd thought I'd never hear from him again. I turned to look at him.

'Dennis?'

He was standing in the doorway nervously fingering his briefcase, not sure whether I was pleased to see him or not. He'd gotten fat.

'Sorry about sneaking in like this,' he said. 'I asked your receptionist not to announce me. I wanted to surprise you.'

'You succeeded.'

Consciously sucking in my own soft stomach, I rose and walked across the room to accept his extended hand. He'd been sweating, he smoked and he reeked of garlic. Finding things wrong with Dennis was an old habit of mine.

'So, Den, when's the baby due?' I said, prodding his huge belly.

'I own a restaurant,' he grunted. His tone was terse — this was only to be expected, I was surprised he was here at all.

'Take a pew,' I said pointing at the designer couch.

I chose one of the armchairs.

I have a large office with a view of the harbour. A workstation runs along one wall, a Hockney print adorns another. A red leather Italian-designed lounge suite and a black lacquered coffee table take up most of the floor space.

The relative luxury of these furnishings was a marked contrast to Dennis's frayed suit, yellowing shirt collar and battered brogues. He looked out of place and I could see that he felt it. I found a degree of satisfaction in that.

'Nice office,' he said looking around uncomfortably.

I wanted to ask him about Annie.

He nervously scanned the top of the coffee table and workstation — the sure sign of a smoker in search of an ashtray. As if to confirm this, he produced a packet of Marlboro. 'Smoke?'

'No, thanks, I gave up. I'm not into suicide.'

He was undeterred. 'Mind if I do?'

Normally, I would have objected and might even have subjected him to a lecture on the dangers of passive smoking, but for old times' sake — or perhaps for the opportunity to demonstrate my superior willpower — I decided to tolerate it. 'Not at all, I'll get an ashtray.'

I made a big show of going to the phone and asking my secretary, Belinda, to bring us an ashtray and tea.

This embarrassed him. 'Listen, don't go to any trouble, Sam ...'

'It's no trouble. Speaking of smokes, how's your old man?'

Back in the days of black and white television, Dennis Dixon and I had been members of a gang of five, known, to some, as 'The Undertakers'. While this name may conjure up images of bad boys in greasy leather jackets, we were in fact a tame, middle-class, sweater-clad group, who, for a brief period, co-owned a hearse. 'The Undertakers' was simply a name coined in jest by our friends. The hearse — an old straight-eight Packard that could go everywhere in top gear — only lasted two summers before dying from lack of proper mechanical attention. 'The Undertakers', however, survived as a group for all the important teenage years.

How we came together in the first place, I'm really not sure. The only thing I am sure about is that while Dennis, too, was one of that gang, none of us ever really liked him.

This was probably to do with the way he looked, as much as anything. He had little piggy eyes, fat wet lips, an off-centre blob of a nose, and ears that stuck out at an angle that only accentuated their difference in size. And while his facial features were larger than life, his arms and legs seemed skinny and under-developed, sprouting like afterthoughts from the corners of his potato-shaped torso. To top it off, he had bad breath and tightly-kinked red hair cut in a way that has never been fashionable.

He tried to overcome his less than attractive appearance with a more than friendly personality, and he had a habit of standing far too close to you when he talked and was effusive to the point of being uncool. For this we teased him mercilessly, especially in front of girls. Which is why I said earlier that finding things wrong with Dennis was an old habit. And not just for me, we all did it. This was cruel, I know, and looking back I'm almost embarrassed by it. Nevertheless, it didn't make any difference to Dennis; he insisted on hanging around with us no matter how badly we treated him. I guess he had nowhere else to go. I think we were the only friends he had, if you could call us that — we were more like parasites than friends. The truth was we were just using him. It wasn't his company we coveted but the things he gave us access to. Among these were his car (our only mode of transport after the hearse passed away), his sister Annie, and his father's grocery store, which we plundered regularly.

Stealing smokes from Dennis's dad was a regular pastime. It was so easy, it wasn't even exciting. If Dennis knew we did it, he never said anything. I think he realised it was part of the reason we let him hang around with us.

Anyway, that's why I asked about his father, now — even though I was more interested in news of Annie.

'Dad's fine,' he said. 'He's retired now. But he still does a bit of work on the side. You'll never guess where ...'

'Surprise me.'

'At Danny's hamburger joint,' he said, waiting for my reaction.

'Like father, like son, like father, eh?' I smiled.

He smiled back, seeming almost pleased that I remembered. Years before, Dennis, too, used to cook at Danny's. He also delivered groceries for his father every day after school and worked in a menswear shop on Friday evenings. Cooking at Danny's was his weekend job. The 'Undertakers' ate there often — without paying, of course.

All these part-time jobs meant that Dennis always had more money than the rest of us. Luckily, he was happy to share it — a practice we encouraged shamelessly. He was usually good for a loan, too, if you could call them loans; I don't know that anyone ever bothered to pay him back. I certainly didn't.

Curiously, though, while my friends and I saw Dennis as a bit of a dork, my father had nothing but respect for his enterprise and energy and would regularly proffer pearls like: 'He knows the value of hard work, that boy; he'll end up a rich man, you mark my words.'

Christ, was Dad ever wrong about that. Dennis was always a mug, one of life's easy marks. One of those poor, naive bastards the whole world takes advantage of. And looking at him now — rumpled and crumpled in the seat before me — I could see nothing had changed.

I could also see that he still hated me. So why was he here?

Belinda arrived with the ashtray and tea. She brought the best cups, the ones I ask her to use when I want to impress people. She obviously thought Dennis was someone important. She even used her deferential tone when speaking to him; I found it hard not to smile.

'I heard you got married, again,' Dennis said, after she'd left.

'That's right.'

'Nice girl?'

'The best,' I lied. Janine was pretty — beautiful even — but in the two years since we'd married she'd turned into a money-munching monster with an unhealthy fascination for her gym instructor. More and more these days I sought the comfort of a sympathetic redhead who worked for an insurance company on the fourth floor of our building.

'You should come over for dinner and meet her,' I said, in a moment of poor judgment.

'I don't think that's a good idea, do you?'

He was right, of course. I tried to change the subject. 'What about you? Anyone manage to drag you to the altar yet?'

He didn't answer right away. He may have been reluctant to.

Dennis had never been what you'd call lucky in love.

When he was young, the few girls who did go out with him were usually just using him as a handbag until someone better came along. Unfortunately, Dennis would fall madly in love with them and end up with heartbreak while they walked off with bracelets, rings, clothes and all the other goodies he'd bought for them during their all-too-brief relationship.

As for sex, as far as I know there was only Noelene, the girl he lost his virginity to — and that was only because we arranged it.

Noelene was in many ways a female version of Dennis, only she used sex instead of cigarettes to gain popularity. She'd leap into the sack with just about anyone. Nevertheless, we thought that even she would draw the line at Dennis. So we decided to offer her an incentive — money. It's not as awful as it sounds. She was already giving it away; we were just trying to make a roll in the hay with Dennis a little more palatable, that's all.

Graham Talbot, the one member of our little group who had been blessed with an embarrassing surplus of good looks and — when it came to matters of the loins — virtually no morals whatsoever, was elected to put the unsavoury proposition to her. He whisked her off to some low-lit den and attempted to break her down with gimlet and soft talk. This nearly backfired when, thinking that he was making a serious play for her, she flung herself bodily upon him. Naturally, he panicked and quickly blurted out the truth — offering her fifty pounds if she'd 'do it' with Dennis.

You'd think an insult like this would have resulted in a slap in the face at the very least, if not a complete sobbing breakdown; but Noelene did neither. We'll never know whether it was the money — fifty quid was a significant amount in the sixties — the messenger or the alcohol, but for some reason, she just laughed and accepted the challenge.

She made her move on a Friday night at a small party at the house of some girl whose parents were out of town. Dennis never stood a chance. By the evening's end the silly bastard was convinced she was in love with him. He certainly was with her — which only goes to show you how gullible he was. I mean, here's a girl who — according to fairly reliable sources — once accommodated half of the First Fifteen on a single Saturday night, and here's Dennis fawning about her like he was her 'one and only'.

And it wasn't just a one-night stand for him; even after she made it clear it was for her. She had been his 'first' and he was never going to forget it. Even though she continued to frolic with other guys, Dennis was always there, waiting to pick her up between heartbreaks. He never judged her and never appeared to get jealous; he was completely, unquestioningly devoted to her. Months later, when she fell pregnant to someone whose name I've forgotten, guess who took her to the school's end-of-year dance? Right — dear old Dennis. In he walked proud as punch, with

Noelene six months pregnant and already big as a house, blushing furiously at his side. Silly bastard.

She left town soon after that; went off to stay with an auntie in the country and I assume to have the baby. She never came back. We soon forgot her, but I'm sure Dennis never did.

Looking at him now, I knew his life had been an endless series of Noelenes.

I repeated my question. 'Well, is there a Mrs Dixon?'

'Been married twice, actually,' Dennis sighed.

'Par for the course these days,' I observed.

'Don't know about par, my last wife was a bloody albatross,' he said. A corny golfer's joke, but that's Dennis.

'That's a shame,' I said, as sympathetically as I could. 'What about your first wife?'

'Oh, you mean Cassaaaanndra!' he said imitating an upper-class accent. 'Stuck up tart. *She* was a vulture — picked my bones clean. Bloody typical, eh? I go chasing birds and end up with a vulture and an albatross.'

'Beats chasing boys,' I said.

'I'll have to take your word for that,' he laughed, but there was no humour in it.

For a few seconds he seemed lost in some private thought and I glanced at my watch.

He noticed. 'Am I keeping you from something?'

'I have a meeting at four.'

'Anything important?'

'Depends upon your point of view. The company's just

been taken over again. That's the second time since I've been here. At four o'clock we meet the new owners, hear the new party line, salute the flag, shit like that.'

'Salute the flag?' Dennis looked confused and groped for another cigarette. He looked increasingly dishevelled and out of place. Obviously, the world of corporate raiders and executive angst was unfamiliar to him.

'You know, they'll want to throw a mission statement at us, or something,' I said, deliberately using corporate jargon. 'I've heard it all before. Our last owners sent in some management experts, chopped off a few heads, painted the walls, rearranged the books and sold us off at a huge profit within eighteen months. I expect it'll be much the same this time.'

He coughed a smoker's cough.

I continued. 'It's the way of the world I suppose; we're making money and that makes us attractive. But these constant boardroom manoeuvres make my job murder, I can tell you.'

He took another quick puff on the cigarette and stubbed it out, waving away the smoke as if embarrassed by his addiction.

'What exactly do you do?' he asked.

'Software and computers. IBM clones, basically. Money's mainly in our service contracts though.'

'No, I meant you yourself, what do *you* do? You said these changes make your job murder. What's your job?'

'Communications Manager.'

'Which means?'

'I deal with media people, arrange cocktail parties and push the advertising agency around a bit.'

'Sounds cushy.'

I lowered my voice. 'Let's put it this way, I've got a top-of-the-line hi-fi system at home, and my restaurant bills are not a problem.'

'Isn't that a bit — you know ...?'

'Why? This company gets great advertising, and I get a few perks on the side. Where's the harm in that?'

'I suppose you're right.'

'Right as rain, mate. Anyway, enough about me, what about you? Making millions?'

'Can't complain.'

'People have to eat, I suppose.'

'Sorry?'

'Your restaurant ...'

'Oh, yes ... of course.'

I could see he'd forgotten telling me he owned a restaurant, I doubted it was true, anyway. As if to confirm this, he didn't pursue the subject any further. He just stared at the floor. The sole was peeling off one of his shoes. He seemed increasingly ill at ease. I guessed he was still trying to pluck up the courage to say whatever it was he'd come to say.

I waited and watched — critically, as always.

Finally he spoke: 'Annie's dead!'

My face turned to ice. I couldn't feel my hands.

'Alone in her car, a hose from the exhaust through the window and one of your old love letters in her hand,' he said, bitterly.

Annie was everything Dennis wasn't — beautiful, confident, fascinating. I'd been in love with her ever since I was old enough to know such feelings. From the speech-stealing infatuation of ten-year-olds to the desperate passion of early adulthood, our love had been absolute.

We were dating at twelve, lovers at sixteen, living together at twenty, married at twenty-four, and divorced before we were thirty.

I still remember how proud Dennis was when we married; his best friend — that's how he thought of me then — marrying his sister. He was in heaven. His wedding gift to us was an entire bedroom suite. Not a shiny, cheap, veneered matching suite from some furniture warehouse, but separate pieces — all antique. He must have spent his life's savings on us. I should have been grateful, but I wasn't. Annie and I were about to move to Australia and I'd hoped to sell all our furniture before we left and make a new start in a new country. Dennis's extravagance ruled this out. This bedroom suite wasn't the kind of thing you flog off at a garage sale; it was the kind you hand down to your grandchildren. So Annie insisted we take it with us and it cost a fortune.

I should explain that Annie was nowhere near as enthusiastic about the shift to Australia, nor the purging of our possessions, as I was. While she agreed to do both, she would have been perfectly happy to live and die in the same New Zealand suburb she'd been born in. The dreams we were going to pursue in Australia were mine, not hers.

Perhaps she hoped I wouldn't find what I was looking for and would eventually want to return home. Perhaps I hoped she would learn to love a life of travel and endless possibilities. In any case, we were both wrong.

We'd been so close for so long, we'd failed to notice that we'd been growing apart for years.

I have no desire to detail the disintegration of our marriage: the dry-mouthed arguments, the disillusion, the panic, the tears — you've heard it all before and our story is no less painful than countless others.

I'm only thankful that in our case there were no children.

I will say, however, that I was the one to end it. I could see no future for two people with such different dreams. I knew we had to call it off before it destroyed us. And I knew we had to do it while we were still young enough to make a new start. There is no kind or easy way to do such a thing, at least none that I could think of, so I just walked out.

Naturally, Annie was devastated. And so was I, although few people seemed prepared to accept that. As far as most people were concerned, I was a heartless, selfish bastard, below contempt and certainly not deserving of sympathy or understanding. The state of emotional exile to which I was subjected, as friends and family gravitated to Annie, only served to heighten my sense of martyrdom. I gathered it around me like a shell.

Dennis's visit today was the first I'd seen or heard of the old gang in years. I'd been too proud and ashamed to make contact myself. Ashamed because, even after all this time, I had never achieved what I set out to do: I'd never pursued my life of footloose adventure. Instead, I'd fallen into the very same settled suburban existence that Annie had craved and I had denied her. Now I was trapped in the wrong life with the wrong woman and not a day went past when I didn't regret it.

I looked at Dennis. He stared back, blankly. He'd never forgiven me for leaving Annie. I'd only spoken to him once since, over the phone, shortly after she had returned to New Zealand. He said I'd destroyed her; he promised to see me in hell for it. Now, perhaps, that time had come.

'It was your fault, Sam,' he said.

'It's been over for years, Den.'

'Not for her.'

'For both of us.'

'Bullshit!'

'Look, this is hardly the time, she's just—'

'She hasn't *just* anything, Sam. She died two years ago.'

'*What?*' I couldn't believe it. 'Why didn't anyone tell me?'

'Why? You didn't care about her. You made that fucking clear.'

'I cared. I loved her. Don't blame this on me.'

'You were all she ever wanted — ever since she was a little girl.'

He lit another cigarette. The fumes annoyed me now.

I looked up to say something and was stunned to see Dennis leaning back in his chair deliberately exhaling smoke in my direction. His whole attitude had changed; his grief seemed to have gone and there was now a triumphant look in his eye.

'She left you a note ...' he said.

I leaned forward.

'I burned it,' he smiled cruelly.

I leapt across the coffee table, grabbed him by the shirt and hauled him to his feet. 'Where is it? You bastard!'

'I told you, I burned it,' he gasped. His breath was foul.

I let him drop back onto the couch. I wanted to smash something.

'I can tell you what it said,' he wheezed as he loosened his collar.

'You read it?' I said in disgust.

'There were only three words: *Sam, I'm sorry*. That's all it said. *Sam, I'm sorry*. Like she owed *you* an apology. It made me sick. As far as I was concerned she didn't owe you a thing. So I burned it.'

'It wasn't an apology, it was a message,' I said.

'What message?'

'I once bought her a T-shirt that had *Love means never having to say you're sorry* printed on it. She said it was dumb. She said that sometimes you hurt the one you love even when you don't mean to, and when you do, you should always say you're sorry. She made me take it back.'

I felt the tears rise in my eyes as I spoke.

Dennis was unimpressed. 'Feeling sorry for yourself, Samuel?'

He was gloating. He revolted me. I didn't need him there. 'Why don't you just fuck off?'

'I'll go when I'm good and ready.'

'You'll go when I say!' I shouted pointing at the door.

He remained seated.

I lurched towards him.

'Don't, Sam,' he warned. 'I don't want to have to sue you for assault.'

I stopped.

He got slowly to his feet. I thought he was going to leave; instead, he began to pace purposefully about the room. 'I'm no use to you any more, am I, Sam? You don't need to sponge money off me, you don't want to bonk my sister or steal smokes from my old man, so I can just piss off, right?'

I didn't answer; this was not the Dennis I knew — he seemed taller.

He went on. 'Tell me, were you just arrogant or incredibly stupid?'

'What the hell are you on about?'

'Did you really think I'd let you rip off my old man like that? Just steal stuff from his shop, when I knew how hard he worked for every cent he had.'

'If you knew, why let us get away with it, why didn't you say anything?'

'I paid for the cigarettes you stole, mate. And every packet of chips, every chocolate bar, every bloody thing you or the others nicked, I paid for. I put the cash in the till later when no one was looking. I only let you think you were ripping off poor, dumb, Dennis's dad because it gave you some kind of thrill.'

'But it went on for years. It must have cost—'

'It was nothing to me. A few bucks here and there, a small price to pay if it meant I could stay close enough to make sure you did the right thing by Annie.'

'Leave her out of it!'

'You must be joking. She was the only reason I hung around and let you treat me like a piece of shit for all those years. *Christ*, even Blind Freddie could see what a self-centred arsehole you were. But for some reason, Annie couldn't.'

'I thought you were happy when we got married.'

'*Happy!* You've got to be kidding. I was bloody shattered. But I wasn't going to let Annie see that. She was so happy I thought she'd burst. You soon put paid to that.'

'I *loved* her!'

'Crap! You loved who you wanted her to be, not who she was.'

'She changed, we both changed, it wasn't my fault.'

'Did you really change, Sam?'

'What's that supposed to mean?'

'Aren't you just the same thieving, selfish bastard you've always been?'

'I'm no thief!'

He raised his eyebrows.

'Okay, so I nicked a few smokes from your old man. It was no big deal. Just kids' stuff. We all did that.'

'You've just finished telling me how you've been ripping off this firm.'

'I'm not ripping off anyone. I'm just getting what's coming to me, that's all. Just oiling the wheels so to speak. No one complains.'

'I never complained, either — did I?'

I didn't need this guilt, especially not from him.

'What the hell would you know about it, Dixon? It's a tough world. You're quick or you're dead. I'm just trying not to get killed in the rush, that's all. Besides, who the hell are you to criticise me? I mean, look at you! *Jesus*, I wish my old man could see you now. He always thought you were going to be such a bloody success.'

'Like you?' he scoffed.

'I'm doing okay,' I said looking pointedly around my office.

'What? Arranging cocktail parties, taking backhanders, you call that *success*? Do me a favour.'

'I don't have to listen to this shit. You said what you came to say, now get out!'

'I haven't finished. In fact, I'm only just beginning.'

He picked up his battered briefcase, laid it on the coffee

table and took out a large envelope, which he handed to me.

It had to be the letter from Annie — I tore it open.

It wasn't a letter, it was a folder containing scores of sheets of paper that were yellowed with age; except for one crisp new sheet with laser printing on it — a statement, made out to me, for $12,340.

'What the hell is this?'

'It's all there.'

I began to leaf through the sheets: page after page of notes, dates and amounts written in Dennis's cramped scrawl; everything I'd ever taken from his father's shop; every cent I'd borrowed from him and not returned; every hamburger I'd eaten at 'Danny's' and not paid for — everything. Some of the writing had faded with age, and many of the early figures were in pounds, shillings and pence, but it was all there. All accounted for. How could anyone be so bloody petty?

'You've got to be kidding!' I laughed.

'Not a bit, my son. That's an itemised account of every cent you owe me, compounded at three per cent a year just to cover inflation.'

'Well, you can shove it up your arse!'

'I was rather hoping you'd be more sensible about this. I don't want to have to take legal action.'

'What? Over a few lousy bucks?'

'Twelve thousand, three hundred and forty lousy bucks to be exact. And if you stuff me around, I'll recalculate the interest, at the bank loan rates that applied during the period. That ought to make it a little more worth your while.'

Belinda had come to the door — no doubt attracted by the sound of raised voices. She tried to catch Dennis's eye. We both ignored her.

'This is because of Annie, isn't it?' I said. 'Some kind of sick revenge.'

'Just pay the money, Sam.'

'Get stuffed. You're not going to sue me, it's not worth the hassle. And in the end it's just going to be your word against mine.'

'You're wrong there, I've got witnesses,' he said.

'Pig's arse! Who?'

'Talbot, Macca and Richo.'

Now I knew he was bluffing. These were the other members of the 'Undertakers' and they'd always been closer to me than him. They didn't even like him; there was no way they would take his side against me.

I laughed. 'Dream on!'

Belinda interrupted busily. 'Excuse me, Mr Dixon—'

'Mr Dixon is just leaving, Lindy,' I said. 'Show him out, would you.'

Dennis stopped her with a wave of his hand. 'One moment, Belinda, please.' He turned back to me. 'Sam, there's a couple of things I think you ought to know.'

Belinda looked across at me, helplessly. I nodded that it

was okay — I wanted to hear what Dennis had to say. 'And what might that be?' I asked.

'Talbot, Macca and Richo, did I mention that they all work for me now?'

He paused to enjoy the look on my face.

I didn't disappoint him.

'A bit of a turnaround, eh?' he continued. 'All the old gang working for me. Even Noelene. You remember Noelene, don't you, Sam? My first *root*, as you so eloquently put it at the time. She manages one of my little printing operations now. Doing a terrific job. She's turned out to be a fine, strong woman. In fact, I'm thinking of asking her to be the third Mrs Dixon. What do you think about that, Sam? 'Dorky' Dixon marrying the village bike?'

Everything I felt was written in my face.

He walked over and patted my shoulder. 'Isn't life a bastard, Sammy?'

'Mr Dixon, please!' Belinda insisted bravely. She was clearly agitated by his refusal to leave.

Dennis glanced at his watch, then smiled warmly at her.

'Yes, Belinda, it's four o'clock. I suppose they're ready for me in the boardroom now. Tell them I'll be right down, would you?' He looked at me. 'You'd better come too, Sammy, my old son. You wouldn't want to miss this for quids.'

LOVE AND MAGIC

Kate watched Brad swaggering towards her and was seized by an all too familiar sense of panic. Mercifully, she was granted a few moments' reprieve when he stopped to talk to a small group of their guests. She was standing next to the musicians — two old men attacking violin and accordion with gusto — so she couldn't hear what he was saying, but she didn't need to; she knew it would be tactless, peppered with sexual innuendo and more than likely embarrassing for those forced to listen. A few watery smiles rippled around the group as if to confirm this.

She sighed and let her gaze wander outside to where a soft drizzle was catching the fire of the setting sun. The beauty of it brought her no comfort.

'Outside! You must be mad. It'll rain for sure,' Brad ranted when she told him she planned to hold his birthday party in the garden.

Far from being disappointed that the rain had arrived, he'd be delighted to be proven right. She dreaded the thought of his gloating.

Her gloomy thoughts were interrupted by a sudden hush in the conversation. She looked up to see a strange bat-like silhouette standing in the main entrance to the marquee. It appeared to flare its wings to shake off a fine spray of raindrops before entering in a swirl of black.

Under lights the new arrival was revealed to be a hunchbacked man dressed in a dinner jacket, bow tie and black cape. And despite the initial pity one might feel at the sight of a body so twisted and bowed, it was plain to see this man wasn't bowed in spirit. Pride and intelligence emanated from his keen green eyes as he scanned their faces.

When he saw Kate, he smiled, and moved towards her.

The others fell into curious silence. Even the musicians stopped playing and watched in fascination as this odd character shuffled across the marquee like a hermit crab.

When he was a few feet from her, he slowly stretched out an arm and, with a snap of his fingers, produced a beautiful bunch of white carnations.

He offered them to her.

Everyone gasped and smiled in the way they do when magic is performed before their very eyes. They gathered closer.

The man's skin was olive and impossibly smooth, giving him an almost polished look. His black eyebrows, which swept back precisely at the base of his high forehead, looked so symmetrical Kate thought for an instant they might be painted on — then she noticed a small scar in the right one and was almost relieved to find it there. His nose, too, was imperfect, bending off to one side above a decidedly sensuous mouth.

She brought her gaze back to his steady green eyes and saw that they now held a look of warmth and amusement. And there was something else ... something familiar. A shadow stirred, briefly, in a rarely visited part of her memory — then it was gone.

Ignoring the curious onlookers and Kate's unblinking scrutiny, the man in black continued to hold the flowers out to her. He encouraged her to accept them with a slight raising of his eyebrows and a mischievous smile.

Kate was convinced that the moment she reached for them, the carnations would be transformed into a rubber snake or something equally horrific. She thought this because she knew he had to be 'Mahmoud the Magnificent', the magician she'd booked after finding his leaflet in the letter box on the very day she decided she'd have live entertainment at Brad's birthday party.

'Please, Mrs Warren, the flowers are for you,' he said.

His voice was warm and slightly accented and she knew she'd never heard it before, yet the feeling that she knew him persisted. However, this was no time to go in pursuit of an elusive memory; everyone was willing her to accept the flowers. Not wishing to spoil their fun (after all, she had hired the fellow to entertain), she reached out fearing the worst.

Nothing happened. No trick, no rubber snake. Much to her surprise and delight the flowers proved to be real. 'Thank you,' she said with obvious relief. 'I love carnations.'

'I know,' he said. 'They're your favourite flowers.'

'How could you possibly know that? And how on earth did you know I was Mrs Warren?'

'Mahmoud knows.'

'Yeah, well, I'd like to know who the hell Mahmoud the chocolate Quasimodo is!' Brad said as he shoved forward to stand possessively by her side.

Their guests fell into an embarrassed silence.

If the magician was insulted, he didn't show it. 'Please allow me to introduce myself. I am Mahmoud the Magnificent, here at the request of your charming wife to entertain you on the occasion of your thirty-seventh birthday.'

He held out his hand.

Brad ignored it.

Kate saw that the hand was horribly scarred; two of the fingers appeared to be webbed together. She found herself imagining that hand sliding across her breast and shuddered unwittingly.

Mahmoud quickly withdrew the hand from her sight.

She blushed. Surely he couldn't have known?

Brad noticed none of this. 'Mahmoud the Magnificent,

my arse. More like Willie the Wanker if you ask me,' he said and laughed.

Nobody else seemed amused.

Mahmoud smiled whimsically. 'Ahhh yes, the clothes ... I am a bit overdressed, I admit. It is a necessary part of the act, I'm afraid.'

'Need plenty of pockets to hide things in, eh?' Brad sneered. He addressed this last remark to the others, not the crippled magician.

They smiled helplessly.

Kate was puzzled: how had Mahmoud known it was Brad's thirty-seventh birthday? She'd only told his agent it was a birthday party; she hadn't said *whose* birthday it was, and no age had been mentioned. He must have asked someone outside before he made his grand entrance.

Brad was talking at her. 'You never said anything about a magician. Tents, magicians, what next — the whole bloody circus?'

The others began to shuffle about uncomfortably. There was a time when Brad's jibes had been amusing, but nowadays they were just bitter and belligerent. His public bullying of Kate was something even his oldest friends were finding impossible to cope with. Kate implored them to ignore it — assuring them it was only the alcohol talking, that she didn't take it to heart and neither should they. But such behaviour is hard to ignore or forgive.

And tonight, despite the occasion, Brad was at his worst: 'Speaking of tents and circuses,' he persisted, 'I told you having the party outside was a shit-house idea. I knew it'd rain.'

Although she'd been prepared for this, Kate hadn't been able to think of a suitable reply.

Mahmoud came to her rescue. 'There is no rain,' he said.

Everyone turned to look outside to what was now a perfect afternoon. Magically, the drizzle and clouds had disappeared.

They looked back at Brad.

'Yeah, well ... lucky for you,' Brad grunted at Kate as he jostled his way outside to assure himself that the rain had really gone.

'Lucky for all of us, I think,' Mahmoud smiled at Kate. 'Now perhaps I can perform my show outside in your lovely garden.'

So saying he scuttled past Brad out into the sunlight.

Kate followed slowly, still puzzled by the certainty that she'd met this fascinating fellow somewhere before.

The others drifted out after her, buzzing excitedly.

Brad was less than enthusiastic. 'I bet this is costing me a fortune.'

'I'm paying,' Kate assured him, expecting no thanks.

Brad ignored her and went to join the others. As he reached the edge of the small crowd that had gathered around the magician, he threw his arm around their neighbour, Tammy Anderson, and drew her roughly into his side. As subtly as she could, Tammy tried to break away, but Brad held her firmly. She looked back helplessly at Kate, who smiled and shrugged. There was nothing she could do. They were both trapped. For Tammy it would only be for a few uncomfortable minutes; for Kate it had been years.

Although most soon realise the folly in it, few women could honestly say they survived their younger years without experiencing at least a quickening of the heart in the presence of that confident and often envied male creature who, by virtue of looks, personality, strength or athletic ability, is acknowledged by all others to be 'the leader of the pack'.

In Kate's case, this affliction had been rather more permanent.

It began one summer in a sunburned beach resort where a high school dropout by the name of Brad Warren had been the undisputed king of the beach. Bronzed, blond, muscular and relaxed, his roguish blue eyes and disarming smile were irresistible to any girl in search of summer romance.

Kate had never seen eyes so blue, or eyes that could promise so much in a single glance.

And as if looks, wit and charm weren't enough, he also played lead guitar with a popular band and sang with a hard-edged voice that stirred her very soul.

From the very first time she saw him, Kate was smitten. And she wasn't alone in her infatuation; the competition for Brad's attentions that summer was fierce. Scores of intelligent, free-spirited girls were reduced to little more than fawning groupies at the mere mention of his name. The lengths they went to to attract his attention bordered on the ridiculous. Kate, herself, was one of the worst.

It was all to no avail, because for most of that summer he ignored her and chose instead the abundant curves and accommodating disposition of a peroxided blonde by the name of Pauline Luke (or 'Puke', as she was unkindly referred to by those who envied her, which included virtually every female for twenty miles in any direction).

Then, one fateful night late in January, Brad abandoned Pauline and claimed Kate. There is no other way to describe what happened.

The last dance for the holiday break had ended. The band was packing up and everyone who mattered was heading for a bonfire party on a small beach a few miles up the coast. There was a touch of sadness about the night — by noon the next day, the Romeos and Juliets of the tented villages and caravan parks would be torn apart as fate and family returned them to homes and lives far from each other. For friends and lovers alike, it was a time for tearful goodbyes and heartfelt promises that could never be kept.

Kate and her friends — many of whom had remained depressingly unattached for the entire holiday break — were standing in front of the local hall hoping to hitch a ride to the beach party. Cars cruised by like chrome-toothed sharks, and hanging from their windows were all the young men who would never be Brad Warren. Accepting a ride with any of these hormone-crazed youths was sure to involve at least a minor tussle with a nervous hand in search of a willing breast. For this reason, among others, the girls had wisely agreed to stick together. They were dallying with an overly zealous red-haired boy called Ralph — who had the use of the family station wagon for the night — when the door to the hall opened and Brad emerged with guitar case in hand and Pauline Puke following a few steps behind. Pauline was crying: 'I'm sorry, Brad. I don't know why I said that. It must have been the wine … I didn't … please …'

One look at Brad's face told you Pauline's pleading was wasted. None of them knew what she had done and none of them cared. Without a second thought for the poor girl's shattered heart, every young woman there realised with predatory glee that Pauline was past tense and the road to dreamland was open.

The night held its breath.

Brad surveyed the weak-kneed feminine huddle before him. Their eagerness was transparent.

After the longest minute, he stepped forward, looked directly at Kate and held out his hand. As if hypnotised, she went to him and fell naturally in by his side. No words were exchanged, none was needed; so complete was her infatuation that a look, a smile and an extended hand were all that she asked for and more than she'd dreamed of.

He claimed her and she acquiesced almost gratefully. Such was the seduction of Kate Hamilton.

Theirs was no ordinary short-term summer romance. It proved deep, lasting and wonderful. Kate couldn't believe she could be so happy for so long. He was the hero and she was his lady. They were the perfect couple. Everyone agreed.

Two years later, when he asked her to marry him, her heart sang.

She was only nineteen and he barely twenty-three.

Her mother cried and her father tried not to get angry. 'The boy's a bloody pop singer, for Chrissake! How's he going to support you? Who does he think he is, Paul Lennon?'

'That's John Lennon, Dad.'

'I don't care if it's Rumplebloodystiltskin Lennon, at least he's making millions, which is more than can be said for this Brad whatshisname.'

In the end, however, her father relented and gave them his blessing along with a cheque for $5000, which was his last, if not most subtle, word on the subject.

A little over five years later, things began to fall apart.

It began when Brad came to understand, as many of us do, that time can be cruel to high school heroes.

For most of his early life he'd been the one others looked up to, the one they envied. He was the 'natural', the leader, the hero. Perhaps it was understandable, therefore, that he tended to dedicate himself to pursuits that came easily to him — sport and music — rather than academic subjects, which took time and hard work, and inspired little admiration from his peers. Besides which, he just couldn't see the point of burying himself in languages and logarithms, or the trials and tribulations of the British monarchy, when such things seemed so irrelevant in his view of the everyday world. So the day he turned sixteen he dropped out of school, leaving his friends to struggle on towards university while he enjoyed the fruits of a musician's life on the road.

For a few years, his lack of education hadn't mattered; he earned good money and had an enormous amount of fun doing it. Moreover, while the band enjoyed a heady time of popularity — aided immeasurably by his cavalier looks and riveting vocals — he was able to maintain his high profile and further cultivate the legend.

He was the one everyone wanted to be, or be with.

This is how it was the summer he met Kate.

In time, though, things began to change. His friends rarely came to the dances and clubs to cheer and envy him any more. They were moving on to new jobs, new interests and new friends. And on the odd occasions their paths did cross, while they always seemed genuinely pleased to see him, after a few minutes' reminiscing their eyes would begin to glaze over. Brad offered them little more than memories of another time — a happier, more carefree time, perhaps, but a time that was past, nonetheless. He had nothing to do with their present or their future.

On the other hand, he himself had no clear plans for the future. He knew by now it wasn't in the music business — he was good, but not *that* good. He needed something more substantial, something with long-term prospects; something he could rely upon and enjoy. Each day he scanned the newspapers for suitable opportunities; casually, though, as if checking his options rather than desperately searching for a future. He applied for a number of jobs, but could never get the ones he really liked.

Invariably, they were looking for people with higher qualifications than someone who'd left school at sixteen to sing in a rock band.

What made things worse was that he often found himself being interviewed by anal-retentive types he had always considered 'nerds' at school. Only now these same nerds held his future in their hands and it seemed to him that they used their power like a form of revenge. Each time he had to suffer their patronising rejections, he was seized by an overpowering desire to punch them. Unfortunately, these dark thoughts tended to show and, as the chip on his shoulder grew, his chances of being hired reduced.

The best he could manage were a few casual labouring jobs and a brief flirtation with a commission-only encyclopaedia-selling job that savaged his pride and earned him barely enough to pay the rent.

Then, inevitably, the band began to fall out of fashion. Bookings dropped off at a worrying rate.

In the end there were weeks when Kate's earnings as a receptionist in a real estate office were well in excess of his own.

Perhaps if he'd set his mind on some vocation, got in on the ground floor and worked his way up, things might have been different, but he found this impossible. To start at the bottom would mean ingratiating himself to lesser mortals in order to get ahead and he just couldn't do that.

Consequently, he was condemned by pride to remain on the outside looking in — with anger.

He was no longer the hero, no longer the one people envied. His glory belonged to another time — like a sports trophy that sits forgotten on the shelf except for those rare occasions when you take it down to remind yourself of a brief, shining moment that has gone for ever.

And the occasions when the old gang would get together to reminisce about Brad's glory days were becoming all too rare.

His legend was losing its shine.

While Brad may have mourned the passing of his prime, Kate did not. She loved the man, not the image. She was more than happy for him to remain a musician all his life, even a poor one, so long as it made him happy. She did, however, understand his torment. She knew how he hated to be beaten by anything or anyone. And — although he never discussed it — she knew that his sense of failure was beating him to death.

She tried to tell him it didn't matter — let the others

have their heavily mortgaged homes, foreign cars and gold credit cards, she didn't need them. They had each other, they were happy, and that was all that mattered to her.

Brad didn't believe her. He was convinced she only said these things to make him feel better. He was certain that, like everyone else, she was merely patronising him.

This feeling only intensified when the real estate company promoted her to sales and she began to earn sizeable commissions. In one month she earned nearly double what he'd earned the whole of the previous year. Within two years she'd earned enough to put a deposit down on their house. Now she took care of the mortgage.

She wanted him to enjoy her success, to accept that her income enabled him to concentrate on his music; but all it did was increase his sense of failure.

Eventually, perhaps inevitably, the alcohol that had for so long fuelled his popular personality began to awaken a darker side to him.

Despite this, Kate tried to help — comforting him through bouts of paranoia and self-doubt, mopping up his vomit and enduring his depression.

But when the months turned into years, with each day bringing a new bout of drunken abuse, when she began to dread his foul-breathed, clammy-handed attempts at lovemaking, when her every gesture of love and support was hurled back at her in a self-pitying fury, she had to face the reality that there was nothing left worth saving.

Now, after two years of unremitting misery, she knew

she had no choice but to leave him, and it was tearing her apart.

True to his stage name, Mahmoud was magnificent.

He began by moving among the guests performing a few simple sleight-of-hand tricks and some incredible feats of pickpocketing.

The late afternoon was filled with cries of amusement and delight as people discovered he had relieved them of their watch, or wallet, or belt, or — in one case — a bra.

At one point he stole Sally Baldwin's engagement ring and caused it to vanish before her eyes. He then produced an egg and assured her that the ring was inside it. But when he broke the egg into a glass bowl there was no sign of the ring. He seemed genuinely dismayed — the trick had always worked before. Sally looked worried. Her husband, Grant, was furious — the ring was worth a fortune. Things became decidedly tense until Mahmoud asked Grant to look in the pocket of his own jacket and, sure enough, there was the ring.

'Fuck me!' said Grant.

'No, thanks,' chorused the others, and hilarity reigned.

The only one not enjoying the show was Brad. During the search for the ring he had been shouting things like 'Look up his bum — I bet the poofter's hidden it up his ring-piece!' and other choice remarks along similar lines.

These witticisms were intended to unsettle the

magician and amuse the others, but they failed in every respect.

Mahmoud alone appeared to accept it in good humour. 'So you think I'm a fake, Mr Warren?'

'I don't think so, mate, I know. This is no kiddies' party, you're out with grown-ups tonight.'

'Aaah ... yes. Children believe in magic, adults do not. That is a shame, don't you think?'

'Why? It's bloody reality, isn't it?'

'What is reality?'

'Wires, hidden trapdoors, mirrors. Trickery, mate — that's the reality.'

'Brad, please—' Kate tried to pull him away.

'It's quite all right, Mrs Warren,' Mahmoud assured her. 'Your husband doesn't believe in magic; this is cause for sadness, not anger.'

'You must be bloody joking!' Brad's blue eyes blazed indignantly. 'You feel sorry for me? Christ, mate, I should feel sorry for you — you pathetic hunchbacked coon!'

The bitterness of his insult stunned them all.

Only Mahmoud seemed unmoved. He looked thoughtfully at Brad as if reaching a decision of some kind.

The sun had dropped below the horizon and the crickets were beginning to serenade the twilight. One of the musicians, bothered by the strained silence, ventured a few nervous notes on his accordion, but a harsh glance from his violin-wielding partner silenced him.

No one spoke.

Mahmoud looked at Kate, sympathy filling his warm green eyes. 'It must be difficult to love a man who does not believe in magic.'

Brad took a threatening step forward. 'What kind of a—'

There was a blinding flash.

Brad leapt back in fright.

When the smoke cleared the magician had disappeared.

Some laughed. Some clapped. Brad looked bewildered.

'Looking for me, Mr Warren?' Mahmoud's voice came from within the marquee. As everyone looked in that direction he emerged, holding before him a large luminous orb — about the size of a basketball — which gave off a soft blue light.

'Nice trick, mate,' Brad said, having recovered his caustic composure. 'A bit of flash powder to divert our attention and you exit stage left. Clever, but not magic.'

Although they thought it unnecessary to say so, few would have argued with Brad's assessment.

Mahmoud seemed to sense what they were thinking and smiled. 'I see I have more than one sceptic in the audience tonight.'

They tried not to look guilty; they had no desire to insult the man, especially since he had developed his skills to such a degree despite his obvious handicaps. Then again, neither should he insult them by expecting them to believe what he did was really magic. It was illusion, nothing more.

'Well, then,' the magician grinned. 'I see I'm just going to have to convince you all.'

He had arrived at the party in a small truck painted midnight blue and covered in white and yellow stars of various sizes. 'Mahmoud the Magnificent' was painted boldly on each side panel in Superman-style lettering and there was a mobile phone number on the doors.

Surprisingly, for one so physically limited, he hadn't brought an assistant to help him. So he'd had to ask some of the guests to help him unload the truck and erect a small low stage in the garden.

Now that the day had settled into lingering twilight, the stage was largely in darkness and you could just make out the silhouette of a large trunk in centre stage, the folds of the gaudily painted canvas backdrop, and the shapes of a few props off to either side.

Holding the glowing orb in front of him, Mahmoud climbed awkwardly up onto the stage, hobbled to the centre of it and stood with his back to them. Then, balancing the orb on the fingertips of one hand, he slowly reached up until his arm was fully extended. Magically, the orb continued to rise, away from his outstretched fingers until it reached a point about eight feet above him. Here it stopped and hovered, its glow gradually intensifying until the entire stage was bathed in an eerie blue light.

He turned slowly and looked directly at Kate. 'I wonder what they'll make of that.'

Kate looked to see how her friends were reacting. They

weren't. There was not a sound — not from them, nor the crickets, nor the birds, nor the neighbours. No children shrieking. No dogs barking. No traffic. It was as if the whole world was in suspended animation.

Except for her and Mahmoud.

'A cheap trick, I'm afraid,' the magician said as he hopped down off the stage, 'but I wanted to talk to you alone.'

Kate stared in horror at her motionless friends. 'What have you done to them? You've hypnotised me, haven't you? This is not happening. It's all in my imagination, isn't it?'

He was now standing close to her. 'Please don't worry, your friends are quite safe,' he assured her. 'They're lovely people, but I'm afraid, thanks to your husband, they're turning out to be quite a difficult audience.'

With an effort she dragged her eyes back to him. 'You did this because of Brad?'

'Well, he does seem determined to spoil his own party.'

'Yes, I'm sorry about that,' she said. 'Sometimes he gets a bit … when he's had too much to drink, you know.'

'You love him very much, don't you?'

'I really don't think that's any of your business.'

'Perhaps not. However, if you're planning to leave someone you love, I think somebody should make it their business.'

Leave someone you love — she felt her heart leap; how could he have possibly known that?

'Let's just say it's magic,' he said, reading her mind.

She found it hard to breathe, as if the air had turned to liquid. The man continued to invade her private thoughts in a way he had no right to.

'Look, Mahmoud, or whatever your real name is, you're a terrific magician. I respect that and I'm sure they do, too,' she said glancing around uncertainly at her inanimate friends. 'Why can't you leave it at that? Why is it so important that we believe what you do is *really* magic?'

'People who don't believe in magic cannot believe in love.'

'And *you'd* know, of course,' she said sharply — and immediately regretted her tone. It was too late. She saw that she'd hurt him in a way Brad had failed to. She began to apologise. 'Look, I'm sorry, I ...'

He was quick to recover. 'It's all right. It's my fault — I've been presumptuous.'

'Yes, you have. But ...' There was no way to undo what she'd said, no words to excuse it. She let it go.

Mahmoud gazed down at his scarred hand, turning it over slowly as if seeing it for the first time.

She noticed that he appeared weary, as if he were hunched by a huge weight on his shoulders rather than a cruel twist of nature.

When he spoke, his voice was quieter, less confident. 'I was in love, once. Platonically, of course, it has to be that way for me ...'

Kate softened. 'Did the girl know?'

'No.'

'Why didn't you tell her?'

'Would you, if you were me?'

She didn't answer.

He shrugged. 'The truth is, I never even spoke to her. I worshipped her from afar, as they say,' he paused, remembering. 'It was many years ago and in those days I was confined to a wheelchair.'

The familiar feeling returned to her again — a blurred image just out of reach. 'Were you afraid she'd be unkind?' she asked.

'No, she could never be unkind, it was not in her nature,' he said. 'She was a popular girl, a happy girl, I'd say, but her eyes were for the handsome boys, not for cripples.'

He said this without a trace of self-pity; it was simply an observation, a fact of life.

Kate could think of nothing appropriate to say.

'That's the reason I became interested in magic,' he said brightly.

She looked suitably mystified.

'I wanted to get attention, to become popular,' he explained. 'A fairly typical wish for a teenage boy, I think. And despite my handicaps, I was typical in most other respects. My first thought was to learn an instrument, but my hand made this impossible. So I chose magic instead.'

'But surely you need to be good with your hands to perform magic?'

'Yes, that's true. It was difficult for me, but I persisted. I found I had a gift for it. Besides, it's only sleight of hand that requires dexterity, not the kind of magic I perform.'

'Real magic, you mean.'

He smiled at the cynicism in her voice, but said nothing.

His calmness only served to further exasperate her. 'You're not going to start all that love and voodoo nonsense again?' she said.

'It's not nonsense — where there is love, there is magic; there can be no love without magic, and without love there is nothing.'

He was beginning to sound like a third-rate philosopher. 'Listen, the last thing I need right now is a guru. If you can read my mind — and you certainly appear to be able to — you'll know that love isn't exactly my favourite subject at the moment. Can't we just leave it alone?'

A look of rejection shadowed his deep-green eyes and for an instant he seemed quite helpless. She recognised that look — she had seen it before. But where? Something stirred and her resolve weakened. For some inexplicable reason, she felt the need to believe him — for his sake and her own. She reached out and took his deformed hand between both of hers.

'All right, if I say I *do* believe in magic, would it make any difference?'

'Only if you mean it.'

She sighed. 'I'd like to believe it, just like I'd like to

believe in Santa Claus, UFOs and fairy godmothers — but how can I? I didn't stop believing in those things by choice, you know, I learned to. Life's like that. You find out the truth and you learn to live with the realities. There's no point wasting your life away waiting for miracles.'

'So you have no time for impossible dreams?' he said.

'No. Do you?'

He was looking down at her hands holding his. After a moment he looked up and she was struck, once again, by the cruel contrast between his handsome features and his distorted frame. 'Oh yes,' he said, almost in a whisper, 'I still have my dreams.'

'Well, it's time you learned that they're just that,' she said, 'just dreams. Sooner or later you have to grow up, face reality and get on with it, otherwise you'll just get left behind.'

'Like Brad?'

She let go of his hand and stepped back a pace in awe. 'You really are incredible, aren't you? The things you know ...'

He didn't say anything, but a feeling of deep compassion seemed to flow out of him and she was drawn to his warmth. He waited.

'I'm leaving him tomorrow,' she confessed.

'But you don't want to.'

'I can't stay. I'll only end up hating him.'

'He loves you, Kate.'

'He might have once,' she said. 'Now ...'

She looked across at Brad, the silence and stillness had taken the anger from him. There was a look of boyish wonder on his face. His blue eyes, so often narrowed in rage and despair, were wide, helpless and innocent. Her heart ached. 'You've seen what he's like. No one could put up with that.'

'I see only a man who has ceased to believe in his own magic.'

'Boy, you don't give up, do you?' she sighed.

'I only state what is true.'

'What if it is true? What can anyone do about it?'

'You must put the magic back into his life. And your own.'

'And you just happen to be giving away free samples tonight, right?'

'You might say that, yes.'

'You'll forgive me if I'm not convinced.'

'If I were to put the magic back into your marriage, would that convince you?'

She said nothing. She didn't need to.

'Then that is what I shall do,' he said.

Within seconds he was back on stage standing with his back to her staring up at the glowing orb. Slowly, he turned with his arms outspread and with a snap of his fingers brought the others back to life.

Completely unharmed, and oblivious to what had happened, they returned to oohing and aaahing and pointing at the floating orb.

Brad pushed his way right to the very front to make sure he got the best view.

'Aaah, Mr Warren,' Mahmoud said spying him. 'Perhaps you'd like to assist me with my next trick.'

'Want to stick a few swords through my head, eh?' Brad joked as he leapt onto the stage.

'No, but I would like to make you disappear,' Mahmoud smiled.

'Wouldn't we all,' someone yelled.

'Get stuffed!' Brad laughed, inverting a finger in the direction of the heckler.

Mahmoud walked over to a brightly painted box that stood on the left of the stage. It was about the size and shape of Dr. Who's telephone booth, which seemed appropriate when he explained what he intended doing.

'I will lock Mr Warren in here,' he said and, as quickly as his curious gait would allow, made his way across the stage and thumped on the lid of a large wooden trunk. 'And I will transport him through space to re-emerge in here.'

'That's what you think,' Brad grinned, his dazzling blue eyes more roguish than ever. He had no intention of co-operating in any way.

The crowd bubbled.

Mahmoud went back to the first box and held the door open.

Brad entered, sceptically. 'Prepare to make a dick of yourself, Mohammed,' he grinned. 'You can abracadabra till the cows come home, I'm not leaving this box.'

Mahmoud was undeterred. He closed the door on Brad's muffled laughter and shuffled purposefully over to the trunk.

The soft downward glow of the orb accentuated the hunch of his shoulders, the folds of his cape and the weaving action of his hands as he turned to address them.

'Ladies and gentlemen! Tonight, for the first time ever, I will endeavour to move two bodies through space simultaneously.'

He stooped to open the lid of the trunk.

'At the very same time Mr Warren is travelling through the unknown to arrive here, I will transport myself from this chest to the box where he is now.'

A ripple of anticipation moved through the small crowd.

'But,' he lowered his voice for effect, 'for an instant in time, we will be as one, our atoms joined in that mystical, marvellous, magical dimension that separates and unites us all.'

They fell silent. Even Brad stopped laughing inside his box.

The orb began to pulse.

Mahmoud climbed into the trunk and carefully, painfully, folded his twisted frame into it.

The heavy lid fell shut with a dull thud.

In that instant, the pulsing of the orb began to increase in intensity until it became impossible to look at.

All at once the night was filled with the sound of

children laughing. The sound came from above them, behind them, beside them — all around. And there was another sound — singing. A boy's voice, sad and alone. So alone.

Then Kate remembered. The crippled Indian boy whose parents owned the fruit shop across the road from her school bus stop so many years ago. There were all kinds of stories about that boy: that he had the face of a dog, hair all over his body, and the hands of an amphibian; that he had to take correspondence lessons because he was too malformed to go to school with normal children. For a long time he was little more than the subject of malevolent rumour. Out of sight, but not out of mind. Then one day, when she was about twelve years old, she heard beautiful singing as she passed the fruit shop early one morning. It was the same lonely voice she could hear now. She'd stopped and looked in. There, at the back of the shop, singing to himself while he carefully arranged oranges on a low display tray, was the boy she'd heard so much about. Not at all like the monster she had imagined, just a small, helpless, hunched boy in a wheelchair. She found herself walking into the shop in the hope of talking to him. But, alerted by the click of her shoes on the tiled floor, he had turned, seen her and wheeled quickly away through a door screened by dangling plastic strips.

She didn't go after him.

In the years that followed, she'd seen him quite often, watching from an upstairs window while she laughed and flirted at the bus stop. She remembered wondering how he got up those stairs. And even from that distance she remembered seeing — or was it feeling? — pain in his eyes and thinking it must be physical. It never occurred to her that it might be the pain of longing for something he could never have.

Despite the teasing of her friends she'd often smile and wave at him, but he would just melt back into the anonymity of his room without returning the gesture.

The uncanny thing was, even though she had never been close enough to notice such details, she seemed to recall clearly that the little boy had emerald-green eyes — just like Mahmoud's.

Suddenly, it was over. The orb ceased to pulse. The night was silent.

With a quiet creak the trunk lid began to lift. Slowly, shakily, Brad emerged, checking himself all over as if to make sure that he was all there.

He looked across to the box he'd been shut into on the side of the stage and shook his head in amazement.

'All done with mirrors, eh, Brad?' Tammy Anderson teased.

Brad just smiled self-consciously.

There was no sign of Mahmoud.

'Where's the magician?' someone asked.

'Show yourself, Mahmoud,' another cried. 'Look in the Dr. Who phone booth thingy, Brad, see if he's in there!'

But Brad didn't appear to want any further part in the

proceedings. He stepped down off the stage and made his way towards Kate.

Urged on by the others, Tammy climbed onto the stage to investigate. She opened the door of the phone booth-like box but he wasn't there.

Others climbed up and began to search the stage for trapdoors or secret compartments. There was none.

'I bet he's in the truck,' someone suggested and went to check.

He wasn't there, either.

By now, Brad was holding Kate in a fierce embrace. 'I'm sorry,' he whispered. 'I'm so sorry.'

'It's all right,' she said.

'I always loved you, only I—'

'I know.'

He began to cry.

Even as she held him, Kate knew that the bitterness had gone from Brad. This had been the magician's gift to her, the gift of a boy who had loved her from afar. He had shown her that before magic can be real you have to believe in it. He'd put the magic back into her marriage and given her another chance at happiness. She wanted to thank him for that. She wanted to tell him she remembered who he was. She wanted to talk to him about so many things. But she never got the chance because he didn't reappear that evening.

And later that night when, in the middle of their lovemaking, she looked up and saw the look of compassion and deep understanding in Brad's emerald-green eyes, she understood why Mahmoud the Magnificent would never be seen again.

GROWING OLD WITH RICHARD

———

The narrow road twisted like a pretzel through the heavily wooded valley. Even on a dry day the deceptive bends had to be negotiated carefully; on a night like tonight — with a cyclone lashing in from the northeast — the going was treacherous.

The driver of the Jaguar travelled this same stretch of road every day, but for all he could see in tonight's conditions he might as well have been blindfolded. The Jag's headlights groped valiantly through the downpour, the bright beams bouncing off saturated tree trunks, tangled lantana, angry little waterfalls and a luminous yellow sign that warned that the road was slippery when wet.

The driver noticed none of this — he had other things

on his mind. Despite the conditions, he drove as if pursued by the devil.

Down near the bottom of the valley, what was usually a small spring-fed stream that trickled tamely through a drain under the road had swollen into a raging torrent that spewed menacingly out across the bitumen on the elbow of a sharp bend. At the speed it was travelling, the Jaguar had no chance: its rear end drifted, the driver overcorrected, the car began to roll.

For a few sickening seconds the valley was filled with the sound of tortured metal and breaking glass. Then there was only the relentless hammering of the rain and the muffled moans of a dying man.

Astrid turned away from the window. *God, what an awful night!* She checked her watch. Richard said he had a few house calls to make after golf and he'd be back by six thirty — it was now ten past seven. She shook her head and smiled a long-suffering smile — running late seemed to be an occupational habit with her husband. If anything, he was getting worse. He never seemed to get anywhere on time these days, especially in the evenings. She'd lost count of how many dinner parties they'd arrived at late, flustered and apologetic; or how many cinemas they'd stumbled into ten minutes after the movie had commenced; and as for church ...

He was never late for golf, though; his tee-off time was sacrosanct.

Sighing with resignation, she absent-mindedly wiped her already dry hands on her apron and made her way back into the kitchen where she turned on the oven light and peered in through the eye-level glass door to check the roast. It was a huge leg of pork, far too big for just the two of them. After a lifetime of buying food for a family, she still hadn't adjusted to buying for just two. Tonight, however, her oversight had given her an ideal excuse to invite the family around for dinner. She was looking forward to that; she missed them.

For years she had looked forward to nothing so much as the day that Emma and Johnny would leave home and she and Richard would be alone again. Now that time had come, she didn't like it at all. She was unprepared for — what was it Emma called it? — her *space*. For the first time in longer than she could remember, she was free to do what she liked, when she liked. She had choices. The trouble was, she didn't know what to do with them. Her days, once so full, were now depressingly empty. She even began to pine for the tiresome, menial, child-minding tasks she had loathed for years. As much as she had moaned about them at the time, she now discovered, to her surprise, that they were the very things that let her know she was needed. Now that she no longer had to do these things for her family, she no longer felt needed. It was a stupid reaction, she knew that, and everyone assured her the feeling would pass; but Johnny had been gone three years now and Emma nearly two, and she still felt the same.

For a time, a kind of madness had come over her — she began moving furniture around for no reason; she dusted and polished until the house positively gleamed; she rearranged the bookshelves — first in alphabetical order, then by category, finally by author; she spent hours cooking banquet-like four-course meals, which she produced ceremoniously every night, until Richard begged her to stop before she killed them both.

Then, in a complete turnaround, she lapsed into lethargy, a period of sloth when she did little except consume endless cups of tea and stacks of popular romance novels. The garden and the house fell into disarray and takeaway meals became the norm rather than the exception. She even developed a mild addiction to daytime television.

Eventually, recognising — with not a little horror — that soap operas now offered more entertainment than her own life, she decided that something had to be done. But what? The children had given her focus; they were her work, her hobby, her passion. Even now whenever she walked past their bedrooms she half expected to find Johnny strewn across his bed like the aftermath of a hurricane, or Emma — neat and tidy Emma — seated at her desk looking out over the garden and tapping away happily at her computer. But those days were gone. For ever. Her children had claimed their independence and in doing so given back hers. But this newfound freedom terrified her. She felt as though she had been abandoned in a wide-open unfamiliar space with no fences, no boundaries, no roads, no maps — only endless horizons and limitless possibilities.

She had never felt so alone.

'Alone, nonsense, what am I, Scotch mist?' Richard said as he bent intently over the putt he was lining up on the living room carpet.

'You know what I mean.'

'Do I?' he said, as the ball rolled towards the little machine that would return it to him if his putt found its mark.

'Over twenty years, Rick, and now ...'

'Peace and quiet!' Richard said and grunted triumphantly as the ball popped back towards him.

'I don't think I'm cut out for so much peace and quiet.'

'You'll get used to it. You'll find plenty to do.'

She made no reply.

He came and sat on the arm of the couch beside her and began tapping the side of his worn carpet slipper with the putter.

She sighed. 'It's okay for you, you've got your work. And your golf.'

'Perhaps you should join a club. What about bowls?'

'Don't be silly. I'm not *that* old.'

'Lots of people play bowls, not just old people. You never know, you might like it.'

'I might, but that's not the point. I need more than that. I can't spend the rest of my life playing bowls.' She swivelled slightly to face him. 'Perhaps I should get a job.'

'What on earth for? We don't need the money.'

'It's not about the money.'

Richard prided himself on being a modern man: he was, for instance, an active and vocal supporter of equal pay for women long before it became fashionable; however, in his heart, he far preferred having Astrid at home doing the wife and mother things that seemed so wrong to many, yet so right to him. It was undeniably a sexist attitude, but one he was perfectly comfortable with. Whereas, the thought of coming home to an empty house and having to prepare meals and do his own washing and cleaning, while Astrid went in pursuit of a career, gave him no comfort at all.

'What kind of job?' he asked.

'I don't know. Anything. I'm not looking for a career — it's a bit late for that — just something to beat the boredom.'

'A lot of jobs *are* boring.'

'Well, I can't mope around here and prune roses for the rest of my life. I'll go batty.'

The tone in her voice told him that the matter required serious consideration, but it was too large a subject to deal with at this late hour. He decided to sleep on it and to try to make some worthwhile suggestions in the morning. With any luck she would have forgotten about it by then.

'You'll be all right, you'll think of something, you'll see,' he said kissing her fondly on the top of the head.

With that he went back to his putting machine, leaving her to gaze wistfully at the empty armchair that used to be Johnny's favourite.

Astrid turned the potatoes and closed the oven door; Carlos would make his famous gravy later — he could cook anything, that boy.

Richard had been furious when Emma first told them she was going to live with Carlos. He'd never denied his daughter anything, but when he discovered that she was going to live — in sin — with a penniless Filipino law student, he had protested vehemently. There was nothing racial in this, simply a father's natural reluctance to accept that his daughter could give herself so completely to any man — let alone one who was far too good-looking to be trusted.

On the other hand, Richard hadn't said a thing when Johnny had moved in with Sarah, a woman who was nearly ten years older than him.

It was Astrid who'd been upset about this.

In the end there was nothing they could do about either relationship. Sometimes, the best way to hold on to your children is to let them go, and as hard as it had been, that's what they had done.

In time, they had become reasonably accustomed to

their de facto in-laws; in fact, Carlos had quite endeared himself to them.

Astrid still had her doubts about Sarah, though.

They were all coming for dinner tonight. With any luck they would stay the night. Lord knows there was enough room. The house was far too big for two. They talked about moving, getting something smaller, an apartment or a townhouse, but the family home was filled with fond memories, and Astrid had developed a deep and meaningful relationship with every tree and shrub in the garden. Besides, there were the future grandchildren to consider — they would need a big house when they came to stay.

She smiled to herself as she made her way into the living room. It seemed like only yesterday that she had been falling madly, irresponsibly in love with a lanky medical student named Richard Howarth; now, here she was, wrapped warmly in a boring woollen cardigan, kneeling carefully on her less than flexible knees, stoking the fire and dreaming about the visits of her as yet unborn grandchildren.

She found a long grey hair on the hearth and tossed it into the fire; hers or Richard's? It was getting hard to tell.

Suddenly, a flash of lightning lit up the room. A deafening crack of thunder followed seconds later. The centre of the storm was moving closer. She shivered, threw another piece of wood on the fire and rocked back to sit on the rug and stare vacantly into the flames.

She worried about Richard driving in the rain — he was getting so inattentive in his old age. Lately, she'd noticed a few dents and scratches in the Jag, which he hadn't said anything about. Then again, he wouldn't — he was very proud of his driving record. 'Forty years and not one prang!' he'd boast proudly, especially to Johnny, who at twenty-two had already had two accidents in his Kombi — although, to be fair, one wasn't his fault.

There was another loud crack in the heavens and the house was plunged into blackness. *Damn!*

Luckily, she was cooking with gas; the dinner wouldn't be ruined.

When her eyes grew accustomed to the darkness, she went in search of candles.

The traffic was backed up for half a mile either side of the accident. As always, a gang of tow trucks had arrived out of nowhere, like vultures ready to fight to the death over the metallic carrion. Tonight they would feast. There had already been a secondary five-car pile-up involving the first few cars that had tried to avoid the Jag lying on its back in the middle of the road. The conditions made sudden braking impossible. More accidents were inevitable. The tow truck drivers were literally licking their lips.

The police weren't so happy. Handling a situation like this was difficult at any time; on a night like this, it was hell. Thankfully, no one had been seriously hurt in the secondary accidents, so there was no need to call in more than one ambulance. The driver of the Jag hadn't been so lucky.

One of the policemen held the licence he'd found in the dead driver's wallet. He hated this part of the job. He read the details over the car radio. Let some other poor bastard break the news to the family; he was going to be up half the night trying to sort out the chaos. What a shit of a night to die.

'No one's home,' said Emma in dismay as they pulled up outside the house.

'No, it's just a power failure,' Carlos said.

'How can you tell?'

'The streetlights are out.'

'Lightning, probably,' said Johnny.

'There's Astrid.' Sarah pointed at the torch-bearing shape walking down the front path towards them.

Astrid was hunched under an umbrella and as she got closer they could see she was carrying two more.

Trust Mum to have spare umbrellas, Emma thought as she leapt out of the car and splashed up the path to embrace her mother.

'Silly girl, you'll get soaked!' Astrid chided.

'Oh, stop panicking,' Emma said as she planted a kiss on her mother's forehead. She was a lot taller than Astrid, more like her father — only in height, thankfully; she hadn't inherited the bumbling, awkward mannerisms that were adorable in Richard but would have been quite unfortunate in a young lady.

Emma took one of the umbrellas, opened it, and made her way back to the car. Astrid followed.

'Where's the Kombi?' Astrid asked when she saw Johnny and Sarah in the car — she had to speak loudly to be heard over the hammering of the rain on the umbrellas.

'Service station,' Emma shouted.

'Not another accident?'

'Give me a break, Mum,' Johnny said as he got out of the car, took the other umbrella, and held it over the door as Sarah climbed out. 'I'm having a head gasket replaced, that's all.'

'Oh, that's all right then,' Astrid smiled, seeming happier even though she had no idea what a head gasket was. 'Hello, Sarah, how are you?' she said as Sarah joined them.

'Fine, thank you.'

'Good to see you, dear,' Astrid said and kissed her quickly on the cheek. It was a polite greeting, but not exactly warm. Astrid still couldn't understand why a thirty-eight-year-old woman would choose to live with a boy nearly twelve years her junior. The only possible reason she could think of made her very uncomfortable. 'Come along, let's get you all inside before you catch your death,' she said adopting a mother's tone.

'Yes, Mommy,' teased Carlos, who was now sharing an umbrella with Emma. He had an intriguing accent, sort of

American-Asian. All Filipinos spoke this way, he'd told them, largely the result of the American television shows they grow up with — God help them.

While she may have had reservations about Sarah, Astrid openly adored Carlos. She often found herself thinking what beautiful children he and Emma would have. She was definitely warming to the whole idea of being a grandparent — although it was rather premature; there had been no mention of marriage from either couple, let alone children. Still, one could always dream.

'Where's Dad?' Johnny asked when they were in the candlelit living room drying themselves before the fire.

'He had a few house calls to make after golf,' Astrid explained. 'I expected him home around six thirty. But, you know your father, once he gets involved in something, he tends to lose track of time.'

'Maybe he tried to call,' Emma suggested.

'Is the phone working?' Carlos asked.

'I never thought to check,' Astrid said. 'Wouldn't it be out because of the power failure?'

'Not necessarily, unless the lightning struck a pole nearby, or something like that.'

'I heard it wasn't a good idea to use a telephone during a thunderstorm,' Sarah said. 'I'm not sure why.'

'But if your father can't get through ...' Astrid worried.

'I'll check,' Johnny grunted. He was back within seconds. 'Dead as a dodo.'

'There, that it explains it,' Emma said.

'I wish he'd use his mobile,' Astrid said to no one in particular. 'I don't even know why he bothers having one, he never turns it on.'

'It's his little rebellion,' Emma said. 'Says he did just fine for years without one and can't see why it's necessary now.'

'The last of the Luddites,' Johnny laughed.

'Lud whats?' Sarah asked.

While Johnny expounded on the little he knew about Luddites, Astrid's gaze strayed to a recent photograph of Richard that sat on the china cabinet among all the other gilt-framed memories. Even though the wear and tear of the years had etched creases into his face, she could still see the handsome, loose-limbed youth who had changed her life. Now he was as much a part of her as she was of him, and she knew that without him she would be less than whole. A chill passed through her. She gathered the cardigan tighter around her shoulders.

'I hope they get the phones fixed soon,' she said softly. 'Your father will worry if his patients can't get through.'

Emma and Johnny looked at each other and smiled — they knew it wasn't the patients their mother was worried about.

'I'm sure they'll have the phones fixed in no time,' Emma assured her.

'No worries,' Johnny agreed.

Eventually, at Astrid's insistence, they ate without Richard. Carlos wanted to go and look for him but Astrid talked him out of it. She didn't know where to tell him to start looking. 'A few house calls' was all Richard had said. He never said with whom — he never did.

Later, when the last of the apple pie had been demolished and there was still no word from him, they were all beginning to worry openly.

He was now nearly three hours overdue.

'Perhaps we should check the hospitals,' Emma suggested.

'Don't even *say* that!' Astrid said sharply.

'I mean, maybe there was an emergency and he had to take one of his patients there,' Emma explained, quickly.

Astrid was embarrassed by her own over-reaction. 'Oh, sorry, how stupid of me. I'm fairly sure he'd be at North Shore if that were the case.'

'Maybe I should go and check?' Carlos offered, not really relishing the thought of such a mission in the atrocious conditions.

'No, if he's had to go to the hospital, it would have to be something really important and he wouldn't want to be disturbed. I honestly don't think we should worry. He's been late before — there's always a good reason,' Astrid said bravely.

'Yes, but three hours ...' Emma said.

Hearing the dangerously contagious sound of panic in his sister's voice, Johnny cut in quickly. 'I'm sure you're right, Mum, he'll be caught up in something important.'

A car came hissing slowly down the sodden street. Astrid got up quickly, went to the window and drew back the curtains. Her shoulders slumped as the car drove on by. She continued staring out at the relentless downpour — if anything, it was heavier now.

'C'mon, Johnny, let's you and I do the dishes,' Sarah said, in an effort to change the subject.

Astrid turned from the window. 'No, leave them. I'll put them in the dishwasher.'

'Nonsense, there's no power, remember?' Sarah said, rising to her feet. 'You sit down and relax. We'll do the dishes and make coff—'

'I said *leave them!*'

Sarah sat back down, plainly shocked.

Emma went to her mother. 'Mum?'

Astrid turned to Sarah. 'I'm sorry, I ...'

'It's all right,' Sarah said, drily.

Astrid went across to her. 'Sarah ...'

'It's all right, really,' Sarah said, but continued to stare stonily at her empty plate.

Johnny's heart went out to them; he understood what was happening, but it was something they had to work out for themselves.

Astrid put a comforting hand on Sarah's shoulder. 'Come on, I'll help you make coffee. We'll let the others go and laze around the fire.'

'Top idea,' Johnny agreed and bolted from the room before the idea of him doing the dishes raised its ugly head again.

Carlos and Emma followed discreetly.

For a while Sarah and Astrid managed to avoid each other in the large kitchen. Astrid kept busy stacking things in the lifeless dishwasher, while Sarah put a pot of water on the stove and ground coffee beans.

Soon the kitchen was tidy and there was nothing for them to do but sit and wait for the water to boil.

Sarah sat on one side of the kitchen table fiddling with the cups she had stacked on a tray along with milk, sugar and a plate of after-dinner mints.

Astrid sat opposite, studying her.

Sarah was a fine-looking woman with high cheekbones, intelligent hazel eyes, and thick, dark, shoulder-length hair framing an attractive, open face. She wore little make-up — just a hint around the eyes and a touch of lipstick. Her beauty was natural, she would age well — not that she was any spring chicken now. And perhaps because of her age there was an air of maturity about her — a confidence. Perhaps it was her confidence that Astrid found so threatening. Here was a woman who was more than capable of looking after her son, and there was no doubt he needed looking after. But why would any woman choose to live with a boy so much younger than her in every way? Why didn't she have a man more her own age? *What was wrong with her?*

Sarah spoke first. 'You're worried about him, aren't you?'

'Richard? Yes, of course I am.'

'No ... well ... yes, of course you're worried about

Richard. What I meant was ... you're worried about Johnny, aren't you?'

'Not really, it's just ...'

'I love him, you know.'

'Are you sure?'

'I'm sure.'

'Have you ever actually *thought* about what you're doing?'

'Of course I have.'

'Well, I can't see why—'

'You don't see why a woman my age would want to get involved with someone so much younger.'

'Exactly. If you want to know the truth, I think it's irresponsible.'

'And futile?'

'That, too.'

Sarah sighed. It wasn't easy explaining what she felt — even to herself. Usually she didn't try, but this was Johnny's mother. 'Do you have any idea what kind of pressure people put on a woman my age who doesn't even have a steady boyfriend, let alone a husband?'

'You're not going to tell me you're with Johnny because of the pressure other people put on you?' Astrid said aghast.

'On the contrary, what they thought didn't bother me at all. I'd simply explain, truthfully, that staying unattached was my choice, that there were things I wanted to do, places I had to see, and long-term commitments, particularly marriage, just didn't fit into my plans.'

'What about children?'

'You see — you're doing it, too. That's exactly what people always say. They just can't seem to accept that a woman might not want a family. It's okay for a man to want to be footloose and family free, but if a woman chooses to do that, she's considered to be some kind of freak.'

'You don't want children?'

'I didn't say that.'

'Well — do you?'

'I don't know.'

'What do you mean, *you don't know*?'

'Sometimes I do, sometimes I don't. I'm just not sure, that's all. And I want to be very sure.'

'You'd better make up your mind soon.'

'I don't need you to tell me that.'

'No, I'm sorry, I didn't mean to ... it's just that Johnny's so young—'

'And soon I'll be too old?'

Astrid looked down at her hands. 'It's possible. There are risks ...'

'Yes, I know, that's something I'll have to deal with if it ever arises.'

'*If*?'

'Yes, *if*.' Sarah waited for Astrid to look up at her. When she resumed, her voice was softer, almost sad. 'You're assuming too much, Astrid. You think I'm in control of all this, but I'm not. I love Johnny, that's all. It's good old-fashioned, uncomplicated, irrational love. Stupid, I know, and often embarrassing as well, but it's love for all that. The problem is, I'm not sure it will be enough.'

'I don't understand ...'

'I'm not sure that it will be enough for marriage, babies, a lifetime together. Do you really think you're the only one who worries about our age difference? Hell, I live with it every day.'

'Johnny says he loves you.'

'Of course he says he loves me — and he does ... for now. But as you're well aware, he's only a boy. You and I know that things can change over time. Stuff happens. Who knows where we'll be in a few years' time? When he's thirty-five, I'll be nearly fifty — nature's not all that kind to fifty-year-old women. Even now my body's not what it used to be — my tits are already beginning to sag a bit.'

'Too much information.'

'Why? Sex is what it's all about, isn't it? Be honest, you think I seduced Johnny, don't you? A shameless old cougar having her last fling with a bit of young stuff.'

'Certainly not. I've never thought anything of the kind.'

'Tell the truth, Astrid.'

Astrid's blush betrayed her.

'Don't be embarrassed,' Sarah said. 'I admit sex is part of it — it wouldn't be much of a relationship without it, would it? But there's a lot more to it than that. For the first time in my life I know what 'in sickness and in health, for richer, for poorer' and all that stuff really means. It's how I feel when I'm with Johnny. And it's *wonderful*. And do you know what's the best thing? He makes me laugh. Sounds silly, I know, but he can always make me laugh and that's a big part of what we have.'

Astrid smiled knowingly.

'Everyone tells me it can't last,' Sarah continued. 'And I'm sure they're right. I don't think Johnny's ever going to ask me to marry him. To be perfectly honest, I'm not even sure I'd accept if he did. I'm not certain it would be the right thing for either of us. But, right now, I'm the happiest I've ever been in my life. It may be the only chance I'll ever have to be this happy. So I'm going to hold on to it for as long as I can. When it's over, it will be over, but it will *never* be wrong.'

Astrid understood — Sarah was right, it's important to make the most of the happy times, God knows they can be all too short. She tried to imagine life without Richard — life without laughter — she couldn't. They had been lucky their love had endured where many had failed. The original heat of their youthful passion may have gone, but in its place had grown a respect, a certainty — a good, honest, compassionate love. They had never had to suffer the mind-sapping deceit and bitterness that had savaged the marriages of so many of their friends. The only threat stalking them was the unrelenting march of time. And even with that, there was the comfort of knowing you had someone to grow old with. She was growing old with Richard and on the whole the prospect didn't seem too awful.

For the first time in a very long time she didn't feel confused, alone or unwanted. She wanted to tell Richard. He would understand and he would be glad. But where on earth was he?

She reached out and took Sarah's hand for the comfort it gave them both. The water boiled unnoticed.

A police car crawled slowly down the street, a torch beam probing out of the passenger window searching for street numbers in the impossible light. It was amazing how few homes had their street numbers displayed; frustrating as hell when you were trying to find a particular address in a hurry.

As he played the torch beam over the unnumbered letterboxes, Sergeant Jim Lawrence was trying to ignore the icy lump in his stomach. He hated doing what he was about to do, but you couldn't just phone — such things had to be done in person.

The lights on the street began to flicker and houses blazed back to life all around them.

'Ah, a little light on the subject,' mumbled Jurd, the pudding-faced constable who was driving.

A quick glance at the few letterbox numbers they could see told them they were at the wrong end of the street but were headed in the right direction. They continued driving at the same deliberate speed; they were in no hurry.

Eventually, they stopped in front of a large Federation-style home that glowed invitingly through the downpour.

'Bloody millionaires,' Jurd said, eyeing the house enviously.

'Not exactly on the breadline, that's for sure,' Sergeant Lawrence agreed. He could never afford a place like this, but he was happy enough with his humble abode. Besides, a huge home and money in the bank is no guarantee of happiness. Appearances can be very deceiving. What you see isn't necessarily what you get. Tonight was another case in point. Jesus, he hated having to wade through the crap of other people's lives.

He noticed a middle-aged woman looking anxiously out of the window, probably the wife. He saw her hunch over as she recognised the police car. Someone put his or her arms around her. Sergeant Lawrence silently thanked God she had somebody with her. It was going to be hard enough breaking the news of the doctor's death; how on earth was he going to tell them about the other body in the back seat — the bruised and naked little girl, with her thin helpless hands bound together by surgical tape?

Astrid sold the house, moved to the Gold Coast and joined a bowling club. Johnny swears he will quit drinking by Christmas. If he does, there's a chance Sarah will come back to him. Emma married Carlos and they are very much in love. They have a son. They did not name him Richard.

The fat man's breath rattled savagely in his throat as he watched the Jaguar slide to a halt and the girl scramble sobbing into it. He smashed his fist into the trunk of the tree that hid him from the road. The bitch! If he hadn't slipped over in the mud she would never have escaped. He cursed aloud as the car's tail-lights were swallowed by the darkness. He pulled the roll of surgical tape from his pocket and hurled it away in fury. His hand hurt. Looking down, he saw that it was bleeding. Despite the cold he was sweating freely. He wiped the torn dress across his forehead and smelled the scent of her. It filled his head with pictures of lacy-edged sheets, fluffy pillows and little white flowers on pink wallpaper. He thought of his mother. He was late for his dinner and covered in mud — she would be furious. He hated to make Mummy angry. He would need to think of a really good excuse.

A BOOK FOR CHARLOTTE

The cruise had been a bad idea from the start. He should have put up more of a fight, argued more convincingly or offered the guys a more attractive alternative. Then again, what other holiday would offer the prospect of hundreds of young women milling about in various states of willingness in a holiday resort from which there was no escape? For this, a cruise ship was without parallel.

'You can't miss,' was the general consensus.

And for hormone-fuelled rugby players not monumentally successful in their endless pursuit of the fairer sex in their day-to-day lives, this delusional carrot was enough to get them to choose a ten days/nine nights South Pacific cruise on the good ship *Fairport* for their end-of-season getaway.

However, for Ben the entire trip been excruciating. His

hormones were in fine working order, but unlike some of his team, he hadn't left his standards on shore. What for them had been a dream trip had, for him, been a nightmare. Days blurred by cold beer and hot sun spent swapping inanities with people too drunk to care. And night after night being kicked out of his cabin by one or other of the three cohorts he shared with who seemed determined to establish who could have sex with the most women in one cruise. A contest within which, apparently, the quality of the conquest was of no consequence.

Even the brief island stopovers that interrupted the cruise had offered little respite: lost hours in tawdry bars packed with sweaty bodies pulsing to Filipino covers of American pop songs, relentless touts in glaring street markets flogging not-so-cheap souvenirs, and dull memories of glass-bottomed boats and parades of kaleidoscopic fish streaming over coral reefs that had seen better days. He couldn't remember being with a single sober soul for days apart from crew members and the occasional older couple that appeared to have booked onto the cruise by mistake and wore looks of bewilderment bordering on terror. He knew how they felt. This cruise had revealed things about some of his friends and the rites of seagoing passage he didn't want to think about and would not be spoken of hereafter. 'What goes on tour stays on tour,' he'd heard people say; now he understood what they meant. In years to come, when many of these currently morally destitute young men and women were married and living in neat brick homes in tree-lined suburbs, he was pretty sure they wouldn't want details of this time of madness dragged into the embarrassing light of day.

He imagined some North Shore mother with her six-year-old son strolling down a supermarket aisle sometime in the future gradually becoming aware of two men smiling at her.

'Patricia?' one of them will say, the light of recognition dawning on his face.

'It is you, isn't it?' the other will ask, the heavier of the two, the one they'd called Davo.

Her face will tell them she remembers, her eyes will say she wants to forget.

'Who're they?' her son will whisper as he edges to safety behind her legs.

'Did Mummy ever tell you about the night she had sex with two men at the same time?' she'll begin.

No, Ben decided, breaking out of his reverie, it's not something you talk about after the event.

And tonight, the last night of the cruise, with disembarkation in Sydney expected around noon the next day, Ben was glad it was almost all over.

He was drowning at sea in a way he could never have imagined possible. He needed air.

Gasping like a fish on sand, he pushed his way through the writhing throng crammed into the Sunset Deck Pool Bar and went in search of a quiet place. His friends wouldn't notice he was gone for some time and wouldn't care when they did. He needed some semblance of peace and time alone to think. He had much to do when he got back into Sydney, priorities to establish. He was slipping back into work mode and was grateful for it.

He felt a marked chill in the air as he walked along the deck. A few people hurried past him towards the festivities in various venues on the ship.

Soon he was alone on a stern deck staring back at the ship's wake as a thick sea mist rolled in across the ocean like steel wool. Swiftly and silently, the swirling vapours enveloped the ship until the distant revelry sounded as if it were from another world.

'Sad it's almost over, or glad?' came a woman's voice from behind him.

Though he was startled by the intrusion, something about the woman's voice reassured him — like an invitation to a fireside chat.

He turned.

There stood the woman he'd been hoping to meet for the entire cruise, the kind of woman he'd imagined when he dreamed of such things, perhaps even the woman he'd been searching for all his life. He'd even known her eyes would be the grey of a fog-bound ocean and would dance in delight as she looked at him.

'Glad, actually,' he said as easily as he could.

'Not your idea of heaven?' she smiled. 'So many women, so little time.'

Her hair, so black he wondered briefly if it were her natural colour, was cut in a short, chic style that framed a heart-shaped face atop what he'd later describe as a ballerina's neck. She had a timeless beauty and a quiet grace, descriptions that floated into his mind as if he were memorising them for a journal he was yet to write.

'I'd rather sip fine wine than guzzle cheap port,' he said, and instantly regretted the lame metaphor.

Undeterred by his inanity, she moved to stand nearer to him at the railing and gazed out at the pale, yellow, smudge of a full moon that was just rising over the unseen horizon.

'I hope the fog doesn't stay with us all night,' she said looking up to check if the sky might clear. 'A full moon on our last night at sea would be too perfect.'

About the only perfect thing on this trip so far, thought Ben, although at this point he was beginning to see the cruise in a whole new light.

'There's been enough lunatic behaviour on this cruise already,' he said. 'God help us if the real nutters come out with the full moon.'

She smiled and drew her wrap a little tighter.

He wondered who would think to bring a wrap on a tropical cruise. He tried to imagine her in a bikini. He couldn't. Her skin spoke of alpine mornings, not tropical afternoons. She must have stayed well protected from the sun during the cruise. And she must have been diligent about it — such flawless skin could only be the result of conscious effort.

If she was aware he was staring at her, she didn't seem to mind.

'Are you with friends?' he asked finally, feeling transparent.

'No, are you?' she said turning towards him.

He noticed she was carrying a book. He wondered why. It was too dark to read out there on the deck.

'I'm with my rugby team,' he said. 'It's our end-of-season holiday. Ten days of bad behaviour. Last year it was Bali.'

'Sounds exotic.'

'Not really; tacky bars and blinding hangovers are pretty much the same anywhere. But it was cheap, you know, after the bombing. Some people thought we were mad going there, but we worked on the lightning-doesn't-strike-in-the-same-place-twice principle.'

He waited for her to say something about the risks of going to Bali as people always did whenever he mentioned it, but she didn't.

'So what's the point of these rugby team trips?'

'Male bonding, team spirit, all of that I guess. For some guys it's just an excuse to get away from home.'

'And you?

'Habit mainly. I go because I'm expected to go. Don't want to let the team down and all that. Silly really. This will be my last one, though.'

'No more holidays with the boys?'

'No more rugby, I'm getting too old. Don't want to be one of those guys you see limping around like old men in their mid-thirties as a result of old footy injuries. Don't want to spend the rest of my life getting worn-out joints replaced. As the song says, you've got to know when to fold them.'

'The song?'

'Yeah, you know, 'The Gambler' by Kenny Rogers — 'You've got to know when to hold 'em, Know when to fold 'em.'

'Oh, like in poker,' she said as if the concept were new to her.

'Exactly,' he smiled. 'And in my case the cards are on the table and they say my best playing days are over, you can bet on that.'

Understandably unimpressed by his pun-riddled explanation, she looked back at the moon, which now hung higher in the shrouded night.

In that soft light she looked surreal and somehow unattainable. The last thought made him anxious. Having been with her for just this short space in time, he knew he didn't want to lose her. Not ever. He wanted to hold her until she would never want to leave. This feeling was irrational and completely out of character, but it had him in its grip. As if reading his mind, she began to move away from him, slowly running her free hand along the railing as she went.

He didn't want her to leave.

'So how come you're travelling alone?' he asked quickly,

and was relieved to see her pause and turn back to look at him.

'It's a long story,' she said.

'I've got all night.'

'Are you asking me to spend the night with you?' she smiled. 'We haven't even been properly introduced.'

Only then did it occur to him he didn't even know her name or she his.

'Ben,' he said. 'Ben Hanson.'

He thought about offering her his hand but she kept her distance.

'Charlotte De Vito,' she smiled.

'Charlotte De Vito ... that's Italian?'

'Originally, yes. My great-grandfather. I'm English. Well, Australian now, I suppose, since we've emigrated.'

'You don't sound Strine.'

'Strine?'

'It's slang for Australian ... a send-up of the lazy way we speak. You know, when an Aussie says Australian it can come out sounding like 'Strine'.'

'Interesting,' she said, but clearly didn't think so any more than he did now.

He could feel her slipping away. She had the look of an animal caught in a clearing trying to decide which way to escape.

In an effort to stop her imminent flight, he nodded at her book, noticing for the first time it was a hard cover, a rare sight these days.

'Good book?' he asked.

'Somerset Maugham,' she said. 'Short stories; I can usually manage to read a whole story before I fall asleep.'

It occurred to him she herself could have stepped out a Somerset Maugham novel. Her clothes, her hairstyle, her make-up and even her mannerisms belonged to another time and place. A more romantic time, one he'd quite like to be in himself if she were there with him. For now he was grateful she was here with him and not flapping about in the main ballroom at the fancy dress party she'd obviously dressed for. But why take a book to a fancy dress ball?

'It's a bit dark out here for reading,' he said stating the obvious.

'Yes,' she said looking at the book as if only now aware of its incongruity. 'I only came out for some fresh air. I must've picked it up through force of habit.'

As if to confirm this, she walked across the deck and put it down on a table that sat between two deckchairs. He took this as a sign that she wasn't planning on going anywhere soon. He tried not to let his delight show.

'So what's the long story?' he asked.

She was clearly puzzled by the question.

'The one that explains why you're travelling on this ship of fools alone,' he reminded her.

'Oh that. Perhaps it was to meet you.'

She didn't sound as if she was teasing him but he knew she had to be.

'Yeah, right,' he said. 'Really, I'd like to know.'

'My, you are the curious one,' she said and smiled in a way that could have meant she was flattered so he chose to believe that.

She looked down at her shoes, pointing one foot out and turning it one way and the other as if to see how it looked at the different angles. It was a nice shoe turned by a delicate ankle but the diversion was obviously designed to give her time to think.

He waited in silence.

Eventually, she appeared to reach a decision. 'Okay. But first ... is there a bathroom around here, do you think?'

'There's one back by the pool. Do you want me to come with you?'

'I don't think that's necessary,' she laughed. 'You stay here and keep an eye out for lunatics.'

She read the disappointment on his face.

'Don't worry. You'll get your answer,' she assured him.

'Okay,' he agreed reluctantly.

'Oh, look,' she said looking excitedly past him. 'The fog's lifting.'

He turned to look and she was right. The fog was dissipating. The moon now hung like a big, shiny gong over the gently breathing ocean, its reflection floating like a cracked yellow pathway to heaven.

'Looks like you'll get your wish,' he said. 'A full moon in a clear sky on the last night of the cruise.'

She didn't reply. He turned to see she'd already gone.

He leant against the railing and began to contemplate the unfathomable ocean.

An hour later he was still sitting in a deckchair hoping against hope she'd come back, if only for the book that still sat on the table beside him.

As the minutes ticked by, that hope faded.

He couldn't imagine she'd forgotten him. She said he'd get his answer and nothing about her indicated she was prone to fabrication. He decided she must have gotten so caught up by something or someone that she couldn't get away.

More than likely she'd been dragged into the fancy dress ball by passing revellers who wouldn't take no for an answer. He'd been subjected to a bit of that on this cruise himself. Some people just can't stand to see others alone. To them, having fun requires boisterous company; they simply can't see how you can have fun by yourself. To them, being alone means being miserable so they're determined to make sure you are never alone. And the more they drink, the more determined they become.

On a cruise ship there is no escape from such people.

He imagined her trapped in a whirlwind of costumed madness in the ballroom below. He picked up the book and set out to rescue her.

The ballroom was a sea of drunkenness. Hilariously costumed bodies whirled and twirled and intertwined and at various times arms reached out and attempted to drag him into some group or another as he passed. A man walking alone, dressed normally and carrying a book was an irresistible target.

'Whadda you meant to be, a fuckin' librarian?' slurred a passing pirate with a bushy red false beard.

'Come back to my cabin and read to me, baby,' hissed a grass-skirted blonde as she wrapped her arms around him more for balance than affection. Her breath smelled of cigarettes and vomit. He broke away from her as quickly as he could.

'Fucking poofter!' she shrieked after him as he hurried away into the crush of heaving humanity, clutching the book to his chest like a secret.

With some difficulty he managed a vigilant circuit of the ballroom before deciding Charlotte wasn't there. Perhaps she'd gone back to find him. This thought had him hurrying back to the stern of the ship, but she wasn't there either.

The wasted moon looked down on his disappointment.

He checked his watch. It was nearly 2 a.m. With some reluctance he decided to give up the search for now and look for her in the morning.

With one last wishful glance at the moon he made his way below, dodging reeling bodies in the corridors holding little hope his cabin would be empty or quiet enough to provide any form of refuge.

As he walked he was aware of the weight of the book in his hand, the substantial feel of it, unlike the paperback thrillers he tended to read when he read at all. He looked down at it and smiled at the thought of her and wondered again where she might have disappeared to — and why.

He didn't see the couple wrestling against the cabin door ahead of him.

'Well, bugger me, it's the librarian!' mocked a drunken voice.

Ben looked up to see the red-bearded pirate from the ballroom fondling the breast of the same grass-skirted blonde he had escaped from earlier. He noticed the word 'Charlie' tattooed on the pirate's forearm. The blonde looked at him briefly with unseeing eyes, then turned her attention back to the pirate.

'Please, no,' she whined, pushing his hand away from her breast.

'Fucking cockteaser!' rasped the pirate and shoved her against the door.

'Hey!' Ben shouted.

The pirate stepped back in alarm.

'You okay?' Ben said to the blonde whose eyes seemed distressingly unfocused.

'Mind your own fucking business!' snapped the pirate.

The blonde began to slide to the floor.

Being a long-time karate exponent hardened by six months of rugby training, Ben was unruffled by the pirate's drunken posturing. 'Don't do anything silly,' he said in way that gave Redbeard cause to reconsider.

He glared at Ben but made no other move.

Ben turned his attentions to the blonde, who was now

passed out on the floor. He knelt, put down the book and reached for her.

Seeing his chance, the pirate lashed out with his right foot catching Ben on the shoulder. Ben rolled with the force of the blow, sprang to his feet and adopted a balanced, crouched pose in one seamless movement.

The speed and agility of the move seemed to shock the pirate into immobility. He made no attempt to continue his attack. Instead his eyes flicked down to a small plastic bottle that had fallen out of his pocket. If he thought about picking it up, the look Ben gave him changed his mind.

He ran.

'Yo ho ho, Redbeard, you gutless bastard,' Ben muttered under his breath.

He picked up the plastic bottle. The label said Rohypnol but it appeared to contain a variety of pills. He assumed they'd all be sedatives of some kind. He'd heard stories of such predators but this was the first time he'd actually witnessed one at work. He put the bottle in his pocket.

'You've just had a lucky escape,' he grunted as he hoisted the blonde to her feet.

'Lucky me,' she murmured with a half smile but didn't open her eyes.

At that point the cabin door opened and a slightly podgy, bespectacled young woman with sleep-tossed hair peeked nervously out. When she saw the unconscious blonde in Ben's arms, her fear vanished.

'My God, Mimi!' she said throwing open the door and glaring at Ben. 'What have you done to her? You bastard!'

Although diminutive in stature, she fearlessly wrested the blonde out of his arms.

'Get your grubby hands off her,' she snapped as she struggled back into the cabin with her comatose friend and laid her gently on a bunk. Her voice softened. 'Mimi baby, how many times have I told you?'

Ben closed the door, picked up the book and went on his way knowing he'd now be looking for the tattooed pirate in the morning as well as the mysterious Miss De Vito.

His cabin mates weren't exactly encouraging.

'Piece of cake, not! There were only about forty-five pirates at the fancy dress ball tonight and half of them were Redbeards,' said Jacko sarcastically. A stroppy, pigeon-toed halfback, he was more distressed by his inability to score on the last night of the cruise than by Ben's harmless little fracas.

'Did you actually see the bottle fall out of his pocket?' asked 'Pedders' Petrovic, a shambolic front rower and ever the law student. 'Could you prove he gave any pills to her? I mean you yourself said you'd seen her earlier and she was already pissed.'

'He's an evil bastard,' Ben insisted without answering the question.

'No argument there, mate,' Jacko said. 'But trying to find the prick before we get off this barge in the morning, well

...' He shrugged at what he saw as the patent futility of the task. 'And I bet the blonde won't remember too much about what went on — even if she wanted to. Far better to use your energy looking for this Charlotte sheila if you ask me.'

'No one's asking you, Jacko,' Pedders said.

'The tattoo should be easy to spot,' Ben said.

'If he's wearing a T-shirt and walking around with his arm stuck in the air,' Jacko countered.

'So tell us about this chick,' Pedders said trying to change the subject.

'Chick is hardly the word I'd use,' Ben said.

'Goddess then,' Pedders offered.

'She have nice tits?' asked Jacko, desperately seeking some kind of sexual gratification for the night, albeit vicariously.

'She had nice everything,' Ben said. 'Buggered if I know how I didn't spot her before last night.'

'Maybe she was shacked up in her cabin shagging some other lucky bastard for ten days,' Jacko teased.

'And nine nights,' Pedders added.

'Very funny,' Ben said. 'You're just jealous.'

'Jealous of what?' Jacko scoffed. 'Thirty minutes of moonstruck conversation you had with some mysterious woman who fucks off and leaves you without so much as a good night and good luck. It's like a bloody fishing story, mate ... the one that got away.'

Pedders, who'd opened the book Ben had left lying on his bunk, looked up smiling. 'Maybe not,' he said. 'Look.'

He held the book up for them to see. On the inside cover, written in a neat hand in fountain pen, were the words:

Charlotte De Vito
14 Granville Parade
Leichardt
Sydney, NSW, Australia

Ben could hardly contain his delight.

'Didn't leave her mobile number,' Jacko said. 'Bitch is playing hard to get.'

'Get fucked, Jacko,' they chorused.

'I tried boys, believe me I tried.'

Everyone laughed, none louder than Ben.

The next morning neither Charlotte De Vito nor the tattooed pirate could be found. Ben was up, packed and out looking by sunrise. He searched among the early-morning risers and late-night stragglers, scoured the sleepy breakfast buffet queues, scouted every gathering place on the ship and scanned every female face on deck as the ship sailed through the heads into Sydney Harbour. Charlotte was nowhere to be seen and the pirate deviate could have been any one of scores of young men wandering the ship in long-sleeved garments.

Somewhat surprisingly, the ship's staff had been uncooperative when he'd asked for Charlotte's cabin number. They stonewalled him, insisting there was no passenger called De Vito, and despite his pleading and protestation would not page her on the ship's PA. Clearly, they suspected his intentions were less than honourable. It occurred to Ben she might have been a crew member herself. Part of the entertainment, one of the domestic staff — a kitchenhand or something; but if any of the crew knew of a De Vito among them, they weren't telling him.

Considering the possibilities and the limited time he had to find her before they disembarked, he decided the search was folly. The important thing was he had her address. He'd even begun to consider the possibility that was the reason she'd left the book behind. Perhaps it had been a deliberate lure.

His heart felt weird when he thought this, but it was a good kind of weird.

Hours later as they disbanded outside customs, despite the constant sledging of his team-mates — who by now had all heard varying versions of the Ben-meets-goddess-on-moonlit-deck scenario — nothing could suppress the 'I know something you don't' smile that ruled his face.

He'd been destined to meet this woman, he just knew it.

And he began to believe there might just be a God.

Despite his best intentions, it was two weeks before he finally found time to set out for Leichhardt in search of Charlotte De Vito. He'd found her phone number in the book and called a few times, but there'd been no reply and, surprisingly, no answering machine. Unlike Ben and everyone else he knew, Charlotte, apparently, wasn't a slave to the inescapable reach of modern-day communication devices. He'd thought, momentarily, about posting her the book, but since returning it was hardly his main agenda, he quickly dispensed with that idea.

So late one perfect, shiny, Saturday afternoon, he found himself driving across town with the book and an explanatory note parcelled up on the back seat of his old Mercedes. If she was home, he'd give it to her in person; if not, he'd leave it in her letterbox. Every part of him hoped she'd be home.

She was.

The very instant he turned into her street, he saw her standing beside a battered furniture removal truck that was parked in front of a large, ivy-covered, terraced home. She was casually clad in a pale-turquoise sweater and jeans and wore the slight disarray of physical effort. She'd obviously been lifting and shifting as much as she'd been issuing directions, which she was doing now to two bouncer-sized Maori men who gave her their full attention while cradling a chest of drawers as if it were a fruit basket.

If anything, she was more attractive in this casual state than she had been when costumed, moonlit and somehow untouchable on the night they'd met. In the soft afternoon light of this suburban street, she looked more real, more desirable, more attainable.

His heart pounded as he parked the car. Just caught her, he thought. She must be moving. Lucky I came today.

He retrieved the book from the back seat and checked himself in the rear-view mirror. He was having a bad hair day but it was too late to turn back.

By the time he'd crossed the street and walked around the truck, the removalists had disappeared and Charlotte was alone on the footpath. She was facing away from him. He was about to say something to get her attention when he heard the sound of a car racing up the street and braking hard.

A car door slammed and a tall, angry, young man strode quickly around the truck towards Charlotte, grabbed her by the shoulders and twisted her around to face him.

'What the fuck do you think you're doing?' he demanded.

The intruder had movie-star looks but his glare was malevolent.

Charlotte seemed rattled but unafraid. 'Go away, Trent.'

The strength in her voice seemed to weaken her aggressor. His voice took on a slight pleading tone. 'I told you she meant nothing to me, baby.'

'Nor did the last one and I'm sure the next won't either.'

'It won't happen again, I swear,' he said shaking her.

'Let go,' she said firmly. 'You're hurting me.'

Ben cleared his throat.

They looked at him.

Charlotte didn't appear to recognise him.

Trent looked quizzical. 'Got a problem?' he snapped.

'Don't like men who push women around?' Ben said offhandedly while looking at Charlotte, searching for some sign of recognition. There was none.

'And I don't like nosy bastards who can't mind their own fucking business,' Trent grunted, but he took his hands off Charlotte.

Something about his tone sounded familiar. Ben looked at him again and immediately noticed a familiar tattoo poking out from under his right sleeve: Charlie ... for Charlotte, of course! This prick had to be the red-bearded pirate from the ship. If so, this was very much his business.

'This is my business,' he said. 'I'm a professional arsehole removalist. No arsehole too big or small. Do you need help removing this arsehole, Miss?'

A smile played at Charlotte's lips but still no sign that she knew who he was.

Trent stepped forward like a gunfighter. He was taller and heavier than Ben and far more sober than when they'd last met.

Ben stood his ground.

Trent stayed out of reach.

'Do I know you?' he said, scrunching his brow like a puppy wary of a kitten.

'Does the name Rory O'Hypnol ring a bell?' Ben said

brightly. 'We met on the *Fairport* a couple of weeks back. On the night of drunken grass skirts.'

Trent's brow puckered momentarily as he struggled with the cryptic references, then in a flash he knew. He wilted slightly and looked nervously at Charlotte, who still had her eyes fixed on Ben.

'*Fairport*. The ship?' she said slowly.

Ben smiled his best smile. 'Yes, ten excruciating days of tropical island torture,' he said, thinking surely she'd remember him now.

Instead she looked at Trent. 'I heard you went on a cruise. Was that it?'

Realising he'd lost the initiative, Trent turned back to Charlotte.

'Baby, ...'

Her response was curt. 'Don't 'Baby' me, Trent. It's over.'

If it was over, she didn't seem upset about it.

'And it's been over for months,' she continued. 'You know that. You shouldn't even be here.'

'Oh, don't tell me you're going to wave the bloody AVO in my face!' Trent almost spat.

That got Ben's attention. He quietly moved closer to Charlotte. She glanced at him curiously but didn't move away.

Trent did.

'I didn't want to get the police involved,' she said. 'You gave me no choice.'

'Yeah, right,' Trent muttered but began to back away.

Ben looked at her as though tacitly asking permission to hurt Trent.

She ignored him and watched as Trent stalked back to his car, slammed the door, raced the engine then peeled away down the street in a cloud of smoking rubber. She kept staring after him long after he was gone.

Ben fingered the wrapping of the parcel.

Eventually, reacting to the noise of his fiddling, she looked at the parcel and noticed her name on it. Before she could say anything the Kiwi removalists reappeared.

'What the hill was thet all about?' said the older of the two.

'Pruck!' said the other.

'Shoulda dropped him, bro,' said the first, looking at Ben.

'Nah, I reckon she could have taken him out herself,' Ben smiled.

The Maoris laughed.

'You boys finished?' Charlotte said bringing them back to the business at hand.

'Yep. Those drawers are un the main bidroom where you sed,' said the older man. 'Enything ulse need doing?'

'No, we're done,' Charlotte said. 'Give or take a few days of unpacking.'

She produced a folded envelope from her jeans pocket.

'Five hundred dollars cash,' she said, handing the envelope to the older man.

'Sweet,' he said.

'Thenks,' said the younger one and blushed.

'No ... thank *you*,' Charlotte gushed, and the poor fellow's blush deepened.

He shambled off to the truck followed by the older man, who thrust the money-filled envelope unceremoniously into his hip pocket.

Ben and Charlotte watched until the big truck with its burly passengers had lumbered off down the street and disappeared around the corner.

Soon there was only the noise of distant traffic and nearby birds to be heard.

Ben was struggling to understand why she would be moving into a house that was already her address? Perhaps she'd moved in with the arsehole until it all went pear-shaped. Didn't matter anyway; she was here, he was here, and the sexual predator was clearly a thing of the past.

'They say moving house is one of the most traumatic things we do in our lives,' he offered as a silence breaker.

'Whoever *they* are, they must live very sheltered lives,' Charlotte said drily.

She had a way of making him feel foolish, yet, inexplicably, he didn't mind. She nodded at the parcel. 'I didn't know couriers worked on weekends.'

He missed her meaning for a second.

She held out her hands for the parcel. 'I'm Charlotte De Vito,' she said.

'Oh, I know,' he said as he handed her the parcel. 'You have no idea who I am, do you?'

She'd already started to tear open the parcel and wasn't really listening but stopped to look at him searchingly. 'Do you need me to sign something ... you know ... acknowledging delivery?'

'No ... oh no. Not at all,' he said fumbling for the right words. 'I'm not ...'

As he drifted off into a helpless silence, she stopped unwrapping the parcel and gave him her full attention. 'You're not what?'

'You mean you don't remember the ship? The last night ...'

'Oh, the *Fairport* you and Trent ... something about grass skirts,' she said, trying to help.

'No ... well, yes, but ...'

'You didn't need to get involved, you know.'

'He told you?'

She looked confused. 'Told me what? I'm talking about just now. He wouldn't have hurt me.'

Ben was dragged back to the present. 'Then why the AVO?'

'Oh, he was out of control one night. On some kind of drug, I think. He stormed into my flat in a jealous rage over some guy he thought I was seeing and smashed up the place. My sister was there and she called the cops. They insisted I take out an AVO.'

She looked at him intently as if trying to gauge his reaction.

He couldn't imagine how such a woman could have ever been involved with such a man. He said nothing but his face betrayed him.

'He wasn't always like that. Or at least he put on a great act,' she said, answering his unasked question.

'And he's a spunk.'

She smiled. 'Yes, he's very easy on the eyes. And it was good for a long time. Then a friend of a friend caught him checking into a hotel down in Melbourne with another woman ... such a cliché.'

'That whole AVO incident might have been a reaction to that, you think? You know, the best defence is attack.'

'Probably. Who knows? He was always dabbling with chemicals, if you know what I mean.'

'Believe me, I know,' Ben said under his breath.

'Dabbled a bit yourself?' she said, misinterpreting his meaning.

'No, God, no,' he protested, realising the conversation was getting way off track.

It occurred to him that if Charlotte thought it unusual to be discussing such intimate matters with a complete stranger, it didn't show. Perhaps she did remember him. He was encouraged.

Then, as though bored with the subject, she looked at the parcel again.

'You're not a courier, are you?'

'No.'

'Then ... how ...' Her voice trailed off. She hugged the parcel to her chest.

The sun had begun to set and it was getting colder.

'Sorry, it's been a long day,' she said. 'I'm not thinking clearly and it's getting chilly out here. Would you like to come in for a cup of tea or something ... if I can find anything? I'm Charlotte, by the way ... but you know that.'

'Ben,' he said, completely deflated by having to reintroduce himself.

She began to walk towards the house.

He decided either she didn't remember their moonlit rendezvous or she had a multiple personality disorder; neither possibility was encouraging. He thought about declining her offer and leaving with his illusions intact. Where once his heart had skipped when he thought of her, it now felt increasingly leaden. The words of a song popped into his head: 'Should I stay or should I go?' Who was it that sung that, The Clash? Yeah, that was it. Great band.

'Coming?' Charlotte called from her front door.

He followed her inside.

There were packing boxes scattered everywhere, at least in the rooms he could see as she led him through to the kitchen.

'Are you just moving in?' he asked as he negotiated the mayhem in the kitchen.

Charlotte plunged her arm into one of the boxes on

the kitchen floor like a child at a lucky dip and emerged triumphantly bearing a packet of tea.

'Yes. You sound surprised?'

He was about to say why he was surprised when a photograph hanging on the wall of an adjoining room caught his eye. He edged towards the doorway trying not to be too obvious.

'Ben,' Charlotte said.

He looked at her.

She held the packet of tea in one hand and a bottle of red wine in other. 'Tea or wine? Best I can do for now, I'm afraid.'

'Tea's fine,' he said. 'White. No sugar.'

She began filling a kettle.

'Do you see something you like in there?' she asked.

'Excuse me?'

She switched the kettle on and began to unwrap the parcel he'd brought.

'Just then ... you seemed to be heading towards the reading room.'

'Yes, I was,' he said walking into what he now knew was the reading room to look more closely at the photograph.

It was her, Charlotte. Looking just as she had on the ship. She was even wearing the same dress and had that same vaguely unattainable demeanour.

'My grandmother,' Charlotte said from the doorway behind him. 'Dad's mum. And before you say it, I know I look exactly like her. Everyone tells me that. I was even named after her. This is her house, or mine now, sadly. She passed on two weeks ago.'

Ben had the inescapable feeling that someone was laughing at him, but in a nice way. He looked around the room and saw it was lined with bookshelves crammed with books.

'She loved to read,' Charlotte said, moving across to one of the shelves.

She was carrying the book she'd unwrapped and seemed to be looking for someplace specific. 'And I'm sure this book you brought me was actually meant to be returned to her,' she said as she found what she was looking for — a space in the books just where she expected it.

'She loved Somerset Maugham,' she smiled, as she pushed the hard-covered book into place with the others by Maugham. 'I think she has everything he ever wrote.'

She stood back and brushed her hands together as if ridding them of dust, more out of habit than need, he suspected.

'Now, Ben who is not a courier, the question is how did you get the book and how did you know to bring it here?'

Ben just smiled as he looked again at the photograph. It was taken at night under a full moon. He felt warm and at peace and had an uncanny sense of arrival.

YIN AND YANG

Simon and Jenny Collins are an unlikely couple. Were you to meet them individually you'd never guess she could possibly be married to him, or vice versa. As it happens, however, they are very much in love — a classic case of opposites attracting.

They met at a party hosted by one of Simon's clients.

After arriving late and enquiring after Charles, his host, Simon was handed a glass of champagne by a rent-a-waiter and directed through some French doors towards a group of people standing on the far side of the swimming pool. As casually as you can when you're at a party where everyone knows everyone but you, he made his way around to join the happy group.

Drawing near, he saw they were gathered around an animated dark-haired woman who appeared to be regaling them with some tale they obviously found amusing.

Charles, who was standing next to the woman and laughing loudest, spied Simon approaching. 'Simon, old boy, I was beginning to wonder where you'd got to.'

Simon hesitated.

'Come on, man, don't stand there on your lonesome. Come and meet Jenny!' Charles said as he placed an enthusiastic hand on the shoulder of the woman by his side.

She, like everyone else, looked at Simon. Her smile was warm.

The others parted slightly to let him through.

Jenny extended a slender tanned hand to him. 'Pleased to meet you, Simon,' she said in a way that told him she meant it.

'Likewise,' he replied, feeling like an intruder.

The others were introduced in turn and although he made a genuine effort to memorise their features for future reference, it was Jenny's face that lingered clearest in his mind. A radiantly healthy face, with honey-coloured eyes that seemed brightened by an inner light.

Maybe she's a vegetarian, he thought, for no rational reason, and, being omnivorous himself, found this concerned him. He wondered why.

Charles interrupted his thoughts.

'Known Jenny since school,' he was saying. 'All us chaps chased her back then. Waste of time, though — she wasn't interested in any of us. Perhaps you'll have better luck,' he added, tactlessly, as his wife, Heather, arrived to tell them dinner was ready.

Simon and Jenny, each embarrassed in their own way by Charles's introduction, were visibly relieved by Heather's timely announcement.

Jenny fell in by his side as they drifted in for dinner. 'Charles is a bit over the top sometimes,' she said.

'Means well, I'm sure,' Simon said, nervously.

She felt his discomfort. 'You look a bit lost,' she said.

'Well, to tell the truth, I don't know a soul here other than Charles, and we only met recently.'

'At work or play?'

'He's a client.'

'And you're ...?'

'A solicitor.'

'Well, Simon solicitor, stick by me and I'll give you the lowdown on everyone here; all their dark secrets,' she promised mischievously.

An evening of gossip was not normally a prospect he would have looked forward to, but if it meant staying close to this captivating woman in the tantalizingly-cut red dress, Simon was happy to accept.

As it happened, she didn't gossip at all. Instead, she spent most of the evening trying to get him to tell her more about himself. And whenever he lowered his guard enough to let her into some private episode in his life, she gave him her full attention.

She was as good at listening as she was at talking, which

was no mean feat. It wasn't simply that she was an extrovert; it was more that she just enjoyed life. She revelled in it. And she appeared to have experienced the best and the worst of it with equal enthusiasm.

During the course of the evening she managed to cast her spell over them all but none more than Simon. He never left her side.

Being naturally shy, he found she was his perfect foil — a one-woman introduction service. By the end of that night he'd met everyone at the party and — mainly because he was with her — they'd welcomed him into their midst as they would an old friend. Although, few could fathom why Jenny should be devoting so much attention to this rather uninspiring stranger. Simon was conscious of this as well and more than a little flattered. However, he was certain Jenny's actions were motivated by good manners rather than any attraction she might have felt for him.

The truth was that not even his closest friends would have described Simon Collins as a prize catch.

Not that he was unpleasant to look at, on the contrary: he was tall and angular with vaguely aristocratic features and searching grey eyes. His smile, though at times inhibited by shyness, was warm and genuine. He was also heterosexual and reasonably well off financially; so in terms of these narrow criteria he was what one would describe as a relatively attractive eligible bachelor.

The problem was that he had such an economy of

speech and lack of flair that he was, to many, a bit, well ... boring. A safe, sober, thoroughly predictable chap who had attended the same school and was now a member of the same law firm and golf club as his father. And no one, least of all Simon, would have been the slightest bit surprised if he eventually married someone his mother recommended. Neither did he feel inclined to break this mould. He was perfectly happy with his lot. He was not by nature an adventurer; he had no desire to explore life's many possibilities, nor — heaven forbid — its temptations. He had never even felt the need to travel. While most of his contemporaries were picking up a crash course in the ways of the world during postgraduate meanderings through Europe, Asia or other more exotic locations, Simon had been content to remain in Sydney getting established in the firm and making an early start in the property market. Safe, sober, reliable and totally innocuous — that was Simon Collins.

Jennifer Goddard, on the other hand, was anything but boring. She very definitely had flair. She was a traveller who had been on the move since leaving school, bypassing tertiary education for the greater training ground of planet Earth. Initially, she paid her way working as a waitress or pulling pints behind bars. Eventually, though, she began to concentrate on her talent as a commercial artist and after some very hungry months in London, was able to get enough work to get by on.

Now, ten years on, she was back in Sydney visiting

family and friends and deciding whether to stay or move on again.

'Do you travel much?' she asked Simon, after giving him a brief but enthusiastic description of her recent trek through the mountains of Morocco on horseback.

'Did once — to Bali. An end-of-season rugby trip,' he said. 'Bit of a boys' bash, you know. Interesting place, I suppose, but a bit too hot and crowded for me. Got dysentery. Nearly died.' It was clear from his tone that he was not inclined to tempt fate in this way again.

Given their differences in interests and personalities, no one would have dreamt that Simon Collins could ever woo and win a prize like Jennifer Goddard. Nevertheless, that is exactly what he did.

After that first evening, he couldn't get her out of his mind. She filled his every waking hour and a good many of his dreaming ones. His concentration at work began to suffer and his once gargantuan appetite dwindled to the point where he began to lose weight.

This all took place during the time of his indecision — that limbo period when he was wondering what to do about her. Infatuation was not an emotion he was familiar with and he thought — even hoped — it would pass and let him return to his normal, comfortable, predictable existence. It wasn't to be; Jenny was in his blood and she was there to stay. Furthermore, when he came to accept this, he wasn't at all unhappy about it. On the contrary, he found it filled him with a kind of heart-stopping joy. And although he was painfully slow to decide what to do about her, once he did, he discovered within himself powers of romantic cunning neither he nor anyone else suspected he possessed.

He pursued her patiently, tactfully, ever so politely, but relentlessly. Nothing and no one could distract him from his purpose. And in time, much to everyone's dismay, it became obvious that Jenny's heart was slowly being won over by this unlikely character.

It wasn't as though he underwent any dramatic personality change to carry out this miraculous seduction; outwardly he remained pretty much the same old pinstriped Simon. Jenny, however, uncovered another side to him — the humorous, gentle, genuine person who sheltered behind his shy and somewhat lugubrious exterior. What attracted her most was the hidden strength she found lurking behind his humble facade. She discovered that Simon Collins was a man of great depth and determination. His apparent humility and reluctance to force his opinions on others was simply an overdose of good manners. Privately, he harboured strong convictions and a fervent desire to see that justice was done, wrongs righted, and the disadvantaged helped to the very nth degree of the law. What's more, unlike many of his dinner party liberal colleagues, he backed up his beliefs with action — giving freely of his time to legal aid and various environmental and charitable organisations. Not that you could ever accuse him of being radical; he was simply a concerned citizen, a man of principle, a rare man.

The more Jenny got to know him, the more she grew to love him. And she came to understand it would be this way for as long as they both would live.

Two and a half years after their first meeting, Simon walked proudly down the aisle with the radiant Mrs Jennifer Collins by his side.

And on that same day, some wag in the back of the church was heard to say: 'The perfect couple — Yin and Yang.'

This is not, however, a perfect world. It is often unfair. So it was that on a dismal winter evening in the third year of their marriage, Jenny Collins had to tell her husband that — according to the opinion of the latest of two specialists — she would never bear children. She was shattered by this news and expected he would be, too. She watched his face for signs of anger, sadness or disappointment.

It was often said that Simon was at his best in tense situations, a quality that had proven an immeasurable advantage in his profession. He had never needed this attribute more. While he was naturally devastated by Jenny's revelation, he was even more concerned with the impact it would have on her. For this reason, in less time than it takes to tell, he resolved never to let her hear or see any sign of disappointment in his words or actions. Perhaps in time, if she wanted to, they could talk about adoption; for now, all that mattered was her peace of mind. As for him, just being with Jenny gave him more happiness than any man should reasonably expect from life. If having no children was the price he had to pay for this, it seemed a fair exchange.

Jenny saw no distress in his face as she gave him the bad news. All she saw was love, unquestionable and unshaken. He reached out, pulled her gently into his arms and held her while she cried.

Later that night she offered to leave him. 'It's not fair on you, Si', or your parents ... you're their only son.'

'And you're my only wife,' he said, gently kissing the top of her head as she lay in the crook of his arm staring up at the ceiling.

They lay like this for some time.

Simon broke the silence. 'We'll travel. Somewhere new each year.'

'Oh, Simon,' she teased, giving him a gentle shove, 'you hate travelling. All I've ever heard about is your infamous bout of Bali belly.'

'I know, but you love charging off to foreign places, and if you were with me, perhaps I would, too.'

She knew he was only trying to cheer her up, but the prospect was genuinely attractive. 'Do you really think so?' she said.

'It's possible,' he said encouragingly. 'Let's try it and see.'

'Oh yes, let's!'

Simon did enjoy travelling with Jenny. Enormously. He

learned to see the world through her eyes and it was a wonderful place. At various times during the next four years he found himself rocking along South American railways, luxuriating in French chateaus, diving on Pacific reefs, and tramping across windswept Scottish isles. And every glorious moment of it was stored in his heart and captured, more tangibly, in a growing stack of photo albums.

In the fifth year of their newly nomadic life, they were on the island of Phuket — off the coast of Thailand — where, due to an unseasonable downpour, they had abandoned their beach-side hotel and were wandering around the town in search of suitable souvenirs to take back to their already over-cluttered home.

Along the way, Jenny was doing what she did best — making friends.

Speaking the local language was something she insisted on attempting in every country. Accordingly, armed with irresistible smile, indomitable spirit and well-worn translation book, she had charmed and amused the locals in every corner of the globe.

Which was exactly what she was doing at that moment.

Watching her working her magic on a tiny, giggling local girl, Simon found himself thinking, not for the first time, what a wonderful mother she would have been. For a single, sad instant, a shadow swept across his heart.

Jenny looked up brightly and swept his blues away. 'Oh,

look, Si — "Antiques and Artifacts",' she said, pointing at a tourist trap across the road.

Before he could respond she was splashing across the potholed road in search of the ultimate souvenir.

He went after her in a futile effort to protect their savings.

'Isn't she just gorgeous?' Jenny enthused some time later as she cradled a dusty, wooden figurine she had retrieved from one of the lower shelves at the rear of the shop.

Somewhere along the line Jenny had convinced herself that the best bargains were to be found hidden at the back of the shops where tourists wouldn't bother to look. It was a curious brand of logic, but she was so committed to it she invariably went ferreting about in the bowels of every store they went into.

On this occasion she'd been rifling about among some dusty ceramic pots when she'd emerged triumphantly clutching the wooden figure of a chubby female of indeterminate age, reclining on her left side against what appeared to be a melon of some kind. The figure's eyes were closed and her plump face wore a secret smile that was both magical and captivating. The figure was about the size of a small child, and when Jenny handed it to him, Simon found it surprisingly heavy.

Unfortunately, and I say *unfortunately* because he hated to be the bearer of bad tidings, Simon noticed a deep crack running down the back of the carving — no doubt the reason it had been relegated to the back shelves in the first place. Fully aware that the shopkeeper was hovering nearby, he pointed sternly at the flaw. 'The wood's split, Jen,' he said.

'Oh, it's nothing. It'll probably bring the price down,' she said, refusing to be deterred.

Simon was well used to dealing with his wife's impetuosity. 'Look, Jen, they probably make thousands of these things on this island. Let's scout around and see if we can find one in good condition. If we can't, and you're still keen, we'll come back and see if we can get this one at a good price, all right?'

'Oh, all right,' Jenny agreed, reluctantly. She knew he was only being sensible, but it broke her heart to put the adorable wooden figure back on the shelf. 'I come back later,' she said, in Thai, to the shopkeeper, who nodded vigorously and tried to steer them in the direction of a gold-plated Buddha, which they neither liked nor could afford.

Jenny declined politely and promised to return; the shopkeeper clearly didn't believe a word of it.

Aware of his wife's strong will and somewhat precipitous nature, Simon walked quickly out of the shop hoping she would follow before she had a chance to change her mind.

She emerged eventually, at a much slower pace.

Later that same day she found the perfect excuse to return for the little wooden figure — she found the ideal partner for it.

As Simon had guessed, there was an abundance of carved wooden figures like the first. They were made in pairs — male and female. The female always reclined to the left, the male to the right. Both wore the same serene look and slept peacefully against melons. Apparently, they were traditional carvings of some sort. Some were painted while others were stained. Jenny preferred the stained versions. However, while there may have been hundreds of them, each was distinctive in its own way — the type of wood, the grain, the hand of the carver, or just subtle differences in the curve of their smiles. Little things in themselves, but such was the personality of these figures — to use the term in its broadest sense — that these little differences made a big difference to the way you felt about them.

And it just so happened that the unmatched male figure Jenny found was exactly the same size and carved in the same wood as the lonely lady they had abandoned earlier. Naturally, she was convinced they were made for each other and it was her duty to bring them together. Leaving Simon with strict orders to buy the male, she hurried back to the first shop to rescue the little lady.

Somewhat bewildered by his wife's apparent obsession, Simon took a moment to study the little wooden figure in his arms. At first he had thought it was simply the soft lines and chubby cuteness of the carving that appealed to Jenny and to some extent himself, but it was more than that — the serene secret smile on the little fellow's sleeping face filled him with an inexplicable sense of calm and wellbeing. He liked that feeling.

Jenny was ecstatic. That night in the hotel she placed the two podgy wooden characters next to each other on the dressing table, polished them lovingly, and promised them each a new coat of varnish as soon as they got back to Sydney. And, never one to forget her manners, she formally introduced them to each other.

'Yin,' she said to the female, 'meet Yang!'

There was great humour amongst their friends when the news got around that Simon and Jenny had brought two funny little wooden carvings back from Thailand and called them Yin and Yang.

Finally, Jenny's agent, Phillip Dawkins, the fellow who'd uttered the infamous 'Yin and Yang' remark at the wedding, was forced to confess.

As you would expect, they accepted the joke in good spirit and henceforth, to avoid confusion, the little wooden figures — who now occupied pride of place on the mantelpiece in their lounge — became known as little Yin and little Yang.

The following year was the best Simon had ever experienced in the practice. Not so much that it was more profitable, which it was, but more that it was so easy. What began as acrimonious litigations quickly developed into benign out-of-court settlements; the most complex contracts were drawn up without a hiccup; and even a couple of divorce cases that had all the signs of being protracted and messy somehow worked themselves out so amicably he began to wonder why the couples were getting divorced at all. It was as though everyone he dealt with had, by some tacit arrangement, agreed to make life easy for him.

Jenny had a remarkable year as well. Not only did she get more interesting and challenging commissions, she also found her work improved dramatically. It was inspired. So much so that during the course of that year she picked up a couple of international commercial illustration awards and her agent, Phillip, was so impressed, that — in an uncharacteristic display of generosity — he offered to sponsor an exhibition for her. That, too, was a raging success.

It was during this time that they both, independently, came to the conclusion that their good fortune was somehow due to the presence of little Yin and little Yang. They never discussed this with each other — for fear of being teased — but whenever either of them was alone with the little wooden figurines, they'd find themselves talking to them as if they were speaking to real people. So it was that, during the course of that year, little Yin and little Yang came to share all the successes, secrets and dreams of Simon and Jenny Collins.

Then, amazingly, Jenny fell pregnant.

Her doctor was astounded. 'It's a bloody miracle' was all he could say.

Simon and Jenny didn't care how it happened; there is no point in trying to rationalise miracles.

'But how?' people would ask.

'Oh, just a little Yin and Yang,' they would reply, and that seemed as good an explanation as any.

Their daughter, Rebecca, arrived whole, healthy and right on time. Where some babies cry constantly and never sleep, Rebecca chuckled when awake, slept soundly when she was supposed to, woke at a civilised hour and — just like her mother — charmed everyone she met. She was a happy and contented baby with the proudest parents in the world.

About six months after Rebecca was born, Jenny discovered that Simon, too, was in the habit of talking to little Yin and little Yang.

She awoke one humid moonlit night to find him gone from their bed, and when after ten minutes he hadn't returned, she began to worry something might be wrong with Rebecca.

She climbed out of bed to investigate.

As soon as she reached the hall and heard Simon's calm voice and Rebecca's happy gurgling coming from the living room she relaxed — whatever the problem had been, Simon obviously had it under control.

She smiled at the thought of the funny serious expression he always wore when talking to his tiny daughter and tiptoed down the hall to spy on them.

However, when she peeked into the living room she

saw that although Simon was cradling and rocking his daughter in his arms, he was actually talking to little Yin and little Yang. There could be no doubt about it.

Furthermore, at one point he even appeared to hold Rebecca up so that little Yin and Yang could get a better look at her.

Strangely, Jenny was a bit uncomfortable with this. It seemed wrong for Simon to be acting this way. While it may have been acceptable for her to talk to wooden carvings — being artistic she could be forgiven a little lunacy — Simon was always so rational; it was one of the things she had come to rely on. To see him talking to inanimate objects was disorientating. It unsettled her. She went to walk away but as she shifted her weight, a floorboard creaked.

Simon looked around. 'Jenny?'

'Did she wake you?' Jenny whispered as she entered the room. Rebecca began chuckling even more enthusiastically upon hearing her mother approach.

'Yes, the little monkey, she needed a change. She'll go back to sleep without any trouble,' Simon replied as he handed Rebecca to her.

'She always does, she's a booodiful liddle lady,' Jenny cooed.

Simon looked ill at ease and vulnerable.

'I saw you talking to them, you know,' Jenny said without looking up.

'Talking to who?'

'You know ...'

'I wasn't, I was just ...'

'Don't worry, I do, too.'

'Really?' Simon said arching his eyebrows. He wasn't sure whether she was just saying this to make him feel better — that was the sort of thing she would do.

'Often,' she assured him.

They stared silently at the serene little figures. Rebecca was breathing softly and evenly on the verge of sleep.

'Sometimes I could swear they're listening,' Simon said.

Jenny couldn't help wondering what his friends would think if they knew that dear old stuffy Simon found comfort in talking to wooden figures and, furthermore, believed they might be listening to him.

'Although, I have to admit,' Simon went on, 'they don't say much.'

They laughed at this and even little Rebecca gurgled away happily as if she understood the joke.

Later, when they were back in bed wrestling with insomnia, Jenny said: 'Si, has it ever occurred to you how good things have been for us ever since little Yin and little Yang arrived?'

'You mean business-wise?'

'And Rebecca.'

'Rebecca?'

'Well, there doesn't seem to be any other explanation, does there? All the specialists were positive it was impossible for me to have children — and here we all are.'

Simon sighed.

'Let's not get too carried away, Jen. They're just a couple of wooden figures, charming and all that, but just cleverly carved teak all the same.'

'Why do you talk to them, then?'

'I don't know.'

'Probably for the same reason I do.'

'And what's that?'

'I think they want me to.'

'Really, Jen—'

'I'm serious, Si, I think it makes them happy to share in our lives. It's like ever since we brought them together, they've been part of our family. Or we've been part of theirs,' she said in a tone that was both earnest and puzzled.

'You haven't been dabbling with the dreaded weed again, have you?'

(Simon didn't forbid his wife's occasional use of marijuana, but neither did he approve; it was, after all, against the law.)

'No, I haven't,' she said indignantly. 'Anyway, you obviously feel there's something out of the ordinary about them, otherwise you wouldn't talk to them, would you?'

He tried unsuccessfully to think of an appropriate reply.

'Well, would you?' she repeated.

'Okay, I admit I do treat them like they're special. I mean they're peaceful-looking little buggers, aren't they? The way they smile ... it's like they know something we don't.'

'Mmmm ... exactly.'

'I don't want you to get the wrong idea about all this, Jennifer,' he hastened to add, a little stuffily. 'I mean, it's harmless, really, the way I talk to them. It's not as though I *pray* to them or anything like that. I just tell them things, that's all — especially good news.'

'And there's been a lot of good news for us recently, hasn't there?'

'Yes, there has. I suppose that's why I've been talking to them more often of late,' he said, happy to seize upon any rational excuse for his irrational behaviour.

'Well, you can say what you like, as far as I'm concerned there's something very special about little Yin and little Yang.'

'All I know for sure is there's something very special about big Yin,' Simon grinned as he rolled over to hug her. 'And my luck changed from the very first moment I laid eyes on you.'

'Flatterer,' Jenny teased, contentedly. 'And I suppose you're hoping you'll get lucky right now?'

'Incredible! You always know exactly what I'm thinking.'

Some weeks later, Simon's law firm held its annual end-of-year function for staff and clients. It was a black-tie affair and, if past years were anything to go by, a night not to be missed. Jenny was really looking forward to it and, although not by nature a party person, Simon was, too.

However, he wasn't at all comfortable with Jenny's choice of babysitter. 'Leigh Goodwin?! She's just a child.'

'She's fourteen, Si. Maggie uses her all the time and she's always been terrific with her kids.'

'Maggie's kids are a lot older, they hardly need looking after.'

'Just get dressed and stop whining,' Jenny said. It was far too late in the day to be having this discussion.

'Have you seen her hair?' Simon persisted, standing at the bathroom door. 'It looks like a packet of exploding jellybeans.'

'We all go through that stage,' Jenny said as she poured herself into a stunning black dress. 'I bet you had a weird hairstyle when you were her age.'

'No, I bloody well did not!' Simon said, grumpily — and he hadn't either. 'She's probably a bloody drug addict,' he muttered as he shuffled back to the bathroom mirror to fiddle unhappily with his bow tie.

'What's that, sweetheart?' Jenny said, trying not to laugh.

'Nothing,' he grumbled.

Simon was wrong, Leigh Goodwin wasn't a drug addict — she was an alcoholic. It had begun innocently enough, just the odd glass of beer when she was a toddler. Everyone found it amusing when little Leigh got tiddly by sneaking sips from Dad's can of Foster's — she looked so comical rolling happily about on the floor giggling. Cute. It was just simple kiddy hijinks, nothing to worry about.

Certainly no one made any connection when years later she started to do badly at school; she just seemed to be so tired all the time, probably a hormonal thing they reasoned. By the time she was eleven, she was in serious trouble and nobody knew, least of all her parents. They drank a lot themselves. They weren't alcoholics, they were quick to point out, just social drinkers who liked to entertain. Consequently, they kept the bar well stocked and never noticed when the odd bottle went missing. In later years, when she began to babysit for extra pocket money, Leigh learned to raid other people's liquor cabinets. She never took enough to be caught out, just a nip or two out of each bottle, but this would quickly add up to a powerful cocktail. Normally, she never drank in the house itself; she'd pour the pilfered liquor into a little hip flask, smuggle it out and drink it later. Unfortunately, on the night she babysat Rebecca, she decided to break the pattern.

This aberration had a lot to do with Rick, her boyfriend, who in response to her phone call, had crept into the house about an hour after Jenny and Simon had left. Rick was nearly seventeen and not normally a drinker, but what he had in mind for this evening required some inhibition loosening for himself as much as Leigh. So when Leigh showed him the flask of mixed spirits she'd siphoned out of the Collins' liquor cabinet, he was quick to suggest that they drink it right away. Leigh protested, briefly — despite her alcoholism, she took her job as a babysitter seriously and didn't want to be caught out should little Rebecca need her — but Rick was persistent. Eventually, she weakened and went to find a bottle of Coke. She drank everything with Coke.

In his hormone-driven enthusiasm, Rick had made two serious miscalculations. Firstly, he had no idea that Leigh was an alcoholic who, once she got started, would simply drink herself into oblivion. Secondly, he hadn't anticipated his own reaction to such a powerful concoction of spirits.

After vomiting for what seemed the hundredth time, he hadn't felt vaguely romantic, and even if he had, the slurring, dribbling creature Leigh had degenerated into would hardly have been the object of his desires.

Somehow he managed to carry her unconscious body into the guest bedroom and, after making a valiant effort to clean up the evidence of their impropriety, fell asleep beside her.

In his hand was a lighted cigarette.

About a mile from home Simon heard a siren behind them. 'Police,' he muttered. 'Probably another false alarm at the Baileys'.'

The Baileys lived in a ghastly pseudo-Spanish mansion a few doors up from them and false alarms from their recently installed security system were driving the neighbourhood crazy.

'No, it's a fire engine!' Jenny said.

Simon pulled over to let the stroppy red machine go by.

They looked at each other.

'No. It couldn't be ...' Simon said.

Jenny was praying.

By the time they got home, their house was beyond saving. Two fire engines, a police car, and an ever-growing crowd of onlookers blocked the street. Simon stopped the car in the middle of the road, leapt out and began to chase Jenny who was already racing towards the flames, screaming. It took two very determined firemen to stop her from hurling herself into the inferno. The heat was incredible, she would have been incinerated well before getting anywhere near the house. She thrashed about in their arms and between sobs tried to tell them that her baby was in the house. They did their best to calm her, but could offer no comfort — whoever was in the house would have died a horrible death. The firemen already knew Rebecca and Leigh were in there, the neighbours had told them that. At this point, no one knew about Rick.

Simon stood off on his own, completely gutted. He watched the fire suck the oxygen out of the night and the happiness out of his life.

In his mind he could see a little girl with her mother's eyes, running towards him. She was laughing. In her hand she held something tiny — a shell? No ... a crab, a hermit crab. He wanted to tell her about that crab, he wanted to tell her about everything.

He cursed God and he wept.

Then the heat and the suffocating smoke brought him

back to the present, forced him away from the pyre and back to Jenny. He put an arm around her. There was nothing to say.

Mrs Asakura, the quiet Japanese lady from across the road, put a blanket around them. Two cups of hot sweet tea appeared from somewhere.

Jenny didn't appear to notice any of this; she continued to stare trancelike as the fire slowly succumbed to the firemen's hoses.

Simon buried his face in her hair and smelled Rebecca there. His mind was filled with her happy soft chuckle, her curious eyes, her promise. Grief wracked his body.

After what seemed an eternity, a fireman emerged from the smoking, puddled, black bones of the house and walked towards them. He was exhausted, shocked and covered in soot and water. He couldn't imagine a worse death than being burned alive; he never got used to it. Unable to meet their eyes, he walked past them and in a trembling voice reported his findings to a senior fire officer and a policeman who stood a little way off.

'We've found two bodies,' he said as quietly as he could.

Jenny let out a silent sob.

'Both teenagers, I'd say,' the man continued. 'One'll be the babysitter and the other's her boyfriend, I reckon. They were in the bedroom ... on the bed. Never had a chance. Looks like the bed caught fire — a cigarette probably.'

'Or something stronger,' the policeman added a little unnecessarily.

Simon moved closer. 'What about the baby?' he demanded.

'There's no sign of her in the nursery,' the fireman said, taking no offence at Simon's tone — he had faced the misdirected fury of grief many times before. 'We're still looking. It's a mess in there.'

'She must be in the nursery. Where else could she be?'

'We're looking everywhere,' the fireman said, not saying what was in all their minds — that they would eventually find Rebecca's tiny, charred body in there somewhere.

Quite suddenly, Jenny seemed to lose interest in their conversation.

'Little Yin and little Yang!' she said, as if reaching a decision. 'Simon, we've got to find little Yin and little Yang.'

Simon heard the disassociated tone of her voice. Probably shock, he reasoned, some sort of hysteria setting in.

Others had the same thought. 'Is there anywhere you can take your wife so she can rest?' the policeman suggested.

Mrs Asakura, who was standing nearby washing her worrying hands over each other, nodded and smiled a mother's smile.

Simon put his arm around Jenny and pulled her head to his chest. 'Go with Yuki, Jen, I'll stay here and—'

With an exasperated grunt, Jenny broke away from him and began running down the side of the property towards the back of the house.

The policeman made to follow, but Simon stopped him. 'I'll take care of her. If you want to do something useful, why don't you do tell these bloody ghouls to push off,' he said, sweeping an arm in the direction of the faceless onlookers whose presence suddenly seemed obscene.

Some in the crowd were offended by Simon's outburst but the policeman understood. He moved off to do as he was asked.

Searching the whirlwind of his mind for words beyond his experience, Simon went looking for Jenny.

Skirting the steaming, hissing pile of bricks and metal that once was their home, he made his way to the bottom of the garden to where the property backed onto a park. Over the fence he could see the adventure playground with the little swings and slides that Rebecca would never use.

Jenny stood clutching the gate staring out into the darkness.

Simon approached uncertainly.

Behind him he could hear the firemen packing up and the cars of the curious moving away. A few firemen were still wearily searching through the waterlogged ruins.

'Jen,' Simon said, hoarsely.

She turned to stare at him, but said nothing.

'Darling, there's nothing we can do,' he said, moving to her.

'Little Yin and little Yang ...' she whispered.

'They're gone, Jen,' he said, holding her now.

'No, they're not! They're looking after Rebecca. I made them promise.'

'I know, Jen,' he said. 'And they will ...'

'No, you don't understand.'

'Yes, I do, darling, please ...' He tried to ease her away.

'Listen!' she said, urgently, gripping his arms fiercely to hold him still.

'What?'

'Listen!'

He listened: a fire truck was driving away, old Jim from next door was telling somebody about someone called Rick, a dog was barking and ... Rebecca! For an instant he imagined he could hear Rebecca's chuckling, distant and surreal. Then it was gone, just a cruel trick of the mind.

He looked at Jenny as something approaching happiness lit up her eyes. 'You heard her, Si — didn't you?'

He felt tears rise. 'Please, Jen, it's just ... night noises. Birds probably.'

Then he heard it again — the unmistakable chuckle of their happy baby.

Jenny saw his head tilt back like a dog trying to catch a scent. 'It's her, Si. It's Becky, isn't it? You can hear her, too, can't you?'

'Yes ... yes, I can!' he said, sure now that it wasn't the

wind, nor birds, nor the wishful thinking of a hysterical mind. He could really hear it — Rebecca's chuckling — coming from the park.

'Rebecca!' he shouted as he threw open the gate and they ran blindly into the park.

Alerted by the noise, some of the firemen came after them bearing torches.

It was one of the firemen who found her — lying in the middle of the sandpit, comfortably nestled in a shallow depression lined with a rug. She was wrapped in a soft pink, woollen blanket and lying beside her, one each side, were two cute, plump, polished wooden figures.

Years later, the fireman would say that the thing he remembered most about those two carved figures was the delightfully serene smiles on their podgy little faces.

Unlike Simon and Jenny, he didn't notice that their tiny wooden feet were covered in sand.

FORGOTTEN HEROES

Billy lay spread-eagled on the imitation Persian rug, his mouth opening and closing as though gasping for air or grasping for words. For an instant his fists clenched and a terrible light sparked in his eyes; then the moment passed and the fight went out of him.

Deprived of a human opponent, Frank began to unleash his fury on the chairs, lampshades, pictures, pottery and other furnishings that filled that innocent room. When he began to attack the walnut-veneered china cabinet she'd inherited from her mother, Mary began to cry.

Slowly, so as not to attract attention, she went across to comfort Billy who had climbed unsteadily to his feet. Together they moved to the safety of a doorway where they stood and watched her husband and his father destroy the things he'd worked so hard to give them.

Minutes later the front door flew open and released Frank into the night.

A blind rolled up at number 47 to reveal the vulture-like form of the neighbourhood gossip, Clarissa Cromwell, squinting out into the street-lighted gloom.

Frank picked up a lump of dirt from his garden and hurled it towards her prying silhouette.

The clod of dirt burst harmlessly but noisily against the window and sent Clarissa shrieking back into her living room to bully her husband from his fireside dreams.

After a time of angry walking, Frank found refuge in a group of ancient oaks that clung to the shoulders of an extinct volcano that loomed above the sleeping suburbs.

He sat heavily and gazed out over the rows of green, blue, white and orange lights that crisscrossed neatly all the way to the horizon — an illusion of order in a world of chaos.

The kids of today, why is it they always have to know everything? Always questioning. Never satisfied. No patience. It all has something to do with too much money, nuclear warheads, computers, junk food, corrupt cops, bullshitting politicians and all the other space-age crap we've got to put up with these days. What was it he'd read recently? The world was about to enter the 'Information Age'. In other words, like it or not, everybody was going to be flat-out minding everyone else's business. And somewhere, in some featureless building protected by electronic eyes, there lurked banks of computers that knew more about you than you knew about yourself. Everything! From the day you are born until the day you die. And they store those things, for ever — especially the crimes.

He wondered if they knew about him and Mabel Stanistreet that long ago summer — she said she was sixteen, but he knew she wasn't.

That was life for him back then — girls, rugby, beer. Work hard, play hard, the important thing was to keep busy. Broader issues like running the country, or the world, were the business of older folk. You trusted them, you respected them, and — if you were a spotty teenager — you certainly didn't question their judgment. Not out loud, anyway. In fact, Frank couldn't even remember being a teenager, not in the laid-back, far-out, anti-every-bloody-thing way the kids were today.

It wasn't as if he were an old man, but for all he had in common with the kids who slouched around the streets propping up walls these days, he might as well have been a hundred.

Nineteen hundred and sixty bloody eight! For some, the sixties had been a time of change; for him it had been a time of panic. His ideals hadn't just been challenged, some were openly reviled — especially by his own children. This endless bloody Vietnam War argument with Billy was typical.

They may have shared the same blood, but the differences in their upbringing had made them strangers.

When Frank was fifteen he'd left school to take a job in a timber yard. Just getting a job seemed enough; nobody talked about job satisfaction. The thing was to get a job and work like hell to keep it. Earning wages to help out at home was important, too. Not that it was asked of you, it was never really discussed; you just did it as a matter of course and with a degree of pride.

He didn't expect his own children, Billy and Debbie, to do this. He'd wanted their life to be easier and he worked hard to make sure it would be.

He loved them.

In the beginning, they loved him, too — spontaneously and unselfishly. He remembered how they'd rush out to meet him at the first squeak of the front gate that would announce his arrival home. Shrieking excitedly they'd fall upon him, their tiny fingers clutching at his trousers, demanding to be swept up into his arms. He'd loved them so much that just holding them close like that stirred up such a fierce pounding in his heart it almost took his breath away.

Slowly, almost imperceptibly, things began to change. As they grew older they found more important things to occupy them: school, sport, friends, television — diversions that became far more attractive than waiting to welcome home a father who came and went each day with monotonous predictability.

When it became clear they'd never be rushing out to greet him with tales of everything that had been important in their day any more, he finally oiled the squeaky front gate — something he'd deliberately avoided doing for years.

Then, when the children were old enough to take care of themselves, Mary took on a full-time job. Initially, she did it to help out with the finances, but it soon became more than that. She loved the stimulation of the workplace, she thrived in it and would never happily accept a housewife's role again. In many ways Frank was happy for her — the extra money was certainly welcome — but another part of him missed being the centre of her world.

It was around this same time that his relationship with the children suddenly became strained and uneasy — almost antagonistic. He never really understood how it happened. It was as though he'd gone out for a long walk and returned to a house full of strangers. Now, instead of being the father they loved without question, he found himself in the role of rule maker and disciplinarian, the one to be feared or challenged according to mood or circumstance. Wide-eyed adoration was replaced by narrow-eyed petulance. Now, far from being grateful for the little he could give them, they came to expect it — as if it were their due — and if he ever failed to provide what they expected of him, they never failed to show their disappointment. At first, this only made him more determined to be a better provider; but when their disappointment gave way to disapproval, and finally to sheer truculence, he began to realise he had created a monster.

He'd tried reasoning with them, tried telling them of the hard times he'd known as a child during the Great Depression, hoping they'd see how well off they were in comparison. It had no effect. They either couldn't or wouldn't relate to his past; they only cared about their present and the fact that other children had more money, more clothes, more travel, more of everything.

Confronted by this self-serving attitude, Frank's powers of reason often deserted him. To him, their disrespect and ingratitude amounted to betrayal. So he fought back clumsily, with anger and sarcasm, as if by belittling them he might devalue their opinions.

Naturally, they misunderstood his outrage; they could not know that he was hurt more than angry, they saw only that he appeared to despise them. The gap between them widened inexorably. Now he was terrified he had lost them altogether and was haunted by a chilling sense of failure.

The truth was, despite what he told the children, Frank didn't remember his childhood as being much of a hardship at all. Looking back it was easy to see just how poor they must have been, but he'd been born into poverty and for the first few years of his life it was all he'd ever known, so there was no sense of loss. He couldn't even remember being hungry. He knew, now, that his parents must have gone without, but somehow they always managed to feed and clothe their children. The food was basic — bread and dripping, soup, and the occasional rabbit stew, and Frank's clothes were always ill-fitting hand-me-downs, but he was happy, warm and loved, and that is what he remembered most.

Sometimes, at night, in the moment before sleep, certain memories would catch him unawares — his parents in hushed, desperate conversations, their momentary unguarded looks of helplessness, the slump in his father's shoulders — stark yet elusive images that would linger in his mind as sharp and clear as if it were happening at that very moment, then disappear as quickly as they came.

Lately, however, these memories were becoming increasingly confused with images he'd seen more recently in books or television documentaries. Now, he wasn't sure whether he'd ever actually seen his mother stealing coal and his father queuing for work, or he'd just put their faces into someone else's photographs.

Nevertheless, he had known nothing of the luxuries his own children enjoyed today, of that much he was certain.

He was also certain that he didn't agree with this conscientious objection stance the kids were taking against the Vietnam War. What kind of bullshit was that?

Frank could still remember the incredible sense of disappointment he'd experienced when, despite volunteering to fight the Japs, he'd been rejected for military service on medical grounds. Twenty-eight years old and strong and healthy in every way except for a stupid hearing problem that had kept him at home. He felt cheated. While others died for their country, he spent the war working alongside women in factories. The sense of shame sat on him like a stain. When the Americans dropped the bomb and Japan surrendered, he stood by the roadside to welcome the homecoming heroes as a mere spectator. His one chance for glory had gone for ever.

The sun found him stretching, yawning and investigating the world through red eyes. His body — aching from an uncomfortable night on cold, damp earth — took a while to find itself. The day smelled good. The sun was warm on his face and for a time he toyed with the idea of staying in this perfect place for the rest of the day. Then a jogger invaded his solitude with the rasp of tortured breathing. Frank looked at his watch — he had plenty of time to get to work. He brushed the dirt from his clothes and shuffled off down the hill.

As he walked he thought of Mary. She would be worried about him, still angry no doubt, but worried nonetheless.

For the first twenty-three years of their marriage they had never really had a serious argument. Even as their relationship had gradually degenerated into grudging co-habitation, they had somehow managed to avoid the unpleasantness of bitter slanging matches. Perhaps if they had wrestled a few of their problems out into the open, things might have been different. But it was a risk he had never been prepared to take. Not just because he was petrified by the thought of losing her, which he was, but also because he was terrified of breaking up his family. He had long since come to accept that bringing up a family might be the only important thing he would ever do in his life. Caring for them and protecting them gave him a sense of achievement and self-respect. He wanted to tell Mary that, wanted to hold her in his arms and tell her how he could feel his family, his life and his pride slipping away and how it scared him to death. But somewhere along the way he'd forgotten how to talk to her and she'd stopped listening.

He tried to think of her the way she was when they first met, tried to capture the smile, the way she laughed at his corny jokes, how her eyes would widen with excitement at the plans they made. They were happy then. Perhaps not dizzily in love in the romance novel sense, but what they had seemed stronger somehow, more permanent — invincible.

Once they had been the best of friends but now they were separated by a distance neither knew how to cross. Whatever passion she had once felt for him had long been replaced by the kind of love that people have for pets. She took care of him, prepared his meals, kept his house, kept him company and, until very recently, had always been faithful to him.

Faithful! What a bloody joke. Dear sweet innocent Mary,

mother of my children, grunting, sweating, smiling — spreading her legs for some expense-accounted prick years younger than her.

He'd tried to understand, but couldn't. He'd tried to leave her, but couldn't. He'd tried to hate her, but couldn't.

It amazed him how everyone had known what was going on except him. Even Billy. It was ironic really; whenever Frank had seen this sort of thing happening to other people he'd always wondered why the betrayed party was always the last to know. He used to think they must be blind or stupid not to notice. Now he knew better.

More lies: she still loved him, it was just that she'd been a virgin when they married and she was curious to know what it was like with another man; it was his fault as much as hers, he'd been drinking too much and lost interest in sex; she needed to feel wanted again. Bullshit — all of it!

More by habit than with any real sense of purpose, he clocked in and found his way to the Dispatch Department where he hung up his jacket, donned a dustcoat and attempted to check the day's first deliveries. It was futile; his eyes wouldn't focus. All he could see was Billy, hands on hips, shouting at him.

'You don't give a rat's arse about what's right or wrong, just how brave you all were back in good old World War Two!'

'Yeah, well, thank Christ we didn't have to rely on you and your gutless long-haired mates back then.'

'That was then, this is now. The world's not at war now.

Why would any sane person want to send their sons away to be scared shitless in someone else's war?'

'Everybody's scared in war. It takes real courage to do the right thing when you're scared.'

'What's *right* about napalming innocent villagers?'

'They're napalming jungles, not villages. No one wants innocent people to get killed, but that's war.'

'Win at all costs, eh? Fuck the morality.'

'At least the Yanks have the guts to fight for something they believe in.'

'Get off the grass! Half the poor bastards are drafted. They join up or they go to jail. Some choice. Anyway, what are they fighting for?'

'For freedom, against communism.'

'Oh, the dreaded *communism*! Some poor bloody poverty-stricken peasants want some kind of equality in their own country. Well, shit, we can't have that, can we? Much better to kill off a few hundred thousand children than let them turn red!'

'They don't *want* to turn red, that's the whole point.'

'How the hell do you know? How many Vietnamese have you spoken to lately?'

It was a futile argument. The real reasons for the Vietnam War were as much a mystery to them as they were to most people.

Frank kept getting it confused with the Korean War — Asia, north versus south, communism versus democracy, America backing the good guys. Okay, so this time it wasn't a popular war, lots of people were questioning it, not only the young. But the world has always had its share of socialist bastards. The way Frank saw it, if the Americans believed there was good cause to be in Vietnam, then New Zealand should be there, too. America was the guardian of world democracy and New Zealand was their ally. That's the way it would always be.

He was going to say something along those lines when he saw Billy's eyes light up, as though he smelt victory and couldn't wait to taste it.

'Have you ever noticed how every time a bomb kills a couple of people in Ireland, the newspapers are full of it?' he said.

'What the hell has Ireland got to do with anything?' Frank answered cautiously.

'Everything. A couple of Irishmen getting blown away is chicken shit compared with the hundreds, perhaps thousands of Vietnamese that get killed every day. But do we hear about them? No way! Why? Because they're only little yellow people, that's why. Just slopes and gooks. It's not like *real* people are getting killed.'

'Jesus Christ! You're not trying to tell me it's a racist war!'

'Well, *isn't* it?'

Frank was not a racist, not now nor ever. He resented the accusation. He was sick of the boy's lack of respect, up to *here* with his smugness and his ingratitude. He worked his arse off to give this spotty prick a good life and all he got in return was this namby-pamby bullshit.

'The *truth* is that all your conscientious objection crap is just a cover-up for the fact that you're just plain gutless. A bloody nancy boy!' he said.

For a moment Billy stood stunned. Slowly, he gripped the headrest of the couch, his voice shook.

'Well ... if you're such a hero, why's Mum leaving you?'

'You fuckin' little—' Frank choked as he lurched towards him.

The boy stood his ground, defiantly. 'Go on, hit me. Show me how brave you are, you pathetic bastard.'

Mary ran in from the kitchen. 'Stop it! For God's sake.'

'Tell him, Mum, tell him!'

Every Anzac Day, Frank attended the dawn parade. In the beginning he hadn't taken part because, despite his wishes, he hadn't ever been in the forces, so he just went along to show his respect. He couldn't remember when, or exactly why, he began marching in the parade itself. It wasn't premeditated, it just happened. He simply drifted into it. He was, after all, around the same age as many of the veterans, and although he had no medals to wear and belonged to no regiment, his presence at the wreath-laying ceremonies seemed right and proper. No one ever questioned his right to be there and with the passing of the years he subconsciously took on the role of an old soldier to such an extent that, in his heart, he became one.

So each Anzac Day he took himself to the dawn parade held at the cenotaph in front of the Auckland Museum. The museum sat on the crest of a hill in the middle of a huge park, and its dignified floodlit facade provided a fitting backdrop for the annual gathering of old soldiers and their memories. In such a setting Frank never failed to experience an intense feeling of belonging, a much needed rekindling of his flagging patriotism, and an almost religious sense of pride in being a New Zealander.

Then, two years ago, this changed.

It started out as a dawn parade like any other. Many familiar faces were there, and a few more were missing — age was their enemy now. Their heads were bowed in silence, each of them alone with their memories.

Suddenly, a group of anti-war protesters ran screaming out of the mist and began to bombard the bewildered veterans with flour bombs.

Some of the old soldiers ducked for cover, others tried in vain to battle their attackers, but the speed and vigour of youth was too much for their tired old bones.

In the chaos, Frank caught sight of an old man standing proudly to attention as if oblivious to the madness around him; a survivor of two wars, he was once again refusing to leave his post. His face was splotched with flour, tears etched down his cheeks; two of his brothers had died so the world could be free to throw flour bombs at old men.

Frank saw red. He ran towards the jeering protesters and began lashing out. Somehow he managed to catch one of them with a kick to the stomach. The force of it felled them both. Frank was first to recover. Rolling to his knees he straddled his prisoner and raised his fist. Then he stopped in amazement — the face he was about to crush belonged to a girl.

'Shit,' he panted.

With the weight of him on her, the girl fought for breath.

The fight went out of him. 'Are you okay?'

'I think so,' she wheezed uncertainly. 'It would help if you got off me.'

He felt embarrassed and slightly ridiculous. 'Sorry,' he mumbled, climbing unsteadily to his feet. His suit jacket was torn.

She made no effort to move.

He offered her his hand.

'Thanks,' she said and grunted quietly as he helped her to her feet.

Still dazed, she swayed towards him. He held her gently at arm's length while she regained her senses.

A pasty-faced youth ran up to them. 'You okay, Shaz?'

'I'm fine,' she said stepping away from Frank. 'Where are the others?'

'They've buggered off. Someone called the cops,' the boy said, nervously shifting from one foot to the other.

'Too gutless to face the consequences, eh?' Frank said.

'Get stuffed!' the boy said and attempted to pull the girl away.

She resisted and smiled apologetically at Frank.

He tried to respond.

She held out her hand. 'Sharon,' she said.

Uncertainly, Frank accepted her hand. 'Frank.'

'I'm sorry about all this,' she said. 'It's only that, you know ...'

She wanted to explain and Frank wanted to understand, but the boy was becoming increasingly anxious.

'C'mon, we haven't got all day,' he snapped and walked away.

Sharon shrugged helplessly, then went after the boy.

Frank watched until they disappeared into the trees.

They didn't look back.

Slowly, the veterans formed back into ranks, the dignitaries took up their places and the ceremony recommenced as if nothing had happened — as if to acknowledge the incident would give it credibility.

Nevertheless, try as he might, Frank could never forget. The injustice of it smouldered inside him still. It confused him as well — because from that day on, whenever he tried to remember Sharon's face, the only person he could ever see in his mind's eye was Billy.

The day moved on relentlessly, deliveries came and went, forms were filled, goods distributed, the work got done. Even in his detached state Frank handled it all with his usual efficiency. On any other day he would have felt a measure of pride in his rock-like dependability; today he felt nothing. Not even the usual parade of drivers with their light-hearted banter and endless grubby jokes could lift his mood. Somehow the security and routine of it all seemed like a lie. He was sick of the lies: a happy family, love, respect, patriotism, a sense of duty, a sense of pride — lies, all of it.

'Pearson wants to see you, Frank!'

Frank looked up to see a chubby pay clerk, standing beside him rubbing his hands together worryingly.

'What for?' Frank asked.

'Buggered if I know. Probably got a rise, you lucky bastard.' The clerk smiled and waddled off in his fat-arsed important way.

After seconding one of the brighter storemen to hold the fort, Frank made his way to the office, wondering what Pearson, the new General Manager, could possibly want. *Rise, my arse*, he muttered under his breath. *It'll be more bloody paperwork, for sure.*

The company had been taken over twice in the last four years, each new regime bringing with it a whole new set of procedures and computer-based administration systems, which always seemed to increase paperwork without noticeably increasing efficiency. Not being one to make waves, Frank complied as best he could, although he was less than impressed when all customers and products had been given computer codes, which he found impossible to remember. Computers confounded him. He was still struggling with metrics, which were another bloody nonsense as far he was concerned, particularly weights and measures. If imperial measurements were good enough for the Americans, he couldn't see why New Zealand had to change to some ridiculous European system. *Bloody bureaucrats!*

Pearson had stepped out for a few minutes, so Frank was asked to wait. Obediently, he settled into one of the visitors' chairs and attempted to read a magazine concerning itself with the latest trends and developments in the international whitegoods market. He couldn't concentrate. He was far too fascinated by the goings on around him. The plush premises of the 'inner sanctum', as the office complex was known, were a stark contrast to the frugal decor of the factory proper. For a start it was quiet. There was no need for office staff to shout to be heard above the roar of the production line. Conversations were carried out in polite, hushed tones, punctuated by youthful laughter. Youth — that was it! That was his overall impression of the people in here — youth and confidence. They carried themselves with an assurance that belied their years — almost arrogance, as if they knew exactly where they were going and how they were going to get there. There was also something in the way they looked at Frank that let him know they thought themselves superior to him. He despised them for it and avoided catching their eyes in case his contempt for them might show.

Pearson arrived in a busy flurry of papers, which he handed to his secretary. 'I want these dealt with by tonight,' he said, and without waiting for any questions, turned to Frank.

'Ah ... Frank. Sorry to have kept you waiting, another bloody emergency, you understand. Come on in,' he grinned, as a spider might to a fly, and waved Frank into his office.

Frank entered uneasily.

Pearson closed the door and went to stand behind his large desk. On top of the desk was a marble pen stand with matching gold pens, a leather-bound blotter, a telephone and a single red folder — a picture of sparse efficiency.

'Sit, please, make yourself comfortable,' Pearson said.

Frank sat in the chair he was directed to; it was smaller, harder and nearer to the ground than was comfortable.

Pearson collapsed into a high-backed leather chair, which rocked back to accommodate the indolent position he adopted.

Frank's chair remained rigid. So did Frank.

Pearson formed his hands into a steeple with the fingertips gently prodding his bottom lip. He gazed thoughtfully at Frank and said nothing.

Frank wondered what was in the red folder.

Finally, as if reaching a hard decision, Pearson leaned forward and sighed. 'How long have you been with us, Frank?'

'You mean working in this factory?' Frank said.

The point of his response wasn't lost on Pearson, who had arrived only eighteen months ago with the latest takeover. He put his elbows on the desk. 'Yes, how long have you been working in this factory?'

'Over twenty years,' Frank said, pushing his shoulders back a little. 'Been here longer than anyone.'

'You must have joined straight after the war,' Pearson said as he looked down at the contents of the red folder he'd now opened.

'A couple of years after, actually,' Frank said. 'Got me first job in a timber yard, then I odd-jobbed around to see a bit of the country, y'know.'

'Mmm ... interesting,' murmured Pearson, although he clearly wasn't the slightest bit interested. He continued to study the contents of the folder with such intensity that Frank found his own eyes drawn to it. He tried in vain to read what was written there.

After much too long, Pearson looked up.

'To be perfectly frank, Frank—' He paused, caught unawares by his unintentional wordplay; if he thought about smiling at it, he wisely didn't. 'I have some rather unpleasant news ...'

Frank didn't hear too much of what was said after that. His mind drifted out to the goings-on outside the window — the traffic choking the road with after-school chaos, the milling grey clouds in an undecided sky.

'... *circumstances beyond our control ...*'

A schoolgirl riding past on a rusty bike, she looked familiar, a friend of Debbie's?

'... *duty to our shareholders ... we reluctantly ...*'

Pearson had a huge pimple above his right eyebrow. A beer bloom, it looked painful.

'... *grateful for your contribution ...*'

The carpet featured repeating patterns of the company's logo. Frank's shoes needed a polish.

'*And a fairly substantial redundancy payment ...*'

'Stick it up your arse!' Frank interrupted.

'Now hang on a minute.'

'Hang on yourself, you smug prick!'

'Look! There's no need ...'

'No need for what?' Frank demanded. 'You and your bean-counting pals march in here with your fancy systems and jumped-up titles and overnight you're all fucking experts. Never mind the people who've been here for years. Never mind all the hard work they've put in to build up this business. It doesn't add up to a bucket of shit to you, does it? It's *business*, that's all. Cut the staff, increase the profits. It's that simple. Nothing personal. Too bad, so sad, see you later, Frank.'

'It's not just you, it's ...' Pearson was trying to get up out of his seat but it rocked and swivelled and refused to let him free.

Frank was on his feet now, leaning across the desk.

Pearson suddenly looked very young and unsure of himself.

'Well, *me* is all I care about, mate,' Frank said. 'Me and twenty of the best years of my life.'

'Be reasonable, Frank.'

'Don't you call me Frank. I'm MR MOSELEN to you, sonny.'

'Okay, *Mr Moselen*, you're fired!' Pearson said defiantly, although he twitched nervously as he said it.

Frank swore in disgust and wheeled away.

Alerted by the raised voices, a small crowd had gathered to stare through the glass door. They pulled back as one as Frank threw it open.

He turned back to Pearson. 'The union isn't going to wear this crap.'

Pearson seemed to regain some of his lost confidence. 'We've already spoken to the union. We've come to an agreement ...'

Frank didn't stay to hear any more. He strode out of the office and across the factory floor, oblivious to the roar and crash of the steel presses and the curious eyes of those who had drifted out of the inner sanctum to gaze after his departing form. Some were shaking their heads reproachfully, some giggled nervously, others were plainly embarrassed for him; too few wore a look of sadness or regret.

Someone called out his name but he ignored it.

He swept back into the Dispatch Department, threw his dustcoat onto the floor and fought his way into his battered jacket. Ignoring the questions and protestations of the bewildered storeman he'd left in charge, he jumped down off the loading bay and walked blindly out across the highway, filling the afternoon with the screech of brakes and the cursing of drivers.

Just as he reached the other side of the road, a bus pulled up to deposit some schoolchildren. Without thinking, he clambered aboard and asked for a ticket to wherever it was going.

The driver frowned but took his money and gave him a ticket to the end of the route.

Children chased each other towards tomorrow, mothers struggled home with too few groceries for too much money, old men dug life into gardens, young lovers wrestled in doorways — Frank rode past seeing none of it.

When the bus reached the end of its journey, he climbed down into a strange street in an unfamiliar neighbourhood and walked hard and fast towards the sinking sun until his lungs were bursting and his legs screamed out for rest.

Somewhere in the distance he could hear them calling. The lucky ones who died as heroes with their truths intact, who would never see how the world they fought so hard to protect could so quickly forget them, who would never have to suffer ingratitude, humiliation and a mind-sapping sense of failure, who would never know the impotency of growing old.

It wasn't an unfamiliar feeling, the one that filled him now. He'd experienced it many times before — in tall buildings, on cliff tops and even once on a footbridge over the freeway — the urge to lean that bit too far ... But always, at the last moment, he'd pull himself together and drive the madness from him. Usually, the power of this feeling, the terrible temptation of it, frightened him; now, he welcomed it like an old friend.

A wind from the south chased a ball of paper across the railway platform and teased at his trouser legs. He shivered and folded his arms tighter. According to the surly stationmaster, the next train through was an express that wouldn't stop at this station. An all-stops commuter train would follow shortly thereafter. Frank felt calm and sure. He heard the express coming. He moved to the platform edge. His despair was complete.

Then a little girl came laughing and skipping out onto the platform. Golden-haired and full of life, she'd run far ahead of her grandmother, who was trying in vain to call her back. Shrieking excitedly at the sight of the approaching express, the little girl turned to urge her granny to hurry. She didn't see the edge of the platform. She didn't see Frank.

She fell.

Frank jumped.

The screams of the bystanders were lost in the roar of the passing train.

The carriages clattered away into the distance. No one spoke.

A few white-faced people moved to the platform edge, afraid to see what they might see. Looking down, they saw the figure of a broken man sprawled amongst the oil-splattered litter beside the tracks.

He was very still. A woman sobbed.

Then the man's shoulders heaved and he slowly rolled over to reveal the little girl safe beneath him. They were both crying and holding on to each other as if to life itself.

Frank didn't notice the frightened faces staring down at him. He was staring up at a tiny speck soaring high above. A skylark.

And the only sound in the world was the sound of its singing — old songs for forgotten heroes.

MY FAVOURITE PLACE IN
THE WORLD

———

This is my favourite place in the whole world — up here, in the fork of this old oak tree. Dad says this tree's been here for years and years — since before he can remember even. He says that when he was a boy, he and his brothers used to play in it, too. But they didn't come here every day like I do, just to sit and think about stuff and watch what's happening all around.

I don't really mean to spy on people, it's just that sometimes I can't help it. The tree's on the top of a hill, you see, so I can see for miles, and I see all kinds of neat things. And some stuff I shouldn't. I saw Doris Martin steal milk out of Tiny White's letterbox — which might sound pretty crook to you, but I reckon he deserved it, because I've seen him pinching the Hurleys' newspaper.

Serves them right, too, because they let Erik, their Great Dane, crap on our front lawn when they're out walking him. I haven't told Dad about this, though, because he said he'll 'shoot the bloody dog!' if he finds out who it is, and you can never tell with Dad — he might be joking but he might not.

The worst thing I ever saw from up here was when Mrs Jackson used to have that ginger-haired salesman bloke round when Mr Jackson was away on work trips. That was a real hard secret to keep, I tell you. That salesman was a real seedy-looking character, if you ask me. Didn't make any difference to Mrs Jackson though, she was crazy about him. He used to park his big Chevy round the corner near old lady Cranston's place, then he'd walk down the hill like he wasn't going anywhere special, and when he got near the back of the Jacksons' place, he'd sort of spin around on his heels, casual-like, to see if anyone was watching. If anyone was around, he'd just walk on and come back a little while later and go through the whole thing again. (He never saw me, of course.) Anyway, when he was sure there was no one about, he'd duck in the back gate and Mrs Jackson'd open the door and grab him and kiss and cuddle him like he was her long-lost brother or something.

Like I say, he never saw me and I'm pretty sure he never saw Mrs Foster either. She's the old bag who lives across the road from the Jacksons. She's always poking her nose through those big green curtains in her front room.

Spying. A bit like me, I suppose; only she's a bitch about it, and I'm not. I don't tell anyone what I see; she tells everyone. And she doesn't always get it right, either. Anyhow, she always seemed to be at the window whenever that salesman came creeping down the road, so I bet it was her that told Mr Jackson about it. Anyway, he found out about it somehow and boy, was he pissed off.

Dad says you should never hit women, but old Jacko sure didn't pay too much attention to that line of thinking. From what I could see, he gave his missus a real hiding. Chased her all over the house whacking her, punching walls and chucking things. She's screaming 'I'm sorry, Jacko!' and he's yelling stuff at her that I couldn't make out — but there were plenty of 'f' words, that's for sure. I could only see little bits of what was going on, but what I could see wasn't good. It was a bit scary, actually. Even worse cos I've known the Jacksons ever since I can remember and they're both nice people — you'd like them, you really would.

The strangest thing was, when it was all over, it was Mr Jackson who was crying. Anyone would think it was him that got the hiding, not her. Pretty soon Mrs Jackson comes over and she's stroking his back and hugging him. Next thing you know they're kissing and doing other stuff that I'm not going to tell you about. People are weird, I tell you. I never saw that seedy salesman again, though. And I never told anyone about what I saw either. I don't even think that nosy bitch Mrs Foster knows about the hiding. I think she was out at the time, which is just as well, otherwise it would have been all over town in a couple of minutes.

That all happened some time ago and things are much better now. The Jacksons still come over to our house for dinner and cards and stuff like that, and they seem real happy these days. She loves him, I reckon, so I don't know why she did what she did. He loves her, that's for sure. Though, I've noticed he doesn't go away so much now.

Anyway, I see a lot of goings on from up in this tree that would really surprise you, but I'll keep them to myself if you don't mind. People have a right to some secrets, I reckon.

My Great-grandma Hansen used to live just over there, in that little wooden house the Martins live in now. She sold it years ago and went to live with my Great-uncle Les and his wife, her daughter, May. Grandma was nearly ninety and getting too doddery to be living by herself, so it was either live with May or go to one of those old folks' homes and Auntie May wouldn't hear of that.

They put Grandma in the front room — the one that used to be Dick's.

Dick was Les and May's son, which made him Dad's cousin, only he was a lot younger than Dad. He'd been born when Les and May were both getting on a bit. 'An accident,' Mum says, whatever that means. I don't know too much about Dick, really. They say he didn't have much of a life because he was always sick and kept to himself a lot. I have to say he was always nice to me, though. He always had something to say that he thought I might find interesting. And he always seemed to be interested in what I had to say, too — which is fairly unusual because I was only a little kid then and you know how little kids tend to babble. But I have to admit, being with Dick was a bit spooky. He spent most of the time in his room with his curtains drawn and when you went in to see him it was like talking to a shadow. You couldn't ever see his face properly, so you didn't know whether he was looking at you or what.

Whenever we went to visit them, Mum would always say something like 'John, why don't you go and say hello to Dick, you know he's always pleased to see you.' (Mothers are always saying stuff like that and putting you in an embarrassing position so you can't say no without looking like a turd.)

Anyway, Les and May would nod and smile at me, cos old Dick was fairly lonely, I reckon — I don't suppose he had too many visitors other than us family. So, what with one thing and another, I'd more or less have to go in and chat to him so as not to hurt anyone's feelings.

But, as I say, being in there with Dick was pretty weird. His room always smelled of medicine and I didn't like to hang around in there too long in case whatever he had was catching. I never knew what his sickness was exactly. No one ever told me. I only know it was pretty serious and everyone was always talking about how Dick was going to die and how it was a crying shame because he was so brilliant and everything. Then they'd start shaking their heads and looking sad and helpless, the way grown-ups always do when the matter is 'in the hands of the Almighty'.

Anyway, they were right; Dick died before his twenty-second birthday. I was sad, I guess, but I reckon if there's such a place as heaven, Dick's got to be a lot better off up there than he ever was down here. Poor bugger.

Shortly after that, Great-grandma Hansen moved in. She stayed in the room most of the time, too. One big difference though: Grandma liked to have the curtains and the windows open most of the time. So it was much brighter when she was in there. It didn't pong so much of medicine, either.

'Fresh air, that's what you need,' she'd say. 'That's the secret, Johnny, lot's of fresh air.' She never actually said what it was the secret to.

When you went to visit Grandma, she'd offer you a blackball from this huge jar she kept by the bed. I don't particularly like blackballs, but old Grandma always got a big kick out of it when you had one — she'd smile like crazy and tell you how she used to love them when she was a kid — so I'd always take one just to make her happy. Only, when she'd hold out the jar, her hands would be shaking so bad I could hardly get my hand in it. So I'd have to try to hold the jar still for her — without making it too obvious. I must have pretty near wore her out the amount of time I used to take trying to get one of those bloody blackballs out of that jar. They were always stuck together so you had to sort of pry them apart with your fingers, which could take a little time, and all the while old Grandma would be trembling and wheezing. It would have been easier if she'd just left the jar on the table and let me help myself, but I wasn't going to tell her that in case I hurt her feelings or something.

Anyway, once I was sucking happily on my lolly, Grandma would lie back against her huge heap of pillows and tell me to sit in this big old armchair by the window. Then she'd tell me some story she'd told me about a zilllion times before. I didn't mind, though, because she was a good old stick and she had nearly a hundred years to look back on, which is pretty awesome when you think about it. And I'd have to say, her stories were pretty interesting, too. Like the time Uncle Les went out after honey and got chased by a huge swarm of bees and was so frightened that he jumped into a river and then remembered he couldn't swim; or how when she was first married, she used to walk the twenty miles from Howick to Auckland just to get a bag of flour; or how she could remember when the stockade up on the hill was a place for the white people to go when the Maoris attacked — and not a place for teenagers to go to drink beer and feel each other up like it is now.

I can see all the land that used to be Grandma's from where I'm sitting now — I can see our house, and Uncle

Les's place, and the Stokes', and the Hurleys', and all the other people on that side of the street. It all used to be Grandma's farm. Dad says that just after the war she offered to sell him a big piece of it for only five hundred pounds. It's worth millions now, he says. He kicks himself sometimes, when he thinks about that. But he said five hundred pounds might as well have been a million for all the hope he had of getting it back then.

Anyway, she was full of interesting stories, my grandma.

By the way, you probably noticed I'm calling her Grandma, even though she was really my great-grandmother. Her daughter, my father's mother, my real grandma, died before I was born. It must be pretty lonely when your children die before you do, I reckon.

In case you hadn't worked it out, Auntie May was Dad's mother's sister — and a lot like her in many ways, people said. Only May was an awful nag and they say Dad's mum wasn't.

To tell the truth, I reckon May was the world champion nagger. 'Les, do this; Les, do that. Les, how many times have I told you not to ...' I guess she had to nag a bit, though, cos Les was a slack bastard in many ways. He could make you laugh, though. A real character, my dad always said. Uncle Les always saw the funny side to everything. Not May, but. She didn't laugh at anything much.

Actually, in lots of ways, they were a weird couple. Les was a messy bloke who loved drinking home brew and playing jokes on people. He had no time for the church or anything to do with it. But Auntie May was always threatening people — especially Les — with the devil. She was Catholic, you see, a full-on God-botherer.

You never saw anything quite so comical as Uncle Les trying to be real good to please Auntie May when old Father Donnelly was in the house. This happened pretty near every Sunday because Auntie May always cooked up a huge roast lunch on a Sunday and she'd always invite Father Donnelly over. Seeing as he was a bit of a freeloader — if you can say that about a holy man — he'd usually say yes. I reckon there were two reasons Uncle Les put up with this. Firstly, because Father Donnelly had been so kind to Auntie May after Dick died; and secondly, and this was the big part, I reckon, because old Father Donnelly didn't exactly hate a drink. In fact, he was a bit of a pisshead. This gave Les the perfect excuse to get stuck into his home brew on a Sunday — something Auntie May wouldn't have put up with normally. On more than one Sunday that I can remember, Uncle Les and Father Donnelly spent the afternoon getting as pissed as farts while Auntie May went about the place crossing herself like crazy, and asking the Lord to forgive them. Some of Father Donnelly's Sunday evening services must have been a hoot, I reckon.

Grandma Hansen was a Catholic, too, so Father Donnelly's visits always gave her the opportunity to confess and do whatever else it is Catholics do when they get a priest behind closed doors. Whatever it was, it was good for her; she always seemed happier after he'd been.

Speaking of confessions, I have to confess I've never even been inside a church. I was meant to go once, for Dick's funeral, but I couldn't do it. That was about the only time I can remember Mum getting a bit tricky about me not going to church. But there was no way they were getting me in there. All that church hoo-ha has always looked a bit up itself for me — people getting all dressed up and putting on that snotty face people get when they're doing something good and you're not.

To be honest, I find it all a bit scary, too.

I watched from outside once — when I was waiting for my cousins Annie and Charles to come out. Boy, what a carry-on — all that standing and sitting and kneeling and singing. The prayers sounded like magic chants to me — like voodoo or something. And what about the way the priests dress up? Reminds me a bit of pictures I've seen of the Ku Klux Klan.

Must be expensive, too, all those big cathedrals with the fancy glass in the windows and the gold and silver and stuff — must be worth a few bob, mustn't it?

I remember how Miss Royston, our teacher in Standard One, was always reading stuff out of the Bible. One day she told us this neat story about Jesus throwing the moneylenders out of a temple. She reckoned Jesus said it would be easier for a camel to pass through the eye of a needle than for a rich man to get into heaven. I thought it was pretty funny that — imagine a camel trying to squeeze through the eye of a needle. He had a lot of stories like that, old Jesus; he must have been a pretty amusing bloke, I reckon. Anyway, Miss Royston said that what he really meant was that God didn't think too much of rich people in general. She said most of the saints, for instance, were poor, and that's the way God wanted it. Well, if that's the case, you'd think he'd have some serious questions about some of those flash churches you see everywhere, wouldn't you?

By the way, the reason I was waiting outside the church for Annie and Charles that time was because they were staying with us for the weekend. They used to come over and stay with us quite often.

Boy, what a wimp Charles was.

It wasn't really his fault, though; his mum, my Auntie Vi, was pretty strict on him. She didn't even like to see him getting dirt on his clothes or anything. In fact, she had so many rules they had to bring a list of do's and don'ts whenever they came to stay. It's true — I swear! She used to write down a list of rules for them. And if they wanted to stay with us for the weekend, one of the rules was that they had to go to church on Sunday.

My parents aren't at all like that. Dad says there isn't a great deal of proof about the whole God thing, really. He says he's heard a lot of rumours about heaven, but he's never met anyone who's been there. I thought that was pretty funny. I tried telling it to Miss Royston — she didn't think it was funny at all. That was the first time I ever heard the word blasphemy and found out that it was serious enough to get you caned by the headmaster. I've given the religious jokes a bit of a miss since then; people can get pretty sensitive about things like that, I reckon.

I mentioned that Charles was a bit soft; well, one day I decided to toughen him up a bit.

Me and my mates had built this big fort out of mud and wood and rocks and stuff at the base of a big pine tree at the back of the football fields. One Sunday, just before his mum came to pick them up, I talked old Charles into getting into the fort to defend it while the rest of us attacked. The idea was to sling a lot of mud up there and get old Charles a bit dirty. Only trouble was, Annie insisted on getting in there with him and that kind of put a bummer on things. There was no talking her out of it, so I made her promise to stay down against the front wall of the fort where she wouldn't get hit.

Pretty soon we were running up the hill hurling blobs of mud for all we were worth and old Charles was chucking it back pretty good, too. But we were better throwers and he was really copping it. He was enjoying himself, though; we could hear him laughing like mad every time he hit one of us.

Then, bugger me if Annie doesn't decide to stand up and sweep the top of the fort wall with a leafy branch she's found in there — like she's doing housework or something. Next thing you know she cops a big hunk of clay fair in the face and it knocks her eye out. I mean right out! So it's hanging there looking back up at her. Naturally, she starts screaming, and pretty soon Charles is screaming, and I'm screaming, and my mates are screaming ...

But that was nothing to the screaming that went on when we got home. Dad gave me such a hiding I thought *my* eyes were going to pop out. And Auntie Vi gave Charles one, too — but that was more for getting his clothes dirty, I reckon. Anyway, they took Annie up to the hospital and the doctors managed to pop her eye back in in no time. Works as good as ever, she says. Pretty amazing, don't you think, the way eyes can pop in and out like that? It'd be a great party trick.

I wasn't too popular for about a million years after that and we don't see much of Annie and Charles any more.

Grandma Hansen had a huge patchwork quilt covering her bed. She made it herself out of thousands of bits of leftover wool. I suppose it sounds really awful to you, all those different colours on the one quilt; but when the sun was pouring in through the windows, that old quilt sure used to cheer the room up. Sometimes — especially when Auntie May wasn't there to tell us not to — Grandma would let me get up on the bed with her. She was only tiny and it was a big bed so there was lots of room.

One afternoon Auntie May and Uncle Les had to go into Auckland for some urgent reason or another, so they rang to see if Mum could come up and look after

Grandma. Mum was out so I said I'd come up until Mum got home. This was a pretty big responsibility for a ten-year-old, but seeing as Mum was due back at five, May said it would be okay. Trouble was, I forgot to leave Mum a note. I didn't worry about it at the time, though; I knew I could always phone her.

After I'd had my usual blackball and Grandma had told me the story about her brother Lloyd and the smuggler's daughter from Kaitaia for about the hundredth time, she asked me if I'd like to get up on the bed with her. It was a warm summer afternoon and we'd had swimming that day at school and I was pretty worn out, so I couldn't get up there quick enough. Then she said she wanted to give me a cuddle. I remember thinking it was strange, because she usually didn't do that, and I have to say I was glad she didn't, because she was so shaky and sick-looking that it made me kind of uncomfortable to get too close to her. But, as I told you, I liked her a lot and wouldn't want to upset her or anything, so I snuggled against her and let her cuddle me to her heart's content. It was pretty nice really. Comfortable. So comfortable that I soon fell asleep.

When I woke up it was dark, but May and Les still weren't home. I found out later they'd called to say they'd be late, but I didn't hear the phone ringing. They'd tried to call Mum as well, but she'd been out looking for me. And panicking, I bet. I'd never been gone for so long before without telling her where I was going. So, what with one thing and another, things were a bit confused there for a while.

I know for sure Grandma didn't hear the phone either. She was dead.

They reckon she died just after I fell asleep. By the time I woke up, her body had gone all stiff and her arms were locked tight around me, but her eyes were still wide open.

I shit myself.

She had me under the arms and I couldn't move up or down. I tried pulling her hands apart and broke one of her fingers. I heard the bone snap.

That's when I saw Grandma and Dick standing together at the foot of the bed. At first they were little more than shadows but I knew it was them. Then they came closer and I could see that Grandma's face was just a skull with blackballs in the sockets where her eyes should have been. Dick had no face at all, just an empty black space. They began to walk around the bed, one either side, calling my name. Grandma was smiling. Then, ever so slowly, she plucked a blackball from her eye socket and offered it to me ...

Uh-oh, here comes Mum! She's got that nosy bitch Mrs Foster with her, and the new postman whose name I don't know. Mrs Foster is pointing at me and talking to that postman at a million miles an hour. (That's the trouble with this oak tree — in winter it loses its leaves so anyone can see me sitting up here.)

'Look, there he is,' Mrs Foster's saying. 'He's always up there. It's not normal, I tell you.'

Mum's not paying too much attention; she doesn't like Mrs Foster any more than I do. Anyway, she doesn't need that old hag to tell her where I am; she always knows where I am. Ever since the night I got trapped in Grandma's arms, Mum's made sure she knows where I am every minute of the day. You can't blame her, I suppose — it must be pretty scary for a mother to have her kid go missing like that.

'Time to come home, John,' Mum's saying. 'We're having your favourite — roast pork and apple sauce.'

'And cauliflower cheese?' I ask. Might as well go for the lot, I reckon.

'Of course!' she says smiling. She's real pretty when she smiles, my mum. 'Come on, Dad's brought you a present!'

A present, neato! I wonder what. A model aeroplane? Jeez, I hope it's a 747, I broke the last one.

I like cuddling Mum. Not many boys like to show affection for their mums, especially when there are other people looking; they think it's a bit sissy or something. I don't. I think it's nice. I even like to hold Mum's hand when we're just out for a walk; it's like we're best friends or something.

Mrs Foster's not my friend, though; she's a bitch. Yeecchhh! We're going to have to walk right past her now. Look at the way she screws up her face when she talks — as if she isn't ugly enough to begin with. She's always going on about me sitting up in the tree — as if it were any of her business in the first place. It's not as if she owns the tree or anything. It's in the park, it's public property; anyone would think it was a crime or something.

'That's him, that's the one I was telling you about,' she's whispering to the new postman. 'He climbs up there every day — been doing it ever since his Great-grandma Hansen died. He was with her when she died, y'know; they say he was trapped in her arms for hours.'

Silly bitch. Hell, I've been climbing up in that old oak tree since way before Grandma died. It's my favourite place in the whole world. Everybody knows that. Everyone except Mrs Foster.

'I mean, it's not normal, if you want my opinion,' she says. 'A thirty-year-old man who still climbs trees, I ask you ...'

THE SWIMMING LESSON

Colin's family wasn't rich. Back in New Zealand they'd lived in a small, two-bedroom home his father had built during weekends. Before that, home had been a shack made out of a Caterpillar bulldozer crate. So the privileged life they now enjoyed in Singapore was an aberration, but an enjoyable one. Now they had servants, a big shiny Chevrolet and a spacious apartment in one of the more sought after suburbs on the island. They had all these things because they now belonged to that pampered group of foreigners known as expatriates: people who, having been transported by fate or ambition to some far-flung colony populated by dusky races, are suddenly elevated to a social status and standard of living far beyond anything they've ever known before. In Singapore at the time of which I write, indulged by servants and a variety of gin-soaked 'Members Only' clubs (which meant, in essence,

'No Natives!'), many 'expats' fell victim to delusions of superiority they were never able to shake off. The British, in particular, were guilty of this. Having been brought up under a class system at home, they naturally created a similar structure to suit their new environment. The result being that the natives were generally placed at the very bottom of the ladder, while even the most bumptious and uneducated English person was elevated to a position of importance. At least in their own minds.

Ironically, while those born to a privileged station in life often know how to treat the less fortunate with dignity and respect, those who have the trappings of privilege suddenly thrust upon them often do not.

The latter can be a very ugly type of person.

Thankfully, Colin's family wasn't guilty of this. His father, a New Zealander of Swedish/Irish/Scottish descent, encouraged a rather more egalitarian attitude. While he wouldn't go so far as to say that all people were created equal — on the contrary, he maintained that some people were clearly fools from birth — he did believe that all people ought to be treated equally. It's tempting to say that he passed this attitude on to his children; but the truth is children are born that way — they have no natural prejudices, they learn them. Consequently, until the time he was eight years old, Colin's attitude to people was the same curious, open-minded one he was born with — simply because he'd never been taught otherwise.

Then he met the boy with the swimming pool.

Even for those used to the climate, the day was punishingly hot. Colin was lying on his stomach on the cool concrete floor with his face only inches away from two large jars he'd placed side by side. Each jar contained a lone male Siamese fighting fish. They were glaring at each other through the glass, their long fins rippling gently, rainbow colours of rage pulsating along their bodies — great amusement for an eight-year-old boy.

He sipped his Coke. The ice rattled. He pressed the glass against his forehead and let the condensation run down his face. Overhead, a ceiling fan whirred valiantly, but his mother — who was lying exhausted on the couch — still fanned herself with a magazine that she had long since given up trying to read. The air moved around them like molasses.

They both looked up at the sound of excited children running up the stairs outside their front door. Colin was on his feet and had the door open before anyone had the chance to knock.

There, panting excitedly on the landing, was Shirley Rankin, her younger brother Kevin, and Colin's best friend, Martin Baistow — a mischievous Australian boy who lived in a bungalow across the valley.

'Wanna come swimming?' Martin said excitedly.

'Yeah! Yeah! Where?' Colin said in disbelief.

'Kev met a kid who's gotta pool. An' he's asked us down for a swim!'

'Yes!' said Kevin, importantly. 'He said I could ask anyone I wanted.'

Without waiting for further details, Colin raced back inside to get his swimming togs.

'Where are you going, mister?' his mother said as he dashed past.

'Kev's met a kid who's gotta pool an' he's invited us for a swim!' he shouted from his bedroom.

'What kid? I've never heard of anyone who's got a pool around here. Are you sure?'

'Sure, I'm sure. Ask Martin.'

'Martin, is he telling the truth?'

'Yes, Mrs Cameron,' Martin yelled, far too loudly, from the door. 'Kev said. Didn'tcha, Kev?'

Being of middle-class English stock, both Kevin and Shirley spoke in a far more adult and precise manner than either Martin or Colin.

'Yes, Mrs Cameron, Shirley was with me,' Kevin confirmed.

'Shirley?'

'It's true, Mrs Cameron. The boy's name is Steven and he lives in that big house the Canadians used to live in,' Shirley said.

'There, see!' Colin said as he raced back into the room pulling up his togs.

'Who's going to watch over you kids? Are there any adults?' his mother worried, following after him as he hurried for the door.

'Their driver will watch us,' Shirley answered, seriously. 'Steven said his mother insisted on it!'

'I'll be careful, Mum, I promise,' Colin said.

She knew he would be. He was an excellent swimmer and really quite sensible despite his tender years. In fact, most of the children were good swimmers — one of the benefits of living in the tropics. She went to the door and looked down at her son's excited face — the chance to go for a swim on a day like this must be like a dream come true, how could she refuse him?

Only ... she had never met these people and you never knew what they might be like.

'Colin,' she said, quietly.

Her tone made him look up at her curiously. 'Yes, Mum?'

'Do you know this boy?'

'No.'

'Are you sure he will want you to come?'

'Yes, yes, he will — truly!' Shirley interrupted. 'He said we could bring anyone we liked.'

Colin could see his mother was unconvinced. This called for desperate measures. 'Pleeeease, Mum, can I? Pleeease!!!' he pleaded as he hugged her and adopted his cutest face.

It worked. To forbid him to go would break his heart; she couldn't do that, even though she had serious reservations. 'Okay,' she agreed. 'But you be careful. And don't you go anywhere near that pool unless an adult is with you.'

'No, Mum, I promise!'

'Yeah, we promise,' Martin said, impatient to be on his way.

'Do all your mothers know about this?' she asked, attempting one last delaying tactic.

'Yes, Mrs Cameron. Mum rang Steven's mother and she said it was quite all right,' Shirley said.

Now Colin knew the way was clear. Shirley never lied — everyone knew that.

'All right then,' his mother said. 'But don't stay too long. And Colin — don't you forget to say thank you to Steven's mother!'

'No, Mum!'

'Bye, Mrs Cameron!'

'See ya, Mrs Cameron!'

Without a backward glance they were gone. With a sigh she closed the door and went back to her fanning and worrying.

By the time they reached the big house at the end of the long drive there were eight of them. They'd picked up the others along the way leaving a trail of bewildered, out-negotiated, but not quite convinced parents in their wake. Steven's mother had received a number of phone calls as a result. The effort must have worn her out because by the time they arrived, she was upstairs taking a nap.

Steven was a happy, peach-faced boy who welcomed

them with a shy wave of his hand and a generous smile. A floppy wide-brimmed hat protected him from the sun. The almost blue colour of his skin told them he hadn't been in the country long.

Kevin did his best to introduce everyone but his attempts were lost in the excited babble.

Ahmad, the Malayan driver charged with watching over them, stood quietly in the background puffing on a clove-scented cigarette.

Steven introduced him. 'This is Ahmad, he's going to look after us.'

Ahmad nodded.

'Hi, Ahmad!' the children chorused, but they were far more interested in the pool than the lifesaver.

'Selamat hari,' said Colin.

'Selamat hari,' Ahmad smiled at him.

Steven was impressed. 'Golly, you speak like a native,' he said.

'You'll soon learn,' Colin said. It was no big deal — all the servants spoke Malay, it was easy enough to pick up.

'Oh, I do hope so,' Steven said. 'Come on then, let's go.'

Steven fell in at Colin's side and began chatting away happily as if he'd known him all his life. By the time they reached the pool, Colin knew that Steven was nine years old, had only arrived four days ago from somewhere near Manchester, his father was some bigwig in a petrol company, and his older sister was in boarding school in

England — where he, too, would be going when he was twelve.

Colin also knew — with a child's unerring instinct — that Steven was a kind-hearted kid who would make a good friend. Better than that, a good friend with a swimming pool!

'Last one in's a rotten egg!' shouted Shirley as she plunged into the deep end.

A few of the others jumped in after her yelling gleefully.

'Geez, I hope Shirl isn't gonna wanna play any of her dumb girls' games,' Martin moaned.

'What sort of games?' Steven asked quickly — he was already quite stricken with Shirley.

'Aw, Swiss Family Robinson or somethin' like that,' Colin said. 'She'll get us to build a hut out of chairs 'n' stuff, then she'll throw rocks 'n' things into the pool and say they're pearls or treasure or somethin', an' we'll have to dive in an' get them for her cos she'll be the princess or somethin' stupid like that.'

'There's no princess in Swiss family Robinson,' Steven said, quite correctly.

'Doesn't matter to her. I tol' you they were dumb games.'

'Yeah, an' sometimes Col 'n' me pretend to be sharks and we swim underwater and rip the princess's togs off so everyone can see her royal bum,' Martin lied.

Steven believed him, though. Now he was really interested. 'Hey, Shirley,' he shouted. 'Would you like to play Swiss family Robinson?'

'Ooooh yes — let's!' Shirley squealed.

Colin and Martin, moaning in unison, fell into the pool as though they'd been shot. The water was wonderful — cool, clear, heavenly. For this they would even play Shirley's dumb games.

With help from Ahmad, they built Shirley a palace out of tables, towels and pool chairs, and she soon had all the boys diving for pebbles as Colin had predicted.

Steven was enjoying every minute of it, especially since Shirley had diplomatically made him the Prince.

On the whole, things were going fairly smoothly until Colin and Martin decided that they would form a raiding pirate party and steal the princess's precious pearls.

Shirley's screaming was enough to wake the dead.

It was certainly enough to wake Steven's mother. The shutters of a window on the top floor flew open and a ruddy-faced woman leant out and squinted grumpily down at them. Sleep had creased her face and her angry red hair was matted to one side of her head by sweat.

'Steven!' she shouted shrilly. 'What on earth is all that noise about?' Her harsh northern English accent cut through the afternoon like nails across glass.

'Sorry, Mum.' Steven said, looking ludicrous in the crown of bougainvillea flowers Shirley had insisted he wear.

Colin sunk silently to the bottom of the pool. From there he could just make out Steven standing on the edge of the pool reasoning with his mother, while the others stood nervously at the shallow end. Except for Martin who swam slowly across the pool until he was directly above Colin's head, then farted.

Colin exploded out of the water shrieking with laughter.

Steven's mother leaned back in horror. 'My God!' she gasped.

'What?' said Steven.

'Who is that?' she croaked on the point of apoplexy.

'Who?' said Steven.

'That boy! That boy there! That *Malayan* boy,' she screeched and pointed a shaking finger at the pool.

Martin and Colin were still giggling helplessly. The others looked to see whom she meant. She was pointing at Colin.

'You boy, get out of the pool this minute!'

Martin stopped laughing. 'She means you,' he said to Colin in disbelief.

'That's not a Malayan boy, that's Colin!' Shirley said, indignantly.

'He's my friend,' Steven added, valiantly.

'I don't care who he is, Steven,' she squawked. 'I've told you time and time again you're not to have native children in that pool. Play with them if you must, but they are not ever to swim in our pool. God knows what diseases they might be carrying.'

Colin understood what was happening — with his black hair and deep tan, he could quite easily be mistaken for local. In New Zealand, people often mistook him for a Maori. Steven's mother had made a simple error, that was all. 'I'm not a Malayan—' he began.

'Colin,' Ahmad interrupted in Malay. 'Go home, Colin. She does not want you here!'

'Why?' Col asked, also in Malay. 'I don't have any diseases — I'm not a native.'

'And I am, so I do?' Ahmad said, raising one eyebrow.

Steven's mother grew impatient with this private discussion in a heathen language. 'Boy! Boy!'

Colin ignored her.

She turned to Shirley. 'Does he understand English? Tell him I want him out of the pool and off this property, immediately!'

Some of the children had begun to cry.

Not Colin, though, he was angry, not sad. He swam to the side of the pool and climbed out.

Martin climbed out as well — much more slowly.

Shirley picked up her towel. 'I'm leaving, too,' she said, quite properly, between sniffles.

Martin nodded in agreement and tried to hide his tears with a towel as he followed Colin around the pool.

'You other children don't have to go,' the woman said, her voice softer — a pleasant contrast to the harridan-like tones she'd employed moments before. 'Stay. I'll have cook bring out orange pop and sausage rolls.'

Martin and Shirley slowed — orange pop and sausage rolls are powerful antidotes for a child's outrage and there was a lot of swimming time left in the afternoon. It was a hard decision.

Colin made it for them. 'You guys stay,' he said quietly. 'I'll be okay,' he added with more conviction than he felt. He felt little, only that his skin seemed to prickle inexplicably.

'Are you sure?' Shirley asked in her motherly way.

'Yes,' Colin said, curtly. Then he looked up at Steven's mother and muttered in Malay, 'A pox on you, shitface!'

'What did he say, Ahmad? What did he say?' she said — it was the first time she had acknowledged the quiet Malayan's presence.

'He said he is sorry, Mem,' Ahmad replied, in English.

This seemed to please her; a sense of order had been restored. Everyone knew his or her place now. 'Well, you tell him this time okay. But, he no come back, or I very angry,' she said, as if bad English might be easier to translate.

'Yes, Mem,' Ahmad said calmly. Then, reverting once more to his native tongue, he said to Colin: 'Shitface ... is that any way for a boy to talk to a whore?'

Colin chuckled delightedly.

The woman interpreted his laughter as a sign of relief — they were simple people, the natives; you had to be firm with them, though, they respect that.

'All right, young man,' she said expansively, 'we'll forget about it this time, but you not come here again, you understand?'

'Yes, Mem. Thank you, Mem,' Colin said in Malay, while backing away humbly. He was smiling and acting cheerfully, but dying inside.

Martin and Shirley didn't understand what was happening. Why was Colin speaking Malay? They watched him go but did not follow.

After rounding the corner of the house, he turned and walked up the long drive without looking back. Off in the distance, shimmering in the afternoon haze, he could see the block of apartments he called home. Suddenly, he needed to be there — away from this strange woman, her swimming pool and her angry voice.

He felt very alone.

Then he became aware that he wasn't alone — he heard the unmistakable pad of bare feet coming up behind him.

It was Steven, still teary-eyed. 'I'm sorry,' he sniffled.

'It's not your fault.'

'She's *my* mother ...'

'Yeah, but mums can be dumb sometimes.'

Steven glanced back at the house and lowered his voice. 'She'll go back to bed in a minute. You could sneak back in if you wanted.'

'Nah — I have to go home now, anyway.'

'Oh ...' Steven studied his feet intently — fat feet on the end of soft downy legs. After a while he looked up at Colin with sad eyes. 'Can we still be friends?'

Colin read the sincerity in the plump face — something important was happening, but he wasn't sure what. He wasn't sure what to say, either, so he answered with his heart. 'Okay, better not tell your mum, but.'

'I shan't, honestly,' Steven said, conspiratorially.

'Mates then, eh?' Colin smiled.

'Yes ... mates,' Steven agreed, uncertainly — not being familiar with this antipodean term of endearment.

There was nothing left to say.

Colin was first to recognise this. 'Well, see you 'round, I s'pose.'

'Yes, I'll see you around ... mate,' Steven said, awkwardly.

Colin turned and walked away.

When he reached the end of the drive he looked back, but Steven had disappeared.

A few minutes later, as Colin was nearing his apartment, he spied a Chinese woman kneeling in the garden by the steps. As he drew nearer he saw that she was picking red chillies off a small bush.

She looked up and smiled.

Colin frowned. 'They're Mrs Rankin's chillies!' he said, sternly.

'She said I could have some,' the woman explained as she stood and brushed a lock of thick black hair from her eyes. Beautiful by any measure, her kind features and gentle demeanour put him instantly at ease.

She regarded him curiously. 'Where are your friends?'

'Um ... oh, they wanted to stay and play one of Shirley's

stupid games and I got sick of it and came home,' he said quietly, avoiding her eyes.

'Are you hungry?' she said.

'Yes.' He was always hungry.

'There's some bean curd in the fridge. The sweet one you like.'

'Neat!' Colin said and bounded away up the steps.

'Make sure you leave some for your father,' she called after him.

'Yes, Mum,' he said and was gone.

A NOTE FROM VINNY

———

Vinny read the note again. It wasn't long and the words weren't fancy, but it said everything he wanted to say. Frowning in concentration, he signed it carefully in big bold letters, then folded it neatly into a small white envelope, which he slipped into his shirt pocket.

He leant back and surveyed the room. Everything was in order, nice and neat. He'd even tidied the drawers of his tallboy and arranged the bits and pieces on top of it in soldier-like rows: shells from the holiday by the sea with Uncle Bruno, Dad's old pen, some interesting rocks — all the things he'd never been able to throw away, all lined up and tidy. He was pleased with his efforts and knew she would be, too. The mere fact that the bed was made would surprise her — he smiled at the thought of that.

The chair scraped rudely on the floorboards as he rose and went to look at himself in the wardrobe mirror. It was the first time he'd worn the red Western-style shirt she'd bought him. It went well with his black jeans and almost new white sneakers. He looked smart — dressed for the occasion, you might say. If she saw him like this, she'd want to take a photograph. She was always taking photographs: of him, of Tony, of flowers in the garden — of things she wanted to capture and hold and keep unchanged for ever. But things have to change; nothing remains the same for ever. Nothing.

He gave his hair a final pat and walked quickly out of the room. The house was quiet, but the others would be home soon. He had to hurry.

He found what he was looking for in her bedroom wardrobe. It was heavier than he'd expected. He heaved it over one shoulder and carried it down to the kitchen where he leant it against the bench and ran himself a glass of water. His throat was dry. When he'd emptied the glass, he washed and dried it and put it back in the cupboard.

That done, he crossed the kitchen, took the envelope out of his pocket and attached it to the fridge with the little pink magnetic elephant Tony had bought her for Christmas. When he thought of Tony, he sighed.

Re-gathering his load, he made his way out through the back door into the blustery, autumn afternoon. A gust of wind snatched the door out of his grasp and slammed it shut with a loud bang. The house shook: plates rattled in the cupboards, coffee mugs rocked on their little wooden pegs, the little pink magnetic elephant fell off the fridge door and the envelope dropped and slid beneath the fridge.

Keeping low against the fence — out of the wind and out of sight — Vinny snuck out to the old wooden garden shed, which huddled against the back of the garage. He loved being in that shed. He loved the feel of the worn wooden handles on the old garden tools and the smell of oil, fertiliser, potting mix and sawdust, which filled his head with pictures of his father. 'You see that, Vinny?' his father would say, holding up a perfect tomato. 'Plant a seed, give it a little love and next thing you know, you got a whole crop of tomatoes. It's a miracle, that's what it is, Vinny. You don't need no fishes or loaves, you don't got to see no people walking on water. You get yourself a little garden, Vinny; you get yourself a garden and you gonna see all the miracles you ever need to see.'

Happy with his memories, Vinny entered the shed and set about jamming the door shut with a plank of wood. When he was satisfied it would hold, he climbed into the cupboard where the long-handled tools were stored and closed the door. There, alone in the darkness, amongst the spades, hoes, rakes and hedge cutters that had belonged to his beloved father, he put the barrel of a rifle in his mouth and squeezed the trigger.

He was nine years old.

Maria clambered wearily off the bus happy to be home and grateful that the French loaf she was carrying had survived the journey unscathed. She was exhausted, her feet hurt, and the handles of the plastic grocery bags cut cruelly into her fingers. What she would give for an hour or so in a hot bath soaking away the day with a glass of chianti and a good book. Afterwards, maybe, she could watch something silly on television while the boys cooked the dinner. Some hope! They would burn the kitchen down first. Although Vinny, bless him, would do his best if he thought it would please her. The thought of her youngest son's eager smile quickened her pace. She hated having to leave him on his own for two hours each day after school, but what could she do? Babysitters were expensive and you couldn't burden the neighbours with such a responsibility. For a while, Guido and Tony had taken turns watching over him, but now that Guido had found a job and Tony was working for Leo in the fruit shop after school, Vinny just had to get by on his own. Still, he was a good boy, very sensible for his age, so there was no real need to worry.

She was pleased that Guido had a job at last; they needed the money and he needed the respect — especially from Tony. While Vinny seemed good with Guido now, was even quite fond of him as far as she could tell, Tony remained hostile. When Guido had been out of work and hanging around the house 'bludging', as Tony called it, things had been very tense; now that he was contributing, things might change.

She wanted the boys to like Guido. It had been two

years since Al died and they needed a man in the house. God knows she did. Guido would never be Al, but he had other qualities: a big heart, warm eyes, a strong body, good teeth, a good-looking man in every respect. Too damn good-looking — she would have to watch him very carefully.

Men! Al, was the worst, God forgive him. A womaniser until the day he died — a fact some weren't too shy to mention to this day. Even his death — a head-on collision in a part of town where he had no business being at that time of the day — was generally believed to be connected with some woman. 'God's punishment!' her mother had said, piously, and perhaps she was right. Even so, God had been overly zealous, in Maria's opinion. For all his sins, Al had been a good father and in most respects a good husband: kind, considerate, hard-working and generous. An even-tempered man who never raised a hand against the children or her. There were many who were worse off. As for his womanising, she was sure he would have grown out of that eventually. Now, he would never get the chance.

Now there was only Guido, who, with all his faults, was better than having no one at all. And, at thirty-seven years old with two growing boys to care for, she had to accept that her chances of finding another man were not good. This scared her more than she cared to say. Not that her looks would let her down. On the contrary, without being vain, she knew she was still an attractive woman. Okay, so there were a few wrinkles at the corners of her eyes, so what? Some added character, that's all. Nothing make-up couldn't hide. As for her figure, she was a little short, perhaps, but her body was trim and her bosom still firm enough to interest the passing eye. So, visually anyway, she had what it takes. She was no Einstein, it's true, but she was no fool, either. She read when she could, tried to stay abreast of things and could hold a conversation on a fairly wide variety of subjects — which was more than could be said for most of the men she'd met lately. Although, to be honest, she'd met very few. That was half the trouble: to find the right man you need more than right shape, you need time, and time was something she had precious little of. Besides, with so many men in this town being either married or gay, the competition for unattached, straight men was fierce. And most of the contestants were younger and riper than her. All things considered, she was lucky to have Guido. She didn't love him, it's true — after Al she doubted she would ever love again — but Guido loved her and that was a start.

By the time she reached their modest, rented fibro bungalow, it was quite dark. The afternoon's gusts had died into a damp stillness and the smell of burning leaves hung pleasantly in the air. It was beginning to get cold; they would need to light the fire. She liked fires. Guido would have to chop wood. He would complain, of course, but he did little enough around the house as it was. A little wood-chopping could do him no harm. In return, she would make minestrone. He would like that. Tony and Vinny would, too. This was also good — it didn't cost so much to fill their stomachs with minestrone and fresh bread.

But ... there were no lights on in the house. Where was Vinny? He was probably watching TV and hadn't noticed that the sun had gone. The kid was turning into a TV addict, but that was the result of having to amuse himself in the afternoons. The guilt rose in her again. 'Vinny!' she called as she stood at the front door. 'Open the door, son, my hands are full.'

There was no reply.

'Vinny!'

Still no answer. Promising herself to be stricter about the amount of television he was allowed to watch, she walked around to the back of the house. On the way she passed the living room; the TV wasn't on. When she reached the back of the house she saw that there was no light in the kitchen, either. But the back door was unlocked so he couldn't be far away.

'That damned kid,' she swore quietly as she put the shopping down on the kitchen table and painfully straightened her blood-starved fingers. 'If I've told him once, I've told him a thousand times to come straight home after school, and *stay* home.' She was angry at herself as much as Vinny. It wasn't his fault. A strong-willed child of his age left to his own devices was bound to become a bit too independent. Next thing you know she'd have a street kid on her hands. On the other hand, he'd never done this before, so perhaps there was a good reason. Maybe he'd gone down to meet Tony. Maybe he'd just fallen asleep in his room. Of course, that's where he'd be.

Vinny was right, the tidiness of his room did surprise her, but not in the way he'd hoped — it scared her. She knew, immediately, something was very wrong. Snakes of ice crawled in her stomach as she walked slowly around his room touching things.

'Jesus, what's Vinny greasing after?' said a voice behind her.

She whirled and put a hand to her heart.

'Take it easy, Mum, it's only me,' said Tony, amusement dancing in his eyes — only twelve years of age and already as handsome as his father.

'You scared the life out of me,' Maria snapped.

'I'm sorry. I didn't mean to,' he said looking forlorn.

She immediately regretted her tone. 'Sorry, it's not your fault. It's this ...' she said, letting her gaze drift over Vinny's uncharacteristically tidy room.

'Yeah, he's got to be after something.'

'Have you seen him?' she said.

'No, I just got home.'

'He's not here and there were no lights on.'

'Well, he was on his way home when he came past the shop.'

'What time was that?'

'Oh, I dunno, early ... about three thirty, I s'pose.'

'And he said he was on his way home?'

'No, not exactly, but where else would he be going? Come to think of it, I thought it was a bit weird him coming home that way. He usually goes down Union Street. And also ... he hung around like he wanted to talk or something, but I was too busy and Leo got pissed off with him being there.'

'So he came straight home?'

'I guess so.'

'Then, where is he?'

'I dunno.'

'What's this "dunno"? You get good schooling and you've still got to say "dunno". You mean you *don't know* where he is.'

'No, I don't. Where have you looked?'

'Nowhere, I just got home myself. Besides, where should I look? This is no time for hide and seek,' Maria said impatiently.

Tony laughed. 'Jeez, I hope he doesn't start that again. He's too good at it. You remember when he hid inside the sack of spuds and ...'

Maria did not miss the sadness that entered his voice as he trailed off into silence. She knew what he was remembering. They had been playing hide and seek one rainy afternoon and Vinny had hidden himself so well they just couldn't find him. They were still looking when Al had come home from work. He helped them look for a while but soon lost interest. 'Aah, to hell with Vinny,' he'd said. 'I'm hungry. What's for dinner?'

'It's nearly done,' she'd replied. 'I was just going to do some potatoes.'

'I'll do them,' he said. 'You keep looking for the midget.'

So saying he'd opened the big sack of potatoes they kept in the corner of the kitchen and found Vinny, balled up inside, shaking with laughter.

Al dragged him out squealing and kicking and a tickling fight ensued, which ended with the whole family rolling about on the kitchen floor.

Maria remembered Al kissing her as they lay amongst the arms and legs of their giggling children. And she remembered the look in Tony's eyes as he watched them. She wondered if she would ever see that look again.

She put her hand on Tony's arm. He gave her a sad smile.

Then he broke away. 'VINNY!!' he shouted as he walked out into the hall. 'Where are you, dog face?'

They searched in all his usual hiding places without luck.

Maria began to get impatient. 'Have a look outside and see if he's hiding somewhere out there just to give us all heart attacks. I'll ask the neighbours.'

'Aww, Mum. I was gonna watch TV.'

'Do as I say!'

Realising that his mother was in no mood to argue, Tony

dragged himself out into the twilight to look for his not-so-long-lost brother.

For the next ten minutes or so, his half-hearted attempts at searching for Vinny consisted mainly of going to various points in the now gloomy garden and shouting things like 'Vinny! You'd better show yourself, son. It's not funny any more. Mum's getting really pissed off.'

He didn't bother checking the shed. They'd both been told a million times not to go in there — too many sharp and poisonous things, Maria said. Tony was happy to obey this instruction, not because he was obedient by nature, but because whenever he went into that shed he always expected to find his father there and only felt sad when he didn't.

Maria had no luck with the neighbours. Mrs Gibson next door and old Jack Arthur across the road had both seen Vinny coming home, but neither had seen him leave. This didn't mean he couldn't have, but Jack had been working in his front garden all afternoon and he was fairly certain he'd have seen any comings or goings. Mrs Gibson thought she'd heard the back door slam a couple of times late in the day — the wind had been strong enough to ruin some of her roses — but she hadn't seen Vinny. They both told Maria not to worry; Vinny was a good boy and he'd turn up soon.

Tony found the little pink elephant lying on the floor. He was attaching it to the fridge when Maria returned, rubbing her arms against the chill.

'Well?' she said.

'No sign,' Tony shrugged, taking a large bottle of Coke out of the fridge.

'Look again!'

'I've already looked everywhere, Mum. He won't be hiding, you know he never misses *The Simpsons*.'

'The little bugger! When I get my hands on him ...'

'Maybe he's at a friend's place.'

'What friends? Do they live around here?' Maria asked.

'I don't know. If you don't, how do you expect me to?' Tony said, indignantly.

'I don't need your cheek, young man!'

'Sorry—'

'Is his skateboard still here?'

'Yes, that's the first thing I checked.'

Maria crumpled into a chair at the kitchen table. She should call the police, but what could she say? 'My son has been missing for an hour!' Hardly enough to start a citywide search. No, better to wait, there was bound to be a simple explanation — and it had better be a good one. Meanwhile, there were things to be done.

Wearily, she got to her feet and began unpacking the shopping bags. Guido would be home soon — starving as always.

Tony went into the living room to watch television. He was back within minutes. 'Can I light the fire, Mum?'

'We need wood. Guido will have to chop some when he gets home.'

'I can do that.'

'I said Guido will do it.'

'So we all have to freeze our tits off till Mister Macho gets home.'

'Tony!'

Tony sulked in the doorway, glaring at her with fierce proud eyes. He wanted to be the man of the house, like his father. He missed Al desperately, and he openly despised Guido for trying to take his place.

She understood. She went to him, gathered his angry body to hers and began to run her thin fingers through his jungle of curls. 'Don't be so hard on Guido, son. He's only doing what he thinks is right. He's not trying to be your father. No one will ever replace your dad. But it's only natural that he should want to be part of this family. He loves me and, well, you know—'

She felt his body stiffen.

'You're not going to marry him, are you?' he said.

'He hasn't asked me yet.'

Tony pushed her away. 'How could you even think about it?'

His rejection angered her. 'It's time you stopped being so damned selfish, Tony. Sometimes I swear—'

'What about Dad? How can you just forget him like that?'

'Your father's dead, Tony. And no matter how much you or I may want to change that, we can't. He's gone and we can't bring him back again. Life has to go on. For your sake *and* Vinny's, I have to consider the future.'

'Your future, you mean.'

'Yes, mine as well. I can't manage on my own and I don't want to. Guido's a good man, a kind man. Why can't you give him a fair go?'

'I don't trust him, that's why!'

'In what way?'

'I don't know … he's always trying to suck up to us.'

It was true. Sometimes Guido did try too hard. It was his clumsy way of trying to get the kids to like him. It didn't work, though; certainly not with Tony. Nevertheless, he was genuine about it, and she knew he was doing it for her sake as much as her own.

'He's just trying to be your friend. Is there any harm in that?'

'I don't want to be his friend. I wish he'd just piss off and leave us alone,' Tony grumbled. He was jealous and protective. He'd been this way ever since Guido had first started staying overnight.

'So you don't want me to remarry?'

'Not to Guido.'

'Would you rather I continued to live in sin?'

'If you want to,' Tony shrugged. 'Lots of people do.'

So young, yet so cynical; it saddened her. 'Your grandmother won't approve, she already wants him out of here.'

'Then do as your mother tells you. You always tell me to,' Tony smiled, tentatively.

Quick to anger and quick to laugh, he was so much his father's son that it tore her heart. 'Oh Tony,' she said, reaching for him again, tears pushing up into her eyes.

'It's all right, Mum,' he said. 'It's just that ... sometimes ...' He squeezed her tightly.

'I know ... I know.'

They stood like that for as long as it took for them to feel better.

Outside, the twilight gave way to darkness, the streetlights smudged in the dew-filled night, a few early stars winked unnoticed, and a small spider ran across Vinny's right eye.

Tony broke the silence. 'There, do you feel warmer now?'

Maria chuckled. 'Get out of here,' she said, giving his hair a final tousle. 'If you're cold, try running down the road to see if you can find your brother. If you find him, tell him I'd like to warm the seat of his pants.'

As much as it would have amused him to be the bearer of bad tidings to his wayward brother, Tony retired instead to the small, crowded living room to watch television. It was even colder now. Maybe now that Guido had a job, they would be able to afford a few electric heaters; the greasy bastard might turn out to be some use after all.

By the time Guido got home, the minestrone was

bubbling happily on the stove. 'Mama Maria! Somethin' smella mighty good,' he beamed as he burst in through the back door bearing a bottle of chianti.

Tony appeared disapprovingly in the doorway. Guido was a second-generation Australian, but now and again he insisted on putting on a phony Italian accent — it annoyed the hell out of Tony. 'Good! Tarzan's home. Maybe we can get some firewood chopped at long last,' he said without a hint of welcome.

For a second, Guido's eyes darkened, then, just as quickly, his face creased into a broad smile. 'And I'ma happy to see-a you, too, Antonio!'

He crossed to Maria and made to embrace her, but she fended him off.

'Vinny's not home!' she said.

'So — what's this? No Vinny, no kiss?'

'I'm worried, Guido!'

'Why? It's not that late,' Guido said, dropping the accent.

'He's always comes straight home after school, you know that,' she said.

'So tonight he didn't. He's a *boy*, Maria.' Guido shrugged as if this explained everything.

'Then where is he?'

'How should I know?'

'Or care,' Tony interjected from the doorway.

Guido glared at him.

'Tony!' Maria warned.

Tony turned away in disgust. 'I'm bloody freezing,' he muttered as he disappeared into the living room.

Maria put a calming hand on Guido's arm. 'Could you chop some firewood, please?'

'Why me? That kid's old enough to do it himself.'

'God! Sometimes I don't know which of you is the biggest kid,' she snapped. 'He won't chop the wood because I won't let him, that's why. Now, would you please just do as I ask.'

'Okay, okay, take it easy,' Guido said, moving towards the back door. 'Just because Vinny's gone walkabout, there's no need to take it out on me.'

Maria turned her back on him and chopped angrily at some garlic she didn't need.

'What the hell!' Guido grunted as he pushed against the shed door. It felt like it was locked. But there was no lock. Something must have fallen against it. Unless ... 'Vinny, you in there? Open the bloody door!' he shouted. 'Vinny! You hear me? Come out of there, you've got your mother worried sick.'

Alerted by his shouting, Maria and Tony were quickly beside him.

'Stupid kid's locked himself in,' Guido explained, as he banged angrily on the shed walls. 'Vinny, I said open the bloody door!'

Maria turned angrily on Tony. 'Didn't you even look in the shed?'

'He knows not to go in there. You've told him a million

times, the poisons, the axe, I just thought—' Tony blustered.

Guido hammered on the shed again. 'Vinny, open the door!'

'Stop it!' Maria said. 'You'll scare the life out of him.'

'I'd like to thrash the life out of him,' Guido growled.

'Yeah, you could just about manage that,' Tony said.

Guido stepped towards him. 'Jesus Christ, I'm sick of—'

'Guido!' Maria warned.

'Well, shit!' Guido rankled but backed off.

Tony took this as a victory.

Maria ignored the pair of them. 'Vinny, baby — please open the door for Mama.'

Tony rolled his eyes. He knew how Vinny hated it when Maria spoke to him like he was still a baby. You couldn't stop her, though.

'Vinny ... honey,' she cooed.

They listened for any sign of movement. There was none.

'Hey, Vinny, stop pissing about. I'm freezing. We gotta get some firewood,' Tony said.

Silence.

'I always said that was a stupid door,' Guido said to no one in particular. 'Why anyone would have a door opening inwards on such a small shed, I don't know.'

They ignored him; he'd mentioned it often and done nothing about it.

'Why won't he answer?' Maria wondered out aloud,

then thought the worst. 'Weedkiller! Oh, God.' She began pushing frantically against the door, but her tiny frame made little impression.

Guido took over. He gave the door a series of angry kicks. The plank shook loose and fell to the floor. The door flew open. They turned on the light. There was no Vinny.

Maria was relieved. 'Thank God!'

Guido remained suspicious; he was sure the plank had been deliberately propped against the door. It was virtually impossible for it to have fallen there by chance.

He opened the tool cupboard.

Looking down he saw Vinny's little body hunched up against the wall. And he saw that the back of Vinny's head was missing. He made a soft choking sound.

'What is it?' Maria said.

Guido tried to push her away.

Tony slipped past them.

Vinny was buried amid a sea of controversy. A horrified nation viewed the suicide of a nine-year-old with ghoulish incredulity; his angelic face beamed out of newspapers and TV screens for weeks on end. No one could believe that such a perfectly adorable child was capable of killing himself; most were convinced there had to be more to it.

In the beginning, public sympathy had been with Maria. But as time went by, her life — past and present — came under remorseless scrutiny. Reports of her Al's infidelity began to leak. Then a series of exclusive 'inside stories' — told, for a small consideration, by people who vaguely knew her — intimated that Guido was only the last in a long succession of lovers. In the end, thanks to a relentless process of innuendo, people began to believe that Vinny's family environment — and Maria's behaviour in particular — was a major contributor to his sad end. Families and friends argued about her. To some she was merely the innocent victim of a procession of personal tragedies, to others she was a promiscuous and irresponsible mother — and many began to openly despise her for it. Complete strangers muttered angrily at her in the street, others phoned to abuse her anonymously. The final straw came when a reliable but unnamed source revealed that Maria had been collecting a solo mother's benefit even though she had a job and was living in a de facto relationship. At that point, public opinion turned inexorably against her. She lost friends and she lost her job. And months later, when in desperation she sought solace in alcohol, she lost her self-respect.

Having successfully destroyed Maria, people turned their attentions to Guido. Gossip ran rife and began to insinuate a very sick portrait of Maria's dark-eyed lover.

Even Maria, her mind softened by months in an alcoholic stupor, began to believe what they said.

'I can't believe you're asking me this,' Guido protested.

'Well, I am,' she slurred.

'How could you even think—?'

'It's not just me. Leo said—'

'I know what Leo is saying. It's crap! How can you even listen, let alone believe it?'

'It goes on all the time.'

'This is *me* we're talking about, Maria. You know me—'

'Do I? Do I really know you, or do I just know the *you* you want me to know?'

'Listen to you, for chrissake — the piss is ruining your brain.'

'Tony says you spent a lot of time in Vinny's room.'

'Tony takes too many pills.'

'He didn't used to.'

'Well, he bloody does now. He should be here supporting you. But where is he? Out on the street, drugged up to his arsehole, with those deadbeat mates of his. The weak little shit.'

'He's not weak, he's broken-hearted. First Al, then Vinny — it's hard for him. He's trying to come to terms with it, that's all. And he's not taking drugs — he promised.'

'Then he's a fucking liar!' Guido hissed. 'Mind you, who can blame him,' he said staring pointedly at the empty glass in front of her.

Maria dragged the glass to her bosom and unconsciously tried to hide it. 'Never mind me, it's you we're talking about. You did spend a lot of time in Vinny's room, I remember.'

'Yes, as it happens, I did. He loved me to read to him, you know that. You encouraged it.'

'I didn't tell you to cuddle him, did I?'

'He cuddled me. Was I supposed to stop him? He was just a little boy. A lovely little boy with no father.'

'You weren't his father.'

'I was better than no one at all. You were never here.'

'That's not fair — I was working, you ought to try it sometime.'

Guido slammed the table with both hands. 'I got fired remember? Retrenched, they said. And all because of this bullshit,' he said. 'Suddenly everyone thinks I'm some kind of sicko. Even you.'

Maria regarded him with the empty eyes of the very drunk.

He turned slightly in his seat, his voice softened. 'Please, don't do this, baby, you're all I've got.'

'Don't "baby" me,' she said in a faraway voice.

'Maria, please — it's not my fault.'

'It was *your* gun.'

He buried his face in his hands, his fingertips tearing at his forehead, his eyes squeezed tightly shut. 'Yes,' he whispered hoarsely. 'May God forgive me, it was my rifle. I left it loaded. That was my fault. I'll go to my grave knowing this. But as for this other business, these horrible things people are saying ... I never laid a finger on him, Maria, I swear. I loved him. And God knows, I miss him.'

'Mrs Gibson next door said—'

'Mrs Gibson is a nosy bitch.'

'She said she often saw you two going down to the park and you'd be holding hands with him—'

Yes, when we crossed the road. It's a busy road. You know how he was.'

She came around the table to lean unsteadily over him. 'It's not natural for a man to hold hands with a little boy!'

'Aaah, to hell with it. I don't have to listen to this shit,' he said and heaved himself to his feet and pushed past her.

She flung herself at his back, hammering at his head with balled fists. 'Don't you push me around, you bastard!'

He hunched over to avoid her blows. She began to kick him. He turned to protect himself and the toe of her shoe caught him in the face.

He shoved her away angrily. She slammed against the wall.

Tony came in through the back door just as his mother slammed against the wall and crumpled to the floor. His pupils were huge in his haunted eyes.

Guido didn't notice him, he only had eyes for Maria — small and terrified, crouching against the wall, shaking uncontrollably. How could they have come to this? His shoulders heaved, he held his hands out towards her — 'God, honey, I'm so sorry, I—'

Tony swung the axe.

Five years later, the landlord sold the house. He'd always let the place fully furnished and although most of the furniture was somewhat the worse for wear, he was able to sell everything to a second-hand dealer for a price that made them both happy. Two men in a large removal van arrived to take it all away. When they moved the fridge, they found a small, yellowed envelope lying in the dust beneath it. The older man picked it up, but he couldn't read, so he gave it to his partner.

'It's addressed to *Mum*,' the younger man explained, as he tore the envelope open and pulled out the note, which was written in a child's unsteady hand on a single sheet of lined paper.

The older man lit a cigarette. 'What's it say?'

'It's from some kid called Vinny. By the looks of his writing he was only a nipper. Sound's like he's running away from home. Says he loves his mum, and someone called Tony, but he wants to be with his dad. Parents must have been separated, I guess.' Reading on, he began to chuckle. 'And the little bugger gives her a bit of marital advice, too, listen: *I wish you wood marry Guido. I no he makes Tony mad sumtimes, but he's kind to me, and he luvs you heeps.*'

'Bloody kids. It's amazing how they cope, isn't it?' the older man said, scratching thoughtfully at his bristled chin.

'Yeah,' the younger man agreed. 'It's a pity his mum never got the note, though, she would have got a laugh out of it, I reckon.'

A SHORT STORY
WITH NO END

I met *him* in a bar in Singapore. It turned out that, like me, he lived in Australia and that was enough for us to form a bond of sorts. We shared a couple of nights on the town and a few too many drinks, and promised to stay in touch when we got back to Sydney. However, as is often the case with holiday friendships, I haven't seen him since.

During our brief time together he told me a story, which, at the time, I thought too cute and moralistic to bother writing down. For some reason, this no longer concerns me. He said it was a story without an end. I'll leave you to make up your own mind about that. Here it is, as I remember it.

I work for a display company located in one of the inner-city suburbs of Sydney. To get to work I travel by train and bus. Sometimes, for the exercise, I get off the bus a few stops early and walk the last kilometre or so to my office. While it's a poor neighbourhood, it's an interesting one. Cosmopolitan. Always busy and full of life. The streets are narrow and steep, and lined with terraced houses that are set so close to the footpath you can see right into them. As I walk I see lonely people sitting in their front rooms watching me watching them; or families gathered around the dinner table all talking at once; or students trying to study in rooms vibrating with heavy metal music. The air is always filled with the smell of coffee and exotic cooking, and the singsong tones of many different languages. On some streets it's unusual to hear English being spoken at all. All of which I find stimulating, and this reinforces my conviction that a population of mixed races makes for a better country in the long run.

This is not to say that it's all roses around there: there are also drunks, drug addicts, dole-bludgers, and sad people who are without work through no fault of their own. Strangely, all these people make me feel uncomfortable, so I avoid looking them in the eye. I cross the street or walk around them as if they were dog shit on the footpath. I admit this is not a good way to react but, to be honest, I find the smell of drunks offensive, drug addicts make me nervous, lazy people make me angry, and the genuinely destitute make me feel guilty. I'm squeamish when it comes to such things. There is no way I could work for the Salvation Army or the Sydney City Mission or any other do-gooder organisation. I don't have the stomach for it. Nevertheless, while I might be somewhat lacking in courage and the milk of human kindness, I do admire these qualities in others. Which brings me to the incident I wish to tell you about.

Around five years ago, I left my studio late one night after working all day without a break. My eyes ached and, having sat crouched over a drawing board all day, I decided to walk for a while to stretch my legs and clear my head.

Not more than a few minutes into my walk, I heard the sound of a man and a woman arguing in some European language I didn't recognise. When I was outside their house I naturally looked in to see what all the shouting was about. They were standing in their front room. The man held a can of beer in one hand and appeared to be threatening the woman with the other. I can't say whether the woman was drunk, drugged or terrified, but she was swaying slightly and leaning against a couch for support. It was none of my business but I couldn't drag myself away. I backed into a darkened doorway across the street, so I could watch without being seen. I was scared of what I might see, but I stayed anyway. I have a similar fascination for snakes.

It was then that I noticed the boy. He was sitting on the front steps of the house with his chin resting on his knees and his arms wrapped tightly around his bony, scabby legs. He wore shorts but no shirt or shoes. His arms were too skinny and his haircut too severe. I guessed he was about seven or eight years old. If he had seen me at all, he didn't show it. He seemed to be preoccupied with a spot on the path by his feet.

I heard something break in the house and looked to see what it was. The woman was now hugging herself as if she were cold, but I couldn't see what had been broken.

At that point a small girl, four years old at the most, came walking slowly down the path. Light from the windows fell across her as she passed — she was curly-haired and delicate, almost angelic in her thin cotton dress. She didn't look into the house; she just walked slowly to the boy and sat down next to him.

He didn't look up or acknowledge her presence in any way.

The woman screamed again. The man hurled his can at her, crossed the room, grabbed her by the hair and began punching the side of her head. She fell to the floor. He kicked her. She stopped screaming.

I was filled with outrage and revulsion and frozen by fear. My skin prickled.

The little girl began to sob. The boy put his arms around her, pressed his face into her hair and said soothing things to her that I could not hear. He did not cry.

I walked away.

For years I carried that memory with me — guiltily. I was never quite sure what I should have done, but I know I should have done something. I did ring the police, the next day, anonymously; but they wanted me to come down to the station, fill in forms, file a complaint and so on, and I didn't want to get involved so I didn't go. In the end I convinced myself it wasn't my business.

You could say that I discovered things about myself that night that aren't all that admirable. On the other hand, I have always treasured the memory of that small boy's act of tenderness towards his sister, and consider myself the richer for having witnessed it.

Nonetheless, true to my feeble nature, I avoided walking down that street for years after that. I guess I didn't want to take the risk of witnessing a repeat performance. It was almost as if I thought that if I didn't see it, it might not be happening. Curious logic, I know, but that's how it is.

Eventually, a few months back, I found the courage to walk that way again — just occasionally. But, even when I walked slowly and deliberately past that house, I never saw any of the family and, thankfully, heard no sounds of beating. I did hear a girl laughing once, somewhere inside the house, but I saw no one. I assumed they'd either found peace or moved away.

Then, not a week ago, I saw them again — not the parents, just the boy and the girl.

Again, it was the boy I saw first. He was on the street demonstrating amazing skills on a skateboard. He must be about thirteen now, not very tall, but wiry and strong-looking.

As I drew nearer, I saw his sister, on the other side of the road with a couple of other girls about her own age.

She's about nine, I guess; all knees and elbows but quite pretty in a waif-like way. Her friends seemed to be urging her to do something, which she appeared reluctant to do. Eventually, she walked across the road to talk to her brother.

After a time of her pleading and him shaking his head stubbornly, he relented and handed her his skateboard.

Her friends squealed with delight and ran over to join her.

She put the skateboard on the path, and with the help of some steadying hands, climbed on and began to wobble — giggling and laughing — towards me. The road at that point is fairly steep and as she started to pick up speed, her laughter quickly changed to shrieks of fear.

Her brother ran after her, yelling at her to stop.

She didn't know how. So she leapt off and fell face down into the gutter. The skateboard rocketed into the path of an oncoming truck.

I ran to the girl. There were minor scrapes on her elbows and knees, but no tears. With an angry flurry of hands she made it clear that she did not need my help. By now her friends were at her side, so I moved away.

The boy came back up the road carrying his shattered skateboard. Ignoring us all, he walked up to his sister and without warning slapped her angrily across the face.

'I told you to be careful, you stupid bitch!' he said.

She doubled up and put her hands over her head to protect herself from further blows.

I stepped between them quickly. 'Stop that!' I growled at him.

His young eyes narrowed in hate. 'Why don't you piss off and mind your own business, you fucking *slope*!' he snarled.

A FOUNTAIN RINGED BY CHUBBY CHERUBS

This is how I remember him: standing on the landing, hands on hips, nostrils flaring, his fat porous face flushed and furious, shouting, 'I don't give a *shit* how heavy it is, I want the bloody thing upstairs, in the boardroom, now!'

Sweat's stinging my eyes, my biceps are popping, my back's about to snap, and if I hadn't been wedged between the wall and a seven-million-ton slab of marble I'd have leapt up the stairs and dropped the fat prick.

Then again, maybe I wouldn't have.

What you have to understand about Bert is that he was a paranoid, megalomaniac bastard. He was short, y'see, and even though I'm only twenty, I reckon I've met enough short bastards in my life to know that they're often megalomaniacs. History proves it: Napoleon, Nero,

Genghis Khan, Alexander the Great — short-arsed over-achievers, every one of them. But at least those guys got the odd important thing done and you have to admire them for that. Bert, on the other hand, was just a mean son of a bitch and he didn't achieve anything worthwhile as far as I could tell.

As you might have guessed by now, I didn't like him. Then again, I don't know anyone who did. Except, maybe, Roger. No, come to think of it, I don't think it was so much that Roger liked Bert, it was more that Bert was the only guy who could stand Roger.

Bert was the chairman of the advertising agency I worked for. He owned it, actually. I suppose he could have just called himself Managing Director but I doubt he'd have thought that sounded important enough. Besides, the title Managing Director would have suggested that he managed or directed something and as far as I could tell he didn't do stuff all — except go to lunch and drink too much. Which was another pain in the arse because when he was drunk, he was an even bigger bastard than usual.

There was nothing he liked better than coming back after a seven-gallon lunch and picking on some poor prick in the agency. He'd sip on his ninth cognac and get himself all worked up about this particular person and what they had or hadn't done, then he'd storm back into the building around 4 pm and proceed to abuse the crap out of them. Which was bloody humiliating because everyone in the office could hear every word he yelled.

After he'd worn himself out, or the person he was abusing had a nervous breakdown or something, he'd waddle back into his wanky wood-panelled office, plonk his lard arse into the padded leather chair behind his huge oak desk and yell for me.

That's right, me. I was the Dispatch Boy, the 'gopher', and the lowliest of the arses to kick. Luckily, my arse was so low he hardly ever bothered to kick it at all. Instead, he treated me like his favourite slave, entrusting me with all kinds of vitally important missions like going out to buy cigars for him or presents for his family — which he always forgot until the very last minute.

You'd reckon he'd get his secretary to do some of that stuff, but *Ms* Patricia Fontaine was above all that. She was above practically everything. All she ever did was file her nails and practise her banana-peeling smile on clients. Jesus, she was a smarmy bitch. She had this particular way of making her eyes light up for guys she wanted to impress — and when she was talking to them she'd slide her bum around on her chair like she was struggling to control a serious case of the hots for them or something. You would have thought she was Marilyn bloody Monroe the way she carried on sometimes.

She was the typical boss's secretary — territorial as buggery. Bert was her territory and if you wanted to get to him, you had to get past her and that was pretty near impossible. She always said it was because Bert was busy and she didn't want him to be disturbed; but she liked to make the point that she could see him whenever she wanted. She'd just waltz in without even knocking. I can still see the way the cheeks of her bum would roll around under her tight knitted skirts as she walked away from me. She had a nice bum, I have to admit. Anyway, she'd disappear into Bert's office and pretty soon you'd hear them whispering and, always, that phony laugh of hers. It really used to get my goat, that phony laugh of hers; it was kind of a restrained cackle — like a chicken being strangled in a library. After a while she'd reappear, smiling, like she was doing you a big favour or something, and she'd tell you Bert was too busy to see you now and she'd let you know when he was free. But she never did. I think she and Bert might have been having it off — though how anyone could do it with Bert is beyond me. He was the ugliest bugger I've ever seen and I've seen some ugly buggers in my time, believe me.

I mentioned earlier that Bert often got me to buy his family's presents for him. Most of the time he'd never even tell me what to get, I could just choose what I liked. More often than not he never even knew what the gifts were himself until they were opened. He trusted me like that. I think it was because his family always liked the things I bought for them. I had better taste than Bert, I reckon.

One time, though, Bert bought a gift himself — he actually saw something for sale in the classifieds and decided it would perfect for his wife, Mary. Needless to say, I had to go and collect it.

It was a white concrete fountain cum birdbath, which belonged to an old Jewish lady in Rose Bay. She said it reminded her of her late husband and she found it too painful to look at. I sympathised with her — it *was* painful to look at. It was about six feet high and consisted of three tiers that were sort of pseudo-Roman in style. On the top two tiers, standing in the middle facing outwards, were all these chubby cherubs holding their dicks and pissing into the basin below. I guess it was kind of funny if you were amused by the sight of chubby cherubs pissing on birds' heads, but not the sort of thing I'd buy for my wife, if you ask me.

It was heavy, too; even though it came apart into five segments, each part weighed heaps. Bert had me haul it piece by piece over to his place in the boot of his Jag.

By the way, even though he said he bought it for Mary, one look at it told you it was really for him. It was the sort of thing only a megalomaniac with no taste could love and Mary was anything but that.

Naturally, she hated it on sight, but tried to pretend she didn't. She was far too well-mannered to ever say she didn't like a gift, even a ratshit one from Bert. And, she was far too kind-hearted to let me see that I'd busted a gut bringing her something she didn't like. So she made out like she was delighted and grateful and all, but I could tell she hated it.

I liked Mary. She was real nice. Good-looking, too, in a rich-lady way. Polite and proper. Not sexy, though. I mean

I couldn't imagine her bonking or anything — especially not with Bert. Hell, just the thought of him groping at her with his stubby, hairy fingers is enough to make me want to throw up. I felt close to her, you see. We had an affinity. After all, I'd bought her last two anniversary presents and I'd taken a lot of time and trouble to choose things I thought she'd like. You might even say I'd put a lot of love into it, which is more than Bert ever did. Of course, I was always glad to do it because, as I say, Mary was a real classy lady and I felt sorry for her having to live with an arsehole like him.

I almost told her once, not about Bert being an arsehole, about me buying her presents and all; but in the end I decided not to. I reckoned she'd be better off believing that Bert still cared enough about her to do that. I'm pretty sure she didn't love him, though, I can't see how anyone could — not even Roger.

Roger was called our General Manager, but he was really just Bert's personal assistant. Poor old Rog, he really was one of life's unfortunates. It was impossible to like him, or even hate him for that matter. He was just *there*. An aggravating part of life — like dog shit on the footpath, or wet dunny seats. What made him even more aggravating was the way he'd try to copy Bert's way of being sarcastic, only it didn't come naturally to Rog; you could tell he was putting it on, and that made it all the more ridiculous.

I never met anyone as nervous as Rog; he was constantly fidgeting and scratching himself and leaping about in sudden movements like a rat on a hot tin roof. And his palms were always damp and his face shiny like it was covered in clear pimple ointment or something.

The reason I say this is because Roger had bad skin. And I mean *bad!* I don't wish to be unkind, but I had trouble looking old Rog in the face sometimes. The poor bugger was covered in pimples — big, bloated red buggers — and they always looked like they were going to pop at any moment.

I remember one time, a few of us arranged to play touch football on a Sunday morning and — even though he wasn't invited — Roger turned up. I would have told him to piss off, only some of the other guys felt sorry for him (on account of him living with his hundred-year-old mother and generally being such an unfortunate bastard in lots of ways), so they invited him to join in. Next thing I know he's tearing around the field like a madman and bugger me if he doesn't turn out to be a damn good player. Pretty soon, I had a severe case of the guilts and began thinking what a prick I'd been and how he isn't such a bad bloke after all. Then — just as I'm developing all these charitable thoughts about him — he goes and peels off his T-shirt and I see that his entire body is covered in huge bloated pimples. Fair dinkum, I nearly threw up! He must have scored twenty tries after that — nobody would touch him.

Naturally, old Rog was pretty chuffed with his performance and tried to get us to make touch football a regular Sunday morning thing, but the rest of us weren't too keen on that — we didn't have the stomach for it.

By now you should have the basic picture about Bert, Roger, Mary and me, so I'll get back to the real point of this story, which has to do with why we were stuck on the stairs with a seven-million-ton slab of marble.

It all began when Bert decided that the main reason our advertising agency hadn't won any new business lately was because our office was a bit shabby. He reckoned our image was dated and we needed something a little more upmarket.

Truth was, our work was no bloody good. All we really needed was better creative people, but Bert was too cheap to get them. He was into property, not people. 'There's no capital gain in Pommy art directors,' he said — and you can't argue with that.

So he went out and found these flash new premises on the sixth storey of a building in North Sydney. It wasn't a new building, just an old one someone had renovated by covering with chrome and reflective glass. But the views were impressive and the rent was low, and that was an irresistible combination to Bert.

The move took place on a Saturday (of course), with the staff doing the bulk of the labour without pay. We also had the half-hearted help of a couple of professional removalists who'd been hired for their truck and their expertise.

Not wanting to lose too much of our precious weekend,

we worked hard and fast, and things had gone pretty smoothly until we got to the last and biggest item — the boardroom table.

I should explain about this table. Bert decided he wanted something special for the new boardroom. 'Something unique,' he said. He had this idea that the personality of an agency should be reflected in its boardroom, which really meant he wanted to reflect his own ego in it.

After checking all the stores and ploughing through stacks of interior design magazines, he announced that he wanted a twelve-foot by five-foot boardroom table made out of green marble with a sandstone base. Now, you have to agree, that's a megalomaniac's boardroom table if ever there was one. Apparently, he got the idea from an art director he knew who'd convinced him that it would be the most impressive boardroom table in town. He was just taking the piss out of Bert, I reckon, but Bert thought it was a brilliant idea.

Pretty soon he had Roger running all over town trying to get the bloody thing made — a task made all the more difficult because Bert insisted it had to be ready in time for the shift into the new offices.

Miraculously, thanks to Roger's fear and persistence, and a couple of hundred bucks in the right hands, it was ready on the day.

Unfortunately, the people who made it would only deliver it to the street outside the building. Getting it upstairs was, to quote their delivery driver, 'Your problem, mate'.

So there we were, in the fading light of a late Saturday afternoon, trying to figure out how to get this monstrosity up into the new offices.

The top of the table comprised two six-foot-long, five-foot-wide, two-inch-thick slabs of marble, which wouldn't fit into the lift and were probably too heavy for it anyway.

By this time the removalists had had a gut full; they didn't give a shit what Bert wanted, they'd only quoted on moving stuff from the old premises; nobody said anything about hauling a humungous green marble table up forty flights of stairs.

Bert tried yelling at them, but they ignored him. So he started picking on Roger instead, saying how it was his fault and he should have anticipated the problem and what was he going to do about it. That was when Roger decided that we, the staff, would carry it up ourselves, piece by piece. This wasn't a popular idea. But seeing as it was Saturday night, and we knew there was no way Bert would let us go until we'd got the job done, we agreed to give it a try.

So there we were, eight of us, even Ms Patricia Fontaine and her beautiful bum, jammed on the fire stairs unable to go backwards or forwards, all trying desperately not to drop or scratch Bert's precious hunk of marble.

As if this wasn't bad enough, I had Roger in front of me, so my head was filled with visions of his pimples exploding out through his shirt and this was making me very nervous. Also, like a lot of pimply people, Rog had a major body odour problem, too, which was pretty overpowering in a confined space, let me tell you.

Meanwhile, as I said before, Bert was screeching away on the landing above us like a maniac.

Pretty soon Rog began to develop a shake in his voice that sounded like he was about to cry.

Macca, our production manager — a man not well known for his patience — suggested we put the bloody thing down until we could figure out what to do next.

We all thought that was a pretty good idea, but Bert was against it because he didn't want to risk scratching the marble on the concrete stairs.

Jenny, the receptionist, offered to let us rest it on her throat if we'd just let her put it down. Bert didn't think that was as funny as we did.

All this time, the two removalist blokes were watching us from the bottom of the stairs and pissing themselves with laughter. Finally, one of them stopped chortling long enough to suggest that we try hauling it up the outside of the building. He said he had enough straps and ropes in his truck to do the job.

Even Bert thought this was a good idea.

Then Roger, bless him, took it a step further by suggesting that we hire a crane on Monday and do it that way.

Unfortunately, Bert wouldn't have a bar of that — he

said he had a journalist coming in to interview him first thing Monday morning and he wanted the table installed before then. 'I want to project the right image from day one,' he insisted.

Macca suggested, under his breath, that Bert could do the interview with his dick in his hand and the journalist would get the right image. Luckily, Bert didn't hear him.

So we decided to go with the removalist's original suggestion.

Somehow we wrestled our load back down the stairs and around to the lane at the back of the building where we wrapped it in blankets and made a harness out of strapping.

After that, one of the removalists took most of the people up to the sixth floor and lowered ropes out of the window. These were then attached to the harness by his mate.

When this was done, the second removalist went upstairs to join the others, leaving Bert and me down on the street.

I'd been given the relatively easy job of controlling the guide rope, which would keep the load from smashing windows on the way up. All I had to do was to stand on the other side of the lane and exert enough force to keep the load from swaying against the building. Compared to the poor pricks above, I was getting off lightly.

Naturally, Bert took the easiest job of all, which was to stand directly beneath the load and let me know when it was getting too close to the building. This left him plenty of breath for yelling orders.

It took two backbreaking loads and nearly three quarters of an hour to get the two tabletop sections up. Then there were only the two sandstone base blocks to go, and they were each considerably lighter.

But Bert was running late for a dinner appointment and Mary had arrived to collect him, and although she was quite prepared to wait, he wasn't. So he decided that, in order to speed things up, we should haul up both base blocks as one load.

We tried to object, but you couldn't argue with Bert at the best of times, and at this point we were too exhausted to do much more than whinge.

In the end we agreed to do what he asked, just to save Mary the embarrassment of watching him carrying on like a pork chop.

The bases were strapped together and the harness adjusted to fit the new shape. When he was satisfied it would hold, the removalist who had done all this went back upstairs to join the others.

The instant the expert disappeared back inside the building, Bert started stuffing around with the harness himself. He reckoned the guy had done something wrong and, needless to say, he knew exactly how to fix it. So he fiddled around retying knots and tightening things until Roger poked his head out of the window and told him to stand back because they were ready to begin lifting.

Try to imagine the scene: it's seven thirty on a Saturday night, a bunch of people are hanging out of a sixth-floor window of a building in North Sydney giving themselves hernias trying to hoist ninety zillion tons of sandstone up the side of the building. Down below there's me, pulling tentatively on a guide rope, and Bert, looking up and barking orders.

Suddenly, the world stopped. I don't even remember any traffic noise. No noise at all. Even Bert stopped yelling — his mouth frozen open. Nothing seemed to move: no cars, no people, no planes in the sky, nothing at all — except the large block of sandstone, which slipped silently out of the harness and dropped through the night to crush Bert like a cockroach.

I don't remember the sound it made when it hit Bert. I mean, without wishing to be macabre, you'd think I'd remember a thing like that, wouldn't you? Bones crunching, guts popping, or something. But I don't recall hearing anything at all. In a way, it's like it didn't really happen.

And that's how it felt. Unreal. Like watching a movie or something. I mean, even in death Bert looked almost comical — all you could see poking out the sides of the hunk of sandstone were his arms and hands, and chubby legs tipped by little white slip-on shoes.

I half-expected him to leap up like Wile E Coyote in a *Roadrunner* cartoon, throw the 'Acme' sandstone block aside and bounce back to his feet.

Then, gradually, my brain began to believe what my eyes saw. Bert was history and someone had better go to Mary, quickly.

Without thinking, I let go of the guide rope. I heard the remaining load thump against the building and for one terrified moment had visions of Mary being shredded by falling glass. Luckily, this didn't happen.

I crossed the road to join Mary. She had her hand over her mouth. I put my arm around her and tried to walk her away. She didn't move. I couldn't think of anything to say.

Now that I was closer, Bert looked less comical — there was blood.

The sandstone didn't have a scratch on it.

Mary didn't cry.

I bet you're thinking this is the part of the story where some old codger gets up at Bert's funeral and makes a speech about how Bert was a war hero, how he'd done lots of work for charity, how he was really a saint at heart, and how we'd all misunderstood him. Forget it. Even the priest had a hard time trying to find anything nice to say about Bert. Fact is, Bert lived and died a bastard. The only decent thing he ever did was to make Mary a wealthy widow.

Shortly afterwards, Mary sold the agency, Roger became MD and I left.

As for the boardroom table, Bert's still got it. It was used in the building of his tomb. Yes, that's right, his *tomb*. Apparently, he requested a tomb in his will — a megalomaniac to the last.

If you don't believe me, you can go and see for yourself. It's up in the Northern Cemetery. Just look for a large tomb with a facade of sandstone and green marble with a fountain out front. A hideous, multi-tiered, white concrete fountain ringed by chubby cherubs with their dicks in their hands.

IRENE'S PROMISE

There was no way we should have let Steve drive. Just thinking about it now makes me shudder. But back then in that wild-eyed, adrenalin-pumping time between school and gainful employment, we took risks like that all the time. Mortality wasn't in the frame. We were invincible.

Sadly, for me, that time has past. I am no longer immortal. Today, bitter experience and rational thought reside in the back of my mind like a pair of disapproving aunts. So much so that even descending a flight of stairs at speed demands a fair measure of caution. My body has lost its resilience. I can feel my bones and they seem increasingly brittle. I fear pain.

So perhaps it's not surprising that a kind of mourning for the someone I will never be again was stirred in me this afternoon when Irene called to remind me of something I'd tried so hard to forget.

'*We gotta get out of disgrace, but it's the last thing we'll ever do ...*' Danno sung lustily while slapping his hands on the car bonnet in time to the music. Changing the lyrics of popular songs was something he was prone to do when he'd had a few. And tonight he'd had a few too many, which meant he was in no state to drive, which meant he had a major problem. I say major because Danno loved his car. No woman ever had more care and attention lavished on her than Danno lavished on Matilda, his flawless Mark II Ford Zephyr.

On Sunday mornings, while the rest of the world slept or indulged in spiritual ablutions, Danno would be slaving over Matilda: washing, polishing, stripping down her engine, or fitting some accessory that was guaranteed to make her go faster or *look* as though she would. Any cash he ever managed to wrestle past the pub was spent on his chrome-piped sweetheart.

Consequently, when he'd announced that he was too pissed to drive, he wasn't thinking about the risk to our bodies and souls, he was simply worried about Matilda.

However, deciding who'd be entrusted with the privilege of driving his six-cylindered obsession was not easy.

Mainly because we were *all* drunk.

Earlier that day, we'd won our rugby match. This might not seem like such a big deal to you, but it was to us. Because, while we loved the game with a passion that was almost primeval, we played it in much the same way —

like a bunch of Neanderthals. We always lost. The only people who ever came to watch us were girlfriends and masochists — often one and the same. But on this particular day we had won, and won handsomely, so all was well on planet Earth.

All, that is, except for Pete Shanahan, who was vomiting violently somewhere in the darkness. Naturally, this ruled him out of the driving role.

I couldn't be considered either. Having drunk too much, too quickly, in the after-match euphoria, I was now trying to steal a little nap in Matilda's back seat. This was not proving to be a brilliant idea — my world was spinning and it threatened to empty my stomach. I sat up, stuck my head out the window and began to suck in the cold night air in long careful breaths.

Hearing the sound of giggling, I looked up to see the remaining two of our group, Irene and Steve, emerging from the dying embers of the party.

Irene, love of my life, wilting willingly into the arms of the wrong man. Despite considerable effort on my part, Irene had failed to respond to my depth, intelligence and subtle charm; instead, she'd joined the long list of helpless females who had fallen prey to Steve's easy-going humour and movie-star looks. I was convinced this was a shameless, physically motivated decision she'd live to regret, but at this point there was no sign of it. All night I'd been tortured by the sight of this hormone-crazed couple huddled in dark corners kissing and groping.

Naturally, the others had noticed as well.

So, and this is only supposition on my part, Danno must have reasoned that — with his mouth otherwise employed for such long periods — Steve would have had less to drink than the rest of us.

'My parents are away, so we're going to my place and you're driving,' he said, tossing the car keys inaccurately towards Steve and hitting Irene in the face instead.

'You stupid prick!' Steve growled, raising his fists. He was caught unawares by his own reaction — Danno was his good mate — but having made the gesture, he continued to waft his fists around in a vague form of threat.

Danno looked confused. It was an awkward moment. Fortunately, they were saved by the belle. Irene, without Steve to support her, slumped slowly to the footpath in a happy-faced heap. (Apparently, she'd found some time for drinking between passionate embraces.)

Steve was caught between the need to punch Danno and rescue Irene.

With admirable presence of mind, I leapt out of the car and went to comfort her myself.

At that moment, Pete, having emptied his stomach in the bushes, vaulted heavily over the fence, spotted the car keys and snatched them up gleefully. 'I'll drive,' he said.

That got everyone's attention. Even when sober, Pete was not a good driver. Steve relieved him of the keys as tactfully as he could and climbed into the driver's seat.

I helped Irene into the back, laying her down with her head in my lap. Danno and Pete squeezed into the front with Steve — Danno issuing instructions as fast as his inebriated tongue would allow.

Matilda was a classic car with effortless power and pristine paintwork. A thing of beauty and the very kind of car that was sure to catch the eye of a passing cop.

'Stay off the main roads,' advised Pete, who was hanging out the passenger window trying to clear his head.

'Yeah,' Danno agreed, 'stick to the back streets.'

Did you ever go to an old amusement park and ride on a Ghost Train? Do you remember how it would twist and turn sharply in the dark, and how each turn would bring with it skeletons, ghosts and shadows leaping at you out of the haunted night? That's exactly how it was on this drive.

'Left here! No right — RIGHT!!' Danno would yell, and Steve would react as fast as he could. It was like this all the way as Matilda lurched, jerked and squealed her way through the back streets in a less than ladylike fashion.

All of this made Irene's head roll about pleasantly in my lap and — desperate to maintain my reputation for subtlety — I struggled to control the natural surges that threatened to make their point felt at any moment.

We were negotiating yet another narrow back lane at an uncomfortable rate of knots when Steve lit a cigarette. What possessed him to do such a thing I'll never know. Matilda was a smoke-free zone — we all knew that.

'Hey — put that bloody thing out!' Danno snapped.

'What? Oh, shit, sorry,' Steve said.

He went to flick the cigarette out of the window, but fumbled and dropped it into his lap. He looked down in panic.

Cccrraannng!!! We careened off a parked car on the right. SCREEEEEEEEE!!! We slid down a car on the left.

For a few million seconds we rebounded from one side of the lane to the other, accompanied by the banshee sound of tortured metal, which was only just audible above Danno's screaming.

Then it was over. A kind of silence reigned, broken only by the bubbling purr of Matilda's engine and some strange choking sounds coming from Danno.

Miraculously, none of us was hurt. Shaken, shocked and shattered, but unharmed.

Steve kept driving, Danno kept whining, and Pete — who'd been hanging out the front passenger window when we hit — kept crossing himself and thanking Christ that we'd hit a car on the right first and the impact had thrown him back inside to safety.

Irene, now sitting bolt upright, was the first to speak. 'Shouldn't we have stopped?' she said.

It was a reasonable question, but we drove a good half a mile before anyone answered.

'We're pissed, they'd throw the book at us,' Steve said, finally.

'Why go back at all?' I said. 'It's two o'clock in the morning, who would have seen us?'

'You can't go around smashing up people's cars and running away just because they didn't see you,' Irene said, sliding away from me and folding her arms in disapproval.

'Stop there! Under that streetlight,' Danno interrupted. Now that he'd found his voice, his immediate concern was to see how badly Matilda was damaged.

'I think we should wait until we get to your place,' Steve said. 'I'll pay, Danno,' he added, 'whatever it costs, I'll pay.'

We knew he meant it. He may have been an outrageously good-looking bastard who would steal your girlfriend at the drop of a bra, but he was a decent bloke at heart.

Reminded of this, Irene softened noticeably. 'Perhaps we should wait until morning, then go back and own up,' she said. 'At least they won't charge you with drunken driving then.'

No, they'll just do us for harmless things like reckless driving and leaving the scene of the crime, I thought, but kept it to myself.

'We'll see,' Steve said, noncommittally.

As it turned out, Matilda had come through it all in remarkably good shape. Under a battery of lights in Danno's garage it became evident that the damage was really only superficial: the chrome strips down both sides needed to be replaced, and the right front fender and left back door would require some skilful panel beating, but the rest of the damage was little more than heavy scratching. Not even a headlight was broken. We'd expected a lot worse.

'She's a tough old tart,' Steve said, slapping Danno on the shoulder in an effort to lighten his mood.

Steve was visibly relieved his stupidity wasn't going to cost him as much as he'd thought.

Danno shrugged him off — he was determined to be miserable.

It was a tense, uncertain time. I felt the chilly pangs of conscience enter the room. No one acknowledged them.

'Anyone for bacon and eggs?' Irene volunteered, knowing that none of us had eaten that night.

'Good idea,' I said. 'I'll help.' I followed her upstairs, not so much to stay close to her (which I had long since recognised as a lost cause), but more to get away from the guilt-ridden atmosphere in the garage.

Pete followed, leaving Danno and Steve leaning against the car not talking to each other. He caught up with me on the stairs. 'Do you reckon we should let Steve take all the blame for this?' he said. 'I mean, in a way, we're all responsible, aren't we?'

Pete was such an honourable fellow. I always felt like a selfish, uncaring bastard around him. If ever there was a guy who would give you the shirt off his back and make you feel like you were doing him a favour by taking it, it was Pete. And there he was, staring right to the rotten core of me, fully expecting a noble response.

He was right, of course we *were* all to blame. Even

Danno. In fact, *especially* Danno; it was his car, so he should have had the sense to stay sober. That's right — it was Danno's fault. The bastard.

I let my mind work on that angle for a few seconds, but it didn't ease the burden. All things considered, sharing the cost of the damage to Matilda seemed only fair. After all, we were already sharing the guilt. What really worried me was the thought of paying for the damage to all the other cars we'd hit. That could amount to thousands. I could see myself paying it off for the rest of my life. We hadn't spoken about this possibility yet. I'm not sure if Pete even had this in mind when he made his magnanimous suggestion. Then again, he probably did — like I say, he was an embarrassingly honourable bastard.

With an empty feeling in my wallet, I nodded my head reluctantly.

'Yeah, okay.'

When we walked back into the garage, Steve and Danno were still slumped against the car avoiding each other's eyes.

I came straight to the point.

'Er ... Pete and I reckon we should all share the cost of the prang.'

Steve looked at me with puppy-like gratitude flowing into his eyes — it was kind of pathetic really, the thought that we might all share the cost had obviously never occurred to him.

'Are you insured?' Pete asked, trying to catch Danno's

attention, which was fixed on some invisible spot on the wall.

'Of course I bloody am,' Danno said. 'Not that it will do us a lot of good, insurance doesn't cover drunken drivers.'

I prefer to think that it was my natural creativity, rather than some inborn criminal instinct, which — in the desperate silence that followed — inspired me to conceive of a plan so simple and devious, it was almost beautiful. 'Let's abandon the car and report it stolen,' I said.

The air turned electric.

Irene clumped away in the kitchen above. Steve slid slowly down the side of the car to sit on the garage floor. Danno raised his bleeding eyes to stare at me. Pete held his breath.

Each of us turned the possibility over in our minds. The chances of anyone having seen us at the scene of the accident at that hour of the morning were remote. Even if anyone had, the best description they could hope to give would be of four or five people in a Mark II Zephyr. If, by some chance, anyone had managed to get the registration number, it wouldn't identify the driver, just the owner. All Danno had to say was that the car was stolen and we'd back him up. It was unlikely that anyone at the party would remember exactly what time we'd left, so all we had to do was establish where we were at the time of the accident and I already had an idea for that. Obviously, if the matter ever got to court, and we were faced with having to perjure ourselves, we would have to reconsider;

but, until that problem arose, a degree of fabrication seemed acceptable. After all, the only ones to suffer would be the insurance companies and that wasn't going to break anyone's heart.

I can't say whether the others followed the same line of reasoning, I only know that one way or another we all arrived at the same conclusion — my plan was a possible way out and, compared with the alternative, a very attractive one.

Danno weakened first. 'Stolen from where?' he asked with an embarrassed, lopsided smile.

'Granny's,' Steve said, referring to a nightclub in town.

'Yes,' I jumped in quickly (it was my idea, after all, and I was determined to maintain the initiative). 'I reckon we should dump Matilda out near Otara, then head into town and hang out at Granny's till dawn. Then, when we leave, we'll make out like we've discovered her stolen and call the cops. It'll be a piece of piss. Cars get stolen all the time, especially at that time of the night. Nobody will think there's anything suspicious about that.'

Deception came so easily to me it was frightening. Moreover, I was sure the plan would work. So were the others.

Everyone, that is, except Irene. When we put the idea to her she huffed and puffed and stared angrily out the kitchen window with her back to us. However, in the end — after some fast persuasion by Steve — she reluctantly agreed to keep our secret. Other than that, she wanted no part in our crime. She put a great deal of emphasis on the word *crime*.

Frankly, her attitude made me nervous: successful crime, like espionage, relies heavily on sealed lips, steady nerves and total commitment to the cause. Irene didn't stand up well in any category.

This thought plagued me as we drove her home and she subjected us to withering looks and turbulent silence.

When we reached her house, I got out of the car with her. 'Irene ...'

'Yes?'

'You won't tell anyone, will you?'

'I said I wouldn't, didn't I?'

'Yes but—'

'Do you want me to promise, cross my heart and hope to die? Would that make you feel better?'

'Well ...'

'Okay, I *promise*. Now go and do what you have to do and leave me out of it.'

All eyes were upon me when I clambered back into the car.

'Well?' said Steve.

'She's cool,' I assured them. 'She won't say a word. She promised.'

'Yeah, well, let's hope Don fuckin' Juan doesn't break her heart or piss her off in any way,' Danno grunted, looking pointedly at Steve.

'It'll make no difference,' I said, with a great deal more confidence than I felt. 'A promise is a promise.'

'And a sigh is just a sigh,' said Pete, with uncharacteristic cynicism.

'And a rose is a rose is a rose,' muttered Steve.

'But all women are Martians,' Danno added, which silenced us all.

After watching Irene strut disapprovingly up her driveway, we set about solving our next problem — how to get into town after we'd abandoned Matilda. However, now that we were in criminal mode, this little complication was quickly solved. We simply stole another car.

It was surprisingly easy. We drove around until we found an unlocked Holden station wagon with a baby seat and some plastic toys in the back. Danno leapt in, did something with wires under the dashboard and we were on our way.

Twenty minutes later we dumped Matilda in a light industrial area that backed onto a public housing estate in South Auckland.

Then we drove into town and abandoned the Holden as quickly as we could. Naturally, we took a great deal of care not to leave fingerprints, to the extent of opening and closing doors with sweater sleeves pulled down over our hands. Danno, who drove, wore gloves.

The calm, dispassionate manner in which I relate this gives no indication of the heart-thumping, dry-mouthed, loose-bowelled state we were in for the entire time. If you ignore under-age drinking, until that night, the closest I had ever come to doing anything remotely outside the law had been raiding neighbourhood fruit trees, and even that used to make my heart pound in my throat. In fact, with the exception of Steve — who had once been involved in a minor encounter with the boys in blue after a fight outside a club — none of us had ever been in trouble with the law. We were your average middle-class Brady Bunch really. Consequently, despite the sense of adventure and camaraderie that was abroad that night, each of us was terrified. No one admitted it, of course; you could just sense it in the forced laughter and the way we refused to look each other in the eye.

Once inside the nightclub, we threw ourselves at the bar and dance floor with manic enthusiasm — as if determined to drink and dance our guilt away. Danno danced with anyone who'd say yes, while Steve tried to evade the attentions of sad-eyed girls who were hoping to end their night on a high note. I wasted a couple of hours buying drinks for a spaced-out blonde who turned out to be with the band. Only Pete — drained by his earlier vomiting and the overall trauma of the evening — elected to adopt a low profile and slid away to sleep in a dark corner.

The crowd got thinner, the music bluesier, the lonely more desperate, and dawn crept closer.

Then it was time.

As we emerged from the club, daylight was pushing its fingers into the sky. The walls of the buildings around us wept from a recent downpour. We walked slowly, four abreast. A few other stragglers were also leaving the club, tired but buzzing, the shriek of electric guitars still ringing in their ears — perfect witnesses for our grand deception.

'Fuck!!' Danno's disbelieving profanity reverberated off the walls. 'I don't fuckin' believe it! Some bastard has stolen my car!' he said as he staggered around convincingly on the spot where his car should have been.

A small crowd gathered.

'Someone stole my fucking car!' he repeated. He had suffered a tragic loss — his car was stolen, his heart was broken and not a person there would have believed otherwise. Even I felt sorry for him.

No one had seen a thing. Everyone was sympathetic. One of the bouncers took him back to the club to phone the cops.

They arrived within minutes.

No one doubted our story for a second. Not then, or ever.

Matilda was found that same day — miles away from where we left her. Ironically, after we'd dumped the car, somebody had really stolen it. Danno was shattered when he heard this; the thought that somebody had actually violated his pride and joy was too much for him to bear.

Unlike us, these car thieves were soon caught, largely because one of them had been in trouble before. They were half-brothers — same mother, different fathers. The oldest, a four-time offender, was only fifteen. They lived on the housing estate. Their mother was an alcoholic. Poor buggers.

This was a complication we hadn't anticipated. The whole idea was that no one would get the blame; now we were faced by the very real possibility that a couple of innocent kids would take the rap for something we'd done. We began to experience a dangerous weakening of resolve.

'You wouldn't believe the cheek of some of these lads,' said the sergeant who rang to tell Danno his car had been found. 'They're trying to tell us your car was already smashed up when they found it.'

'Found it?' Danno said, trying not to choke.

'Yes, they say they found it out near some factories in Otara.'

'Maybe they're telling the truth?'

'Possibly but not likely. They're born liars, these kids, they'll say anything to get the bleeding hearts feeling sorry for them. No, I reckon we've got the little buggers fair and square. I only hope we manage to scare some sense into them before it's too late.'

'Yeah, but still ...' Danno's conscience wasn't easily salved.

'Don't you worry about them, son,' the sergeant said. 'By the looks of all the scrapes and paint marks on your car, I'd say these kids bounced off more than one vehicle during their little joyride. There's a good chance there'll be witnesses and more charges to come.'

By the time Danno related all this to us, he was convinced the sergeant was right; there would be witnesses, but to *our* crime, not theirs.

His paranoia was contagious. We were finding it hard to live with the lies. No one volunteered to confess, though. Instead, with the haphazard pragmatism of occasional villains, we adopted a 'let's deal with it when it happens' attitude.

But nothing happened. Days, weeks, then months went by and, incredibly, according to the police, not one person came forward to report their car being damaged by a hit-and-run driver. As a result, the charge against the brothers who had stolen Matilda amounted to little more than joyriding, and much to our relief, they got off with probation.

As for us, we nearly went mad waiting for bad news that never came.

It was uncanny, as if the entire incident had never occurred. As though it only existed in that haunted place where all our dark secrets lurk, ready to rise up at any given moment to remind us that none of us is as innocent as we might pretend to be.

And for nearly twenty years that's where my guilt had remained, dormant and undisturbed — until today.

I hardly ever see the others now, because I moved away and because that's often just the way life is. Even the best of friends go through changes and find new rainbows to chase. We still write to each other occasionally: light-hearted newsy letters, written with the easy familiarity of those who have been close enough in the past to understand each other's need to get on with the future. Danno is an actor living in England — you will have seen him on television. (I haven't used his real name, of course.) The others still live in New Zealand. Pete has a beautiful wife who loves him to death, four perfect children, a highly successful law practice and a weight problem. Steve sells cars, is still a bachelor, still in great shape, and still irresistible to women. Irene has become quite famous as a television personality and — you'll be pleased to know — she's married to a man whose most endearing qualities include depth, integrity and subtle charm. Unfortunately, it's not me. I live in Australia, where I hack out a living as a writer.

Perhaps it was my vocation that inspired Irene to ring me today. Her call came as quite a surprise; other than the odd Christmas card, I hadn't heard from her in years.

It never ceases to amaze me how, even after all this time, talking to her can reduce me to adolescent babbling: 'Irene ... God! ... Irene. It's been ... what, must be ... um, how are you?'

'Couldn't be better,' she laughed, amused as always by my confusion.

'And Martin ... and the girls?' I asked. She has two lovely daughters but I can never remember their names.

'Kirsty and Claire are fine,' she said. 'Growing up fast. They're already getting phone calls from nervous young men.'

I heard the tease in her tone and was reminded of how I used to struggle to control the shake in my voice whenever I called to ask her for a date — usually unsuccessfully. I felt the tremor threaten even now. 'Nothing changes,' I said — another vacuous remark for her to remember me by.

'Tom,' she said, changing the subject. 'Remember the night we smashed into all those cars?'

'I wish I could forget it,' I said as the memory reached down through the years and took a grip on my stomach.

'Well, I think I'm about to ease your conscience,' she said, then added tersely, 'although *you* of all people don't deserve that.'

'I'm listening,' I said, ignoring the reprimand.

'You remember I told you we'd bought a big old house in Herne Bay?'

I remembered, vaguely, that something along those lines had been conveyed to me in her last Christmas card. Domestic details are not my strong suit, but I answered with conviction. 'Yes.'

'Well, you'd never believe it, but the house backs onto the very same lane that we had the accident in.'

I began to whistle the theme from *The Twilight Zone*.

'Exactly,' she said. 'Spooky. And here's the part you'll like. According to one of our neighbours, an old chap called Sam who's lived here all his life, the house we're living in now used to be a brothel. Quite a classy one, apparently, frequented by all sorts of leading lights — politicians, sportsmen, captains of industry — men who had a lot to lose if they were ever exposed.'

'An interesting choice of words,' I observed and immediately regretted it.

She ignored me. 'And the cars we ran into—'

'Belonged to brothel customers who had no desire to be tumbled — so to speak,' I said completing her revelation for her.

'Correct,' she said. 'Sam remembers it well. He said he'd never seen so many famous men in one place at one time. All running about in the street, some only half dressed, all dreadfully upset. He wanted to call the police, but was talked out of it. In fact, someone slipped him a hundred dollars to say nothing. He said one of the politicians went to great lengths—' she giggled at that, but quickly gathered herself. 'He said one of the politicians went *out of his way* to convince him it wouldn't be in the national interests to get the police or press involved.'

'So the grubby old bastards were as scared of being found out as we were.'

'Right!'

I could feel two decades of guilt lifting off my shoulders — I could also smell a story. 'Did this fellow Sam tell you who any of these famous men were?' I asked, trying not to sound too obvious.

'Yes.'

'And?'

'Sorry, Tom, I promised not to tell.'

'Yes, but surely—'

'Forget it, Tom. A promise is a promise.'

DEAR AMY

Dear Braveheart,

Forgive me for being cheeky and writing to you. I know it is more usual for men to approach women on this site but I did not know if you would find me here because there are so many women to choose from. So I am making the first move. I am not always so bold.

I like the things you say in your profile and I like the way you look. You have a kind face so I would like to ask you a question. It is easy to love someone who is young and beautiful but will you still hold my hand when I am old and wrinkled? Will you be able to kiss me if I am dying of a contagious disease? That is what I believe true love is. I saw love like that when I was a nurse. That is the love I seek. That is why I am here. How about you?

Amy

Dear Amy,

You are clearly a lady who looks at life in depth. I understand what you mean about love that lasts beyond initial attraction and I agree. Especially since I am no longer a young man and certainly not in as good physical shape or health as I like to think I once was.

You ask why I am here? In short I have a good life that I think would be better shared.

While I live in Australia, I write to you now from a small villa in France that I am renting with a friend. France is a very beautiful country. Not just Paris, which is deservedly famous for being a romantic city, but the French countryside, too. Wildflowers and lavender fields are blooming now where I am in the south. It's a wonderful sight to see. And an experience that I think would be better shared. That is why I am here on this site.

My name is Joe. I am pleased to meet you.

Kind regards,

Joe

Hello, Joe,

Amy is just my online name. My real name is Ying.

I can only dream of travelling to such places as France. It sounds very beautiful, I love the thought of wildflowers in the fields and lavender is one of my favourite colours. I have heard of Paris but only know there is a big tower there and a river.

I live a far more humble life. I live in the same city I was born in. I married my high school sweetheart and we were happy until our daughter was born abnormally small. She was normal in every other way but it still upset my husband. He blamed me. He began to drink and sleep with other women. I had no choice but to leave him. This meant I lost face and so did my family. I left my job as a nurse and drove a taxi to earn more money. I did this for twenty years. Now that my daughter has started work, I have taken an easier part-time job. I drive a school bus for deaf and blind children. They are my little angels. I love them and I love my job.

I live in a city called Wuhan, have you heard of it? Over ten million people live here. I have never been overseas but did once have a holiday on the island of Hainan that I enjoyed very much. You may have heard of Hainan chicken. Do you like Chinese food? I am a good cook.

Your new friend,

Amy

Dear Amy,

In my country you would never 'lose face' for divorcing a man who treated you badly. I admire the way you did what you had to do to raise your daughter on your own.

I have been married twice and have one son and two grandchildren.

Yes, I do like Chinese food and love Hainan chicken. However, I am also a good cook, so I am not looking for a woman who will cook and care for me. I am searching for a friend and lover to share my adventures.

Tomorrow I leave France for a few weeks in Italy. I am going to an area called Tuscany, have you heard of it?

What does your daughter do for a living? Has her small size been a problem in her getting a job?

In closing, can I ask you a favour? Your profile photos are very impressive but you look far too young for someone who is 51 years of age. Obviously they are professional photos prepared by your agency. I would be grateful if you could send me a snapshot taken by a friend. I know this may sound distrustful and I also know there is a great deal more to a real connection than attractiveness alone, but believe me when I tell you that I have had some unpleasant surprises with online dating before.

Sincerely,

Joe

Hey Joe,

Do you know the song by Jimi Hendrix called 'Hey Joe'? My daughter, May Ling, played it to me. She said it is an old song but I had never heard it. We did not hear much Western rock music in China when I was young. It is very popular with our young people now.

My daughter has her own business, a little shop that sells everything from hats and ice cream to cooking pots and soft drinks. She works long hours and loves her work. She has many friends. She is a happy and bright young woman. I am very proud of her. It was she and her friends who encouraged me to look online for a husband overseas. A woman of my age is not much of a prize in China. There are so many beautiful younger women here. Many who would be interested in a man like you. I imagine a few have already approached you on this site. Am I right?

I am sending you two photographs that were taken last week when I was staying at a friend's house for her daughter's wedding. They were taken just before I went to bed and I am not wearing make-up. I hope they don't scare you away.

I had never heard of Tuscany but my daughter May Ling looked it up on the Internet. It looks like a very beautiful place. I like the shape and colours of the rounded hills and ploughed fields and the red tiles of the farmhouses. I would like to see such beauty for myself one day.

Fondly,

Ying

(Hello, Joe,

My name is Li Gan. I am the agency interpreter who translates Amy's letters. I just wanted to tell you that she is really a natural and beautiful lady who is funny and friendly. You do not need to be suspicious about her or her motives. She is an honest and good woman. I want you to know that.

Your friend,

Li Gan)

Buongiorno, Ying,

I am now in Italy. I apologise for my silence. I've had some computer problems, which is why I have not contacted you for so long. I am not very good with computers but the problem is fixed now.

Thank you very much for the photos. I am far more comfortable with the 'real' you. I like your smile. You are very attractive and in excellent shape. You must exercise regularly and eat healthy food. I could learn a thing or two from you in that respect. I need to lose weight.

Another question: It says on your profile that you are learning English. Does that mean you cannot speak English? I believe you need an interpreter to read my letters and write to me. Is that correct?

Ciao,

Joe

Dear Joe,

I am so glad to hear from you. I thought my last photos had scared you off.

I had to search for the words 'Buongiorno' and 'Ciao' online and like you I am not very good with computers. I need my little angels and my daughter to help me with such things. May Ling knew they were Italian words. Do you speak any other languages besides English, Joe?

I do not speak English but I am eager to learn. However, it is expensive for adults to take English classes in China whereas children in school learn for free. All my little angels speak English and they have been teaching me but I must confess I am a poor student.

However, I have a friend who married a man from America and after only two years she now speaks English very well. They live in a place called Dayton, Ohio. Have you heard of it?

Don't worry about your weight, I do not like skinny men, they cannot be trusted.

Joe, you travel a lot. Is this part of your work?

Warm hug,

Ying

Hi, Ying,

I am now in New York staying with my American friends Bruce and Judy. Travel is not part of my work, it is just recreation. I do it for fun.

In actual fact I have retired from full-time work. But in my life I have been lucky enough to make a living doing the things I love to do ...

Hey Joe, you writing to that woman in China?

Yes.

She's a looker.

Men. Is that all you can say, Bruce? 'She's a looker.'

Well, she is, Jude.

She is but have you not noticed something else about her letters?

You've read her letters?

Joe let me read them.

Joe?

It's chick stuff, Bruce.

You don't think I have a feminine side.

Not sure I want to see it actually. What should I have noticed, Judy?

She never asks about what you own, your job, your house, how wealthy you are — nothing material at all.

She asked about my work.

She's just curious about your travel, that's all, who wouldn't be?

What's your point, hon?

Well, the last thing Joe needs is some woman who's after his money. And that's what people think motivates a Chinese woman looking for a Western husband.

Isn't that all a bit stereotypical, Jude?

I'm just saying. That's what many of your friends are going to think.

I don't care what they think.

I'm not thinking about you, I'm thinking about her. People will talk.

Maybe ... but we're getting way ahead of ourselves. I've never even met the woman. This is all just pen pal stuff.

And how long are you going to keep that up?

I don't know.

You pay for these letters to be translated, right?

Yes.

So if you don't mean to do something about it, like actually meet the woman, it's simply an expensive pastime, right? Pointless.

I guess. I don't know. I'm writing to a couple of others, too.

A couple of others ...Why?

Eggs in one basket ...

Jesus, Joe.

What do the *others* look like?

Bruce!

Want to see? Here ... that's Cindy and this is Mia, real name Ling Ling.

Sounds like a Chinese bicycle.

Bruce! ... They're attractive. What are their letters like?

Not as good as Amy's ... Ying's. Nowhere near as good actually. Maybe she has a better interpreter.

No, it's more than that. Trust my woman's instinct. Ying's the one for you.

You think I should meet her?

Or stop writing. Don't string the woman along. That'd be cruel and pointless.

Bruce, what do you think?

She has a point. Face it ... nothing else has worked for you.

There are a few more things I'd need to know about her first.

Then ask. Find out what you need to know and then go see her or not. Just don't drag it out forever.

... in the magazine industry in which I worked for thirty years.

I retired from working full time six years ago and these days I mostly write for fun. I am hoping to write books that might sell and provide me with a small income.

I am sure that you will now be thinking that I must have retired at a very early age so I have a confession to make: I am actually 62 years of age, not 57 as it says on my profile. I am sorry about this lie. However my profile pictures are recent. The lie has been in the words, not the pictures.

I also have to tell you that I have been talking to other women online but have now decided that I would like to talk to you exclusively.

This brings me to ask you some questions: Are you talking to anyone else online? Have you met anyone else or do you plan to? I hope you don't now think of me as overly intrusive as well as deceitful.

With respect,

Joe

Dear Joe,

I'm disappointed that you feel you need to lie about your age. Is this vanity? I know women lie for this reason. But I will forgive you because your photos are recent.

I am not surprised that you have been talking to other women. That is quite common. I myself have corresponded with more than one man at a time, but am not doing so now.

Since I began this online search I have met two men: one from Britain and one from the USA. The British man did not look like his photos at all. I do not mind bald men but he sent a picture of a strong-looking man with a full head of hair then turned out to be old and balding and very overweight. He had lied about his age and he smelled bad.

The American was tall, handsome and charming but turned out to be a real playboy. I discovered he was also here to meet another woman from Wuhan. But he did not know we were both with the same agency so he was caught out. Sadly, I found out after he had seduced me. I hope you do not think less of me for that.

I understand why you ask such questions. I hope my answers do not shock or disappoint you.

Hugs,

Ying

(Hi, Joe,

It is Li Gan again. I advised Amy not to tell you about the American man, but she insisted she must tell you the whole truth. This is what I meant when I told you she was a good and honest woman.

Your friend,

Li Gan)

Dear Ying,

I'm sitting in a Business Class lounge at Los Angeles airport waiting to connect with my flight home. It is crowded and noisy. I cannot believe so many people can afford to fly Business Class with their children.

Please do not worry about your mistake with the handsome American 'playboy'. We all make mistakes. My past is riddled with them. I imagine it was painful to discover that you had been deceived.

Ying, while travelling these past weeks I have come to a decision. I have decided to sell my business in Sydney and move back to live in New Zealand. This is a move I have been contemplating for some time. I would like to live in the area around Queenstown, which is in the South Island of New Zealand. It is a beautiful place surrounded by mountains and lakes. I long for peace and space as I get older. A home with vegetable and flower gardens perhaps. Can you imagine such a life? It would be very different from the one you know now.

How does your daughter feel about the possibility of your moving overseas and far away from her?

I must go now. They have announced my flight is boarding. It will take a great many hours to get to Sydney and I lose a day because we cross the dateline. I hate long flights.

Fondly,

Joe

My dearest Joe,

I did not even know what Business Class is. My agency interpreter, Li Gan, explained it to me. He also explained about the dateline. You are very lucky to afford such luxury. I have never been on an airplane. I would like to one day. Perhaps when I come to visit you?

I understand from what you say you do not like children and crowds? If so, you would not like my job of driving excitable children on a bus through the streets of Wuhan.

I tell my little angels about you. They want to know more. You would be amazed how deaf and blind children can communicate. They are so happy despite their handicaps. It warms my heart. And they are clever as well. They get very fed up when I fail to remember the English words they teach me.

May Ling found Queenstown for me on the Internet. It is very beautiful. I love mountains.

It must be wonderful to live in a place where the air is so clean. In China we have terrible air pollution although our leaders assure us they are working to fix it. I also love flowers and vegetables but I am not a gardener. There has been no opportunity to have a garden in my life. I would love to learn to grow things. I would work hard at that. Are you a gardener?

Joe, I am excited to tell you I will soon have a new home. I bought a small apartment in a building that is still being constructed. It will be ready for me to paint walls and choose my *tiles and light fittings in three months' time. I saved many years for this. It will be winter by the time I move in.*

I notice that the mountains in Queenstown were covered with snow. Does it get very cold there?

I did not know you owned a business, Joe. I only knew you were retired. As I learn more about you I can see that you are wealthy and must be accustomed to a finer lifestyle and a far more sophisticated kind of woman than I am. Surely you know many beautiful, educated and wealthy women, Joe. Why are you talking to a Chinese bus driver?

Yours,

Ying

And the reason we're all gathered here today is?

Joe has a problem.

He's got the pox?

No, it's the Chinese woman.

She has the pox?

Get serious, Grant, he's thinking of going to China to meet her.

Really?

Really.

So you're not just chucking in your business and moving back to freezing Enzed, you're going marry some Chinese chick.

I'm going to check her out, yes.

Didn't you say she couldn't even speak English?

She'll learn.

The way you talk, she'll never get a word in anyhow.

Brett, you're not saying anything. What do you think?

They say the definition of madness is doing the same thing over and over and hoping for a different result.

And?

Well ... nothing else he's tried to date has worked. At least this is different.

It's different all right.

So how can we help? Need someone to carry your bags?

It's something she said in her last letter about her world being so different to mine.

And ...?

She drives a bus. Before that she drove a taxi for twenty years.

Didn't you say she once was a nurse?

Yes.

Well, she's clearly no dunce. And she has balls. And from what you've told me she has a big heart. And that stuff she said about what true love is, I liked that.

Me too.

She's easy on the eyes, too.

So you think I should check her out? You think she'd fit into my world? I mean, would you guys accept her?

Mate, what kind of question is that? Who among us would even think about such things?

No, I don't mean I'm worried about her race. It's just ...

That she might be a bogan is what you're thinking. You

fucking snob! If you think that, why keep writing to her? Besides, from what you've told us she has real class — the kind that really matters.

What if it's just her interpreter? A kind of Cyrano de Bergerac scenario.

Is her interpreter a man or a woman?

A man. And he's written to me separately a couple of times to say what a good woman Ying is.

Then believe it. Have faith.

All you've got to lose is the travel cost.

What if she asks him for money?

Don't give her any.

That's what Peg thinks.

What does Peg think?

She says all the wives are worried this woman is just after your money ... and Australian citizenship.

New Zealand you mean.

Whatever.

Judy in New York warned me about that.

That she'd want your money?

No, that people would think that. So she'd never really be accepted or trusted.

Nah, she would, mate. If she's the real thing, the women would get over it. They're just being ... women, you know. They've been trying to match you up for years without success. They just don't want to believe this woman could be any better than anyone they tried to set you up with.

You kidding, remember Josephine?

Who will ever forget Josephine?

Mad as a cut snake. Whose brilliant idea was that?

Peg's.

Say no more.

Hey, that's my wife you're taking about.

You know what I mean. Peg hates that I'm single. Thinks I'm a bad influence on you.

You end up with a hot Chinese chick waiting on you hand and foot and you'll be a bad influence on us all, mate.

Dear Ying,

I am not a gardener but, like you, I would like to learn now that I have the time.

Please do not worry about the differences in our world. My mother came from a poor family. Our family was middle class at best. While I may be wealthy in your eyes, money plays no part in the choice of the company I keep. Yes, I do know a number of clever and wealthy women but the fact that I am still looking tells you I have not met anyone I would like to spend my life with.

I do not think of you as a simple bus driver. I think of you as a kind-hearted, honest, attractive and courageous woman who has made the best of a hard life. I admire that.

Yes, it does get cold in Queenstown in winter. It sometimes snows in the town but most often only on the mountains, which attracts skiers from all over the world.

However, since I do not ski, I will often travel abroad during winter.

Ying, have you told your family about me? I have told my friends about you.

Warm hug,

Joe

Hi, Joe,

Thank you for your nice comments. I feel much better after reading them. I like to think I have done the best in my life. I always put my daughter first and sacrificed much to do so. That is why she is so supportive of my search now. She likes you very much, Joe.

I have told my two sisters and brother about you. My parents are no longer with us. My father died ten years ago and my mother passed away just after May Ling opened her shop. I was glad she lived to see this because she was the one who looked after May Ling when I was working as a taxi driver.

I understand that you would live in Queenstown in the summer and travel in the winter. Where would you go? France? Tuscany? I would love to see those places.

Are there any Chinese people in Queenstown?

Do you think we will ever meet, Joe? I could save money and come on a holiday to Australia — or New Zealand.

I know I am being forward saying this ... tee hee.

Your cheeky friend,

Ying

The first leg of the flight, from Sydney to Guangzhou, in Business Class on China Southern Airlines, was far better than he'd anticipated. Then again, what had he expected — rice and beans and severe-visaged cabin crew in military uniforms? He was surprised, even alarmed at his prejudices in this regard. China is a giant awakened and, with leisure pursuits like tourism, was catching up to the rest of the world rapidly. Yet, like so many others he knew, he expected it all to be just a little bit below par. Hence a massive modern international airport and a top-flight airline with efficient friendly service in the air and on the ground were something of a surprise. The only thing that really met his dour expectations was the thick, grey smog that enveloped Guangzhou airport while he waited for his connecting flight to Wuhan. If anything, it was worse than he'd imagined.

He glanced down at his iPad and read Ying's last email for the umpteenth time.

Darling Joe,

I am so excited about your arrival. I cannot keep my heart still. I have been given the week off from my job so we can spend time together. My little angels say they will miss me but they wish me the best. My sister Jean will drive the bus for the week. Her husband Yang has loaned me his car to drive you around in. I will meet you at the airport. I will wear a red scarf so you can recognise me.

Li Gan is sorry he cannot be there to act as interpreter when we meet. He has to return to his village for that weekend to attend a family wedding. He will join us on the Monday at your hotel.

I will be able to take you to see my apartment when you are here. Perhaps you can help me choose tiles and colours for my walls?

Joe, I do not want you to worry. I know that we might not be attracted to each other in person and I am quite ready for this. I know you are a good man and not a playboy and only have good intentions in your heart. At the very least we can be friends, OK, Joe?

I am grateful and flattered that you are coming so far to see me and meet my family.

Warm hugs and kisses,

Ying

Placing the iPad back in his carry bag, he checked his watch again. This two hours layover was a drag. The transfer lounge was grey, sparsely furnished and, after briefly sharing the small space with a Chinese businessman who stared steadfastly at the floor for the whole time, he was now the only occupant. He'd forgotten to bring a book and hadn't downloaded any onto his iPad. He'd given up trying to connect with the airport Wi-Fi. Whether the problem was his technical incompetence or just a weak Wi-Fi signal, he didn't know. There was nothing to occupy him but his growing paranoia — inner voices that were louder still in the quiet of that solitary space.

You'll know within a nanosecond if she could be the one, you always do. No ... you know far too many good things about her to make an instant judgment like that. Good things. Qualities you admire. You can't keep making choices with your penis. Look where it's gotten you to date. Nowhere. How are you going to talk to her? What if the translation apps don't work? Her whole family is in on this. Maybe they see you as a golden goose. What are you going to do for a whole week? See the sights? Make plans? Talk about the future? Buy an engagement ring? Will you have sex? Should you even try? What's the Chinese position on such things? She had sex with the American playboy ... no one gets married these days without a test drive, not even in China. Jesus ... marriage! It sounds so permanent. Guess she wouldn't entertain the idea of just living together. No ... she's with a marriage bureau you idiot, not a rental agency. And there'll be visa issues if things go well. I'll need advice on that score. How in the hell do you get yourself into these predicaments, Wilson?

May Ling stepped carefully along the dimly lit corridor. The builders had left junk all over the place. There were puddles everywhere and pieces of wood that seemed to have no purpose leaning against walls. They kept assuring her mother the apartment would be finished on time but she found it hard to believe. The walls of this corridor hadn't even been painted yet. This stop and start process had been going on for months. It made no sense to her. She'd tried to get to the bottom of it, tried to get some confirmation of an actual completion date, but no one took her seriously. They rarely did at first, one of the many downsides to being as small as she was. People saw her as a child and too often treated her like one. Especially stupid and arrogant men like these builders.

She knocked on the door. Ying answered holding a slightly tattered American home decoration magazine in one hand. She held up a double-page photo of a tiled bathroom.

Do you like this colour?

It's white.

Yes. I know, but do you like it? And the tiles?

Very nice.

May Ling closed the door behind her and produced a huge WELCOME card she'd made for Joe that was nearly as big as she was.

Ying was delighted. She pointed at the large hand-painted words.

His name?

Yes.

The hearts and flowers ... you don't think that will be too much?

They're just decoration.

Still ... I don't want him to feel pressured.

Just take the card, Mum.

Ying admired her daughter's handiwork as she placed it on the unfinished kitchen bench. Everything was unfinished but the apartment was definitely taking shape. You could see its potential.

Are you nervous? May Ling asked as she walked across to look out of the panoramic living room window.

Of course I am.

Have you been practising with the translation app on your phone?

Yes.

Don't forget to keep the sentences simple and short. Don't get complicated or the words could come out all wrong.

Yes, dear.

The ever-present smog choked the sky and reflected dully on the man-made lake below.

That lake smells awful, May Ling said wrinkling up her tiny nose. I bet those idle-boned builders have been pouring paint and God knows what else into it.

It wouldn't surprise me.

Ying came to join her at the window. Somewhere behind the smog, the sun was going down. There was no heating in the apartment.

So Mum, if this works out, will you be happy to exchange the view of high-rise buildings and a poisoned lake for the mountains and crystal-clear water of New Zealand? The hills of the upper Yangtze for the hills of Tuscany?

Or the lavender fields of France, Ying smiled.

Imagine, May Ling sighed as she took her mother's hand.

Let's not get ahead of ourselves, sweetheart. He might not fall for me. Or vice versa.

Or he might smell, giggled May Ling.

After two tortured hours in transit, Joe boarded the Airbus flight to Wuhan. The sun had long since disappeared. By the time he arrived it would be near to midnight. He'd be exhausted and in no mood for conversation, even if that proved to be possible. He should have refused Ying's offer to meet him at the airport. But how could he?

Somehow he slept for most of the flight and was awakened by the announcement of the imminent landing. His throat was dry. The tiny flutter of excitement in his gut was nullified by an irrepressible sense of dread.

The plane came to earth with a thump. So did he. This was it: Six months and countless words all leading to this very public meeting in a place far from home.

Wuhan airport was much larger than he'd expected. There was so much about China he did not know. Clearly, this was a city of size and significance. Over ten million people, she'd said. Far bigger than Sydney so why should the airport's size and sophistication surprise him? He should have done some research before coming. More groundwork was needed in every respect. But it was too late now.

Even at that hour of night the airport was buzzing with excited voices and countless comings and goings. Not a word of English could be heard.

Ying was somewhere out there beyond the exit doors, which opened and closed as passengers exited to reveal blurred glimpses of those awaiting loved ones. He tried not to look in that direction and focused on the luggage conveyor belt, hoping his bag would be one of the last to emerge. He wanted to delay the inevitable for reasons he didn't quite understand. His bag was one of the first to emerge, its bright orange PRIORITY tag waving defiantly. He let it go around twice before he claimed it.

Having already cleared immigration in Guangzhou, there were no more possible delays. Slowly he made his way towards the doors and out into the waiting throng and began to look around for a familiar face and her red scarf.

He saw her in an instant. Waving. Smiling. Jumping up and down behind taller people who had pushed forward for a better view. She carried a hand-painted sign that said 'WELCOME, JOE WILSON' with hearts and flowers all around.

When she knew he'd seen her she pointed towards the exit doors beyond the throng. The word 'EXIT' was in English. He smiled and nodded to show he understood.

As he weaved among the other arriving passengers wheeling suitcases or wrapped in welcoming arms, he wrestled with the heart-chilling impact of that first glimpse of her. It was only for an instant and from a distance but in that nanosecond he knew with immutable certainty she wasn't The One.

This was an all-too-familiar reaction. It had happened (or not happened) many times before. Endless cyber conversations leading to the cold, hard reality of a meeting in person that was always, for him, a disappointment. The feeling of something approaching love he'd cultivated in months of virtual courting failing to manifest itself when he first laid eyes on them. And, as irrational as it was, if he did not instantly feel what he needed to feel, he knew he would never feel it. Was it fear or instinct? What was it he was looking for that he never seemed to see in that first heart-stopping instant? Was it even reasonable, or was it a form of madness? An unrealistic expectation? A delusion based upon the thousands of fantasy-laden, the-minute-I-first-laid-eyes-on-her moments in all the romance movies he'd ever seen? Was he expecting the woman of his dreams to arrive accompanied by orchestral backing? This was real life, not some perfect scripted moment on the silver screen.

He wanted to turn back and lose himself in the crowd. To end it before it could begin. But his feet kept dragging him on towards the distant door. He felt heavy. He could feel her watching his every step, probably mystified by his sedate pace and the fact that he wasn't looking back at her with the same level of effervescent joy. To ignore her any longer would be cruel and insensitive. He dragged his eyes up to find her again. There she was, shadowing him from the back of the huddled masses lining the path to exit. She was grinning from ear to ear: So very happy.

Self-loathing enveloped him. I am not a good man. I have done a bad thing and it's going to get worse.

She broke through the crowd and ran to him. She embraced and kissed him on the cheek. Hello, Joe, she said and laughed at his patent shock at being greeted so enthusiastically. She had a wonderful laugh. It broke his heart to hear it.

May Ling do, she said holding up the sign with his name and the flowers on it. You like?

I like.

She seemed pleased. She hooked her arm through his. Come, she said and with surprising strength urged him towards the door.

She wore a red beret, red scarf and padded red jacket over a white T-shirt, blue jeans and black boots. Red must be a favourite colour. Her black fur-lined gloves looked like driving gloves. Despite the bulk of her winter clothing it was easy to see that her body was slim and well proportioned. She was also taller than he'd expected. Her thick black hair cascaded down her back. Her cheekbones were the kind women kill for. Her eyes sparkled cheekily, the tiny crinkled lines at the corners the only hint of her age. She had perfect teeth. He could tell she was not a smoker, something he had never thought to ask before now. One of many things he hadn't asked before now.

The night air took him by surprise. It felt cold enough for snow though none could be seen on the surrounding car park. They walked in silence for about a hundred yards, her arm still looped through his, her face turned upwards towards his. Though aware of this, he looked straight ahead.

Wait, she said, stopping suddenly. Me car. You wait.

To emphasise the point she placed a hand on his chest to make it clear he was to stay where he was.

He'd rather have kept on walking than wait in the cold. No, I come, he said.

She either didn't understand or didn't care. Wait, she insisted and scampered off into the gloom with the WELCOME card wobbling beside her.

He watched her go. She had long legs and a perfect posterior. An arse to die for, some would have said. Her photos had not lied. He knew most men would take a chance on her on this basis alone let alone the other fine qualities he knew she possessed. He also knew he never would. The cold of the night took a grip on his heart.

What he would have to say to her could never be said

through electronic translation devices. He cursed Li Gan for not being there.

The car lights approached rapidly and the vehicle screeched to a stop alarmingly close to him. Good driver, she grinned as she climbed out of the car and went to open the boot. He wheeled his suitcase around to the back of the car while she rearranged the various boxes, tools and items of clothing the generous brother-in-law, Yang, had left in there. With some quick rearrangement, his suitcase fitted in easily.

She slammed the boot and scurried around to hold the passenger door open for him.

He thanked her and climbed into his seat. The car rattled a little when she slammed the door. It was not a new car but in good condition. A Toyota of some kind, not a model he was familiar with.

Ying climbed in and accelerated away before he had time to find his seat belt, which was lodged firmly down between the seats, a sure sign it was not often used.

When they stopped to pay the parking fee at the exit, he remembered he had no Chinese money but she was happily chatting away to the young man in the payment booth and handing over the required amount before he had time to say anything. The young man laughed at something she said. He wondered if they were talking about him.

Then they were on their way at some speed. There was little traffic about, probably because it was now past midnight. A light rain had begun to fall, hardly more than a mist but enough to make the road slippery. She held the wheel in a competent and relaxed way and kept her eyes fixed firmly on the road.

You hotel? she said.

Yes, hotel.

Hotel where?

I don't know ... oh, you want the name of hotel?

You hotel?

Marco Polo.

Makoporo?

Marco Polo.

Wait.

She produced a mobile phone and with one hand on the wheel hit the speed dial with her thumb.

Joe noticed large pieces of pomelo peel on the dashboard. He leant forward to pick one up.

Smell, she said.

He picked up a piece of peel, put it to his nose and sniffed.

She laughed.

Smell, she repeated making a sweeping motion with one arm.

Then he understood that she meant the peel was there as a deodoriser for the car.

Oh, he grinned.

She didn't react. She was now talking to whoever had answered her midnight call. Among the excited and happy chatter he heard his name and 'makoporo'. By the slowing of the car and the concentration on her face, he assumed she was getting directions.

She ended the call, smiled at him and put her foot down with purpose. We go.

They were soon flying down the freeway at something close to the speed of sound.

Hotel soon, she assured him.

Hotel safe, he prayed.

There appeared to be nowhere to park outside the hotel. Two uniformed security gorillas approached the car wearing forbidding looks. Joe saw this as the ideal opportunity to end the night there and then and offered to get out and see her the next day. She wasn't listening; her attentions were on the parking Nazis. She smiled and laughed and waved her hands about. Within seconds their foreboding looks had given way to laughter and they unlocked a chained-off area and guided her into a space which required the car to have two wheels up on the kerb in order to leave room for other vehicles to pass by.

Joe was a mere spectator throughout.

The foyer of the Marco Polo was impressive in the way hotels of that ilk always are. It oozed quality. Given that the cost had been so cheap for a five-star hotel, he'd assumed the star rating standard in China must be less rigid. Communist stars, so to speak: a straw pallet and pot to piss in being the benchmark. He lived with the illusion that China was so backward that it would take years for it to move forward. He would soon discover he was wrong. His respect for China in general and Ying in particular was in for a major overhaul.

The young man who greeted him at reception could have been a fashion model. He looked as impeccable as his English sounded.

Welcome, Mr Wilson, did you have a good flight?

A long one. Two flights to be exact.

Yes, a layover in Guangzhou, I assume?

Correct. Two bloody hours.

Then you will be pleased to hear you have been upgraded to a Premier King suite.

No extra cost?

Not at all.

Sweet.

Are you here for business or pleasure?

Joe glanced back over his shoulder to where Ying was madly thumbing the keys of her mobile phone. Neither, he said. More like family matters.

The receptionist didn't miss a beat. We have you booked as a single, is that still the case?

Yes. Absolutely.

I see. You're on the tenth floor, he said, as he handed

over the key card. I'll give you a spare key just in case. The porter will bring up your bag.

I have no money to tip with, Joe said. Haven't had a chance to get to a money machine.

There is an ATM near the elevator, but there's really no need to tip.

As he turned away from the reception desk, Ying fell in at his side and held up the screen of her phone. She had her own translations app and below the Chinese text he read in English, Can I come up to see your room?

He hesitated before answering.

She began furiously thumbing again. I not stay long.

He smiled and made a yawning motion. Tired, he said.

More thumbing. OK. You sleep. I see you tomorrow morning at 10.

If she was disappointed, it didn't show.

He was grateful. Relieved. He walked her slowly to the front door. They paused awkwardly on the threshold.

Stay, she said and kissed him quickly on the cheek. For the first time he noticed she wore no perfume or lipstick, just some lip gloss. She smelled faintly of shampoo and soap. Then she was gone through the revolving door. He did not stay to watch her drive away but was confident that she'd run the parking guys around like marionettes. Clearly charm was her strength. Insight, too, if her agreeing to leave so quickly was any guide. Once again he felt a chill in his heart. The self-loathing returned as he made his way to the lift.

His suite was luxurious. Everything he could want for and more. The Wi-Fi was speedy but he was far too tired to read all the emails that had accumulated during the day.

He stared out the window without taking much in. There was a wide river bordered by a well-lit riverside park on the near side and neon-edged tall buildings on the far side, the reflections of the latter adding a Las Vegas-like garishness to the scene.

He drew the curtains, stripped and fell into the bed without showering or unpacking. He was exhausted but sleep did not come easily. When it finally did, it hit like a hammer.

It was 9.15 am by the time he drew back the curtains to reveal the slow-moving river below shrouded in fog or smog, it was hard to know which. A light coating of snow had fallen onto the surrounding rooftops and park. It was like looking out into a black and white photograph: black, white and every shade of grey. The skyscrapers on the other side of the river were now more shadows than shapes, their neon outlines gone with the dawn.

As he emerged from the shower, his room phone rang. It was reception calling to say Ying had arrived. She was early.

He said he'd be down in five minutes and he was.

The red scarf remained but today she wore a black jacket, black beret, black T-shirt, blue jeans and the same black patent leather boots as the night before. She was carrying a cord-handled paper bag of the kind you get from clothing stores.

He kissed her awkwardly on the forehead. She seemed pleased with that.

For you, she said holding up the bag but not giving it to him. Room?

She was clearly determined to see his room. Perhaps she'd never been in a five-star hotel before.

He nodded. She grinned happily.

On the way up, the elevator stopped at the first floor cafe to admit a group of young women. The smell of bacon wafted in after them. They themselves reeked of wealth. It was apparent in the cut and quality of their clothes, the shape of their shoes, and in the easy confidence with which they moved in the surroundings. Their eyes moved quickly from curious glances at him to a slow appraisal of Ying: vinyl jacket, cheap woollen scarf, patent leather boots and jeans of no significant brand. If Ying noticed their disapproving scrutiny, she didn't care. She seemed excited just to be heading up to see his room. The feeling that she didn't fit was his alone. One of the young women spoke to him in English.

American?

New Zealander.

Oh, my brother went to university in Dunedin. He

loved it. He's a doctor in Shanghai now. She smiled a perfect smile. She was gorgeous, educated and in her element, which Joe knew was the whole point of her talking to him, because clearly Ying was not. Out of respect for Ying, he just smiled back and didn't attempt to carry on the conversation with the urbane beauty.

With a final patronising look at the bus driver by his side, the privileged beauties left the lift on the eighth floor.

Joe was relieved.

Ying's only reaction was to loop her arm through his and smile. Beautiful girl, she said, without a hint of malice.

When they entered the room, Ying ignored the salubrious surroundings and began to unpack his bag and fold and arrange the few clothes he'd brought into drawers and onto hangers. Nothing he could say would dissuade her from this domestic activity.

She then emptied out the paper bag she'd brought. In it were some mandarins, a packet of oolong tea and a pair of dark brown thermal long johns.

You, she said holding the underwear out to him. Cole, she added pointing at the snow outside.

He started to laugh. You want me to wear long johns?

Cole, she said and patted his thin jeans to emphasise the point.

You, she repeated. And again held out the thermal underwear.

She wasn't going to take no for an answer.

He took the brown bundle from her and went into the

bathroom. Miraculously the woolly leggings fit, but he looked ridiculous. Catching a glimpse of himself in the full-length bathroom mirror, he began to laugh.

You okay? Ying asked.

Okay, he laughed. Just silly.

When he emerged from the bathroom feeling decidedly snug around his nether regions, she had peeled a bowlful of mandarins and made a pot of tea. She'd also typed another message on her phone. We meet Jean in park.

As he mulled this over she added, Park beautiful.

OK, he smiled, even though the thought of getting further immersed in this tangled web by meeting her family members held no appeal at all.

They only had a one-hour window within which to meet Jean since she had taken over Ying's bus driver duties for the week. The park was not, as he'd originally thought it would be, the one by the river below, it was a much larger one on the far side of the city.

Ying drove with a calm confidence, Joe rode in a state of barely restrained panic.

When he'd arrived the night before, the city streets had been pretty much deserted. Today, in complete contrast, the traffic was like nothing he had ever experienced before. Not so much that it was bumper to bumper, which it was, more in the way the vehicles were being driven. It bordered on anarchy. The motorists of Wuhan drove in much the same way they might ride bicycles: turning and stopping at will, signalling at the last moment if at all, drifting from lane to lane at random and happily driving the wrong way up a one-way street if the need took them. It wouldn't have surprised him at all to have seen a car take to the footpath. And amongst it all were countless pedestrians and cyclists meandering through the rivers of traffic with no fear for life or limb. Not a cop to be seen anywhere, not that any official intervention could hope to sort out such chaos any more than a baby might untangle a fishing line.

Yet, incredibly, Ying navigated through it all without once using her horn and he didn't see a single sign of road rage in the entire forty-five minutes they were on the road.

The day was grey and the park was not beautiful but crowded and ordinary. Winter still had the grass in its grip so the ground underfoot was drab and often muddy. A few cherry trees struggled valiantly to blossom providing rare photo opportunities for the determinedly cheerful family groups gathered there. The park layout was uninspired. The surrounding lakes in which Ying told him, via her translation device, she often swam in during the summer months were hemmed by litter-strewn, broken reeds. The thought of immersing himself in those suspect waters at any time of the year didn't appeal in the slightest. In the centre of the park stood a tawdry stage upon which performers wailed out Chinese folk songs to a largely disinterested audience. The music, though, was pleasant in its way and entirely appropriate for the setting. Here and there were busts of People's Party personalities including, of course, Chairman Mao.

The highlight of the park was Jean. Bright, boisterous and, remarkably, freckle faced, which he didn't think a Chinese person could be. (Another misconception smashed.) And she obviously enjoyed food as much as she enjoyed life. Not to say that she was obese, she was more Rubenesque, and clearly not impressed with her sister's sylphlike figure, which she said was far too skinny as if seeking Joe's confirmation of this.

She had more English than Ying, though not enough for any kind of in-depth conversation, and keen eyes that looked searchingly at him from the outset. Within a heartbeat of them meeting, those eyes had seen that Joe was not in love with her sister and as they meandered through the park struggling to converse with simple words, he noticed her constantly searching her sister's face to see if she knew it as well.

However, as far he could tell, Jean gave Ying no hint of what she'd detected. Breaking this hard news was to be his responsibility and his alone.

He could tell this without them exchanging a word on the subject. He could also tell that Jean did not think the less of him for it. Such things happen. There is no fault to be assigned. Only heartbreak.

When Jean said goodbye there was an extra squeeze in her hug that seemed to say, my sister is a good person, be kind.

Ying was loved and she *was* a good person, there was no doubt about that. She was lovely in every way. But that didn't change a thing.

What he had to do and say was not going to be easy.

Dear Judy,

I know you don't want to hear this, but Ying is not the one. I knew it from the first moment I saw her. And that certainty has only increased throughout this first day.

She's attractive, vivacious and judging from the way she charms everyone around her, it's clear she has a great personality. When she's around, laughter is never far away.

Today, after we met her sister Jean (in a park of no particular appeal), she took me for a quick noodle lunch (she insisted on paying) after which we made a brief visit to a local market where she bought vegetables and fish.

Everywhere we went she had people smiling happily as they did her bidding. It was easy to see that people from all walks of life like her instantly. Men particularly.

On the other hand, I can't understand a word she says, any more than she can understand anything I say. And her ability to retain English words is non-existent. Today I tried to teach her the words tree and lake. We were surrounded by trees and lakes but when we'd walk past one or the other, mere minutes after my teaching her the word at the previous one, she simply could not remember it. She'd laugh at her own stupidity and she has a delightful laugh. However, there is just no way I could even begin to cultivate a relationship with someone who is just so foreign in every way. Even if I felt what I need to feel — and I don't.

I like her. I like her a lot. But it's nothing that comes close to love. And never will be.

By the way, I knew Jean could see how I felt from the moment we met so there's every chance she's telling Ying what she detected even as I'm typing this.

But it is such a delicate subject I can't possibly broach it with her myself without an interpreter present. It would be too cold, clumsy and insensitive to attempt to do so with the translation software on our phones.

However, we aren't due to see our interpreter Li Gan until Monday — the day after tomorrow — so I have two more days in which to maintain the charade.

I feel deceitful doing what I'm doing, even though Ying always made it clear she understood the magic might not be there when we met.

The problem is I get the feeling that she feels for me what I can't feel for her. Perhaps I'm kidding myself. Perhaps it's just my ego that gives me that sense. I hope so.

Best to Bruce and tell him, no, I'm not going to just shag her anyway.

Much love,

Joe

The next day was full and busy. Were it not for the chaos on the roads and the smog, there were vast tracts of Wuhan that reminded him of the outer suburbs of some of the Eastern European cities he'd visited. Many of the roads were relatively new and wide, and the bleak monochromatic tones of the cityscape definitely had the feel of a European winter. A new subway system had recently been completed in record time but the scars in the city overhead were yet to heal. In some places it looked like the aftermath of an earthquake.

Knowing that he was interested in art, Ying took him to the Wuhan Art Gallery, the contents of which were surprising and thrilling. The neighbouring museum was impressive in its way as well, though not quite so thrilling.

Instead of using her mobile phone to take photos, as most people do these days, Ying carried a 35 mm camera and insisted on his posing for happy snaps at regular intervals. Naturally, she often asked him to photograph her as well. By the end of the day, his little pocket Canon was filled with images of her posing by various points of interest, smiling, doing star jumps and generally enjoying herself to the fullest.

Their inability to converse on any meaningful level made no difference to her. She was happy just to hold his hand and occasionally to hug him for no reason. The more she did this, the worse he felt. The word 'cad' kept cropping up in his mind. An old-fashioned word but perfect for the role he felt he was playing.

Thankfully, her determination to show him the city chewed up the hours and when it was obvious that he was weary towards the end of the day, she seemed happy to drop him off at the hotel before the rush-hour traffic made it impossible for her to get home in time for her weekly dinner with May Ling. Much to his relief she did not invite him to join them. Perhaps she didn't think he was ready to be confronted with her 'smaller than normal' daughter, or perhaps it was vice versa. Regardless, he was grateful for the respite despite the fact that she'd been easy company all day, albeit far too affectionate for his liking. Her happy and natural disposition only made things worse: the better she was, the worse he felt.

My dear hopeless, lost cause Joe,

I can't tell you how disappointed I am for you and for Ying. But please do not toy with her heart. As we both know — and knew before you even left for the Orient — she is a good woman who does not deserve to be treated badly by you or anyone else.

I appreciate that you are waiting for Li Gan to return but please do what you have to do as soon as you can. Say it kindly but say it soon. Every day you delay will only add to her possible pain. She will have had her hopes up with you coming all the way to meet her and, in the same way you can sense she is a good woman, she will know in her heart you are a good man. She will love that in you and that feeling might only grow if you delay the inevitable.

You simply must be cruel to be kind.

I know you will do your best to find the right words. I pray that you will.

Love,

Judy

PS I won't pass on Bruce's advice, you can just imagine ...

Joe dined in the hotel that night. He avoided the cafe with its sumptuous international buffet and chose instead the more up-market à la carte restaurant. Saturday was clearly date night for Wuhan's well-heeled set and the restaurant was filling fast. Nevertheless he managed to get a corner table and spent a couple of hours eating, sipping tea and half-heartedly wrestling with a cryptic crossword while surreptitiously studying the passing parade of diners.

Of particular interest to him were three mixed couples: all European men with Chinese women. One pair looked to be in their sixties and comfortable and familiar with each other in a way that suggested they'd been together for a long time.

The younger couples were far less comfortable. There

was a slightly unnatural sense about the way they interacted. Would-be Chinese brides and their visiting mismatches, perhaps?

In one case a pixie-sized, delicate-featured woman seemed keen to impress her somewhat less attractive companion. She was doing most of the talking. He was saying little but had the look of someone who'd won the lottery. He was lucky to be with her and he knew it.

The other couple appeared to be struggling to find any connection at all. The woman kept looking around the room as if searching for a more attractive alternative or the nearest exit. The guy had a disproportionately large and constantly moving Adam's apple and seemed fascinated with his hands.

He couldn't hear what any of these couples were saying but it seemed clear that they were conversing in English. He wished he could do that with Ying. Then again, would it make any difference? Would it give them any chance of a future together? No. The thing that was missing for him was beyond language. However, the language barrier gave him good reason to rationalise his decision. A woman who didn't speak English would struggle in his world. He'd need to be with her virtually every minute of the day. Simple things like shopping would be an ordeal for her. He was too old to be a babysitter and she was too good a woman to have to suffer the indignities she would surely suffer in a land and life so foreign to anything she had ever known. International travel would be even more of a challenge. It would be like travelling with a child.

He found it easier to focus on these potential problems rather than the simple truth that the real problem was, as it so often was for him, that the magic simply wasn't there. Whether he should even be looking for magic at his age but settling instead for the love and loyalty of a good woman was moot. Settling for anything less than his own idea of perfection just wasn't in his nature. He might go to his grave alone and strapped by his delusions but at least he would have been true to himself.

He signed the check and headed up to his room for an early night. Tomorrow Ying planned to show him her new apartment. She was so proud of it and he could understand why. As far as he could tell she wanted his advice about paint colours. This was the kind of advice a wife might want.

Sunday dawned brighter than any of the previous days. The roads had a little less traffic but were still treacherous in Joe's view. He would never be able to drive in this city. The ride across town involved a mix of wide freeways and narrow one-way streets and on more than one occasion they had to avoid vehicles driving the wrong way on the latter.

Somehow they survived the drive and Ying parked the car in a designated parking area out front of an apartment block that was pretty much a mirror image of the buildings that surrounded it. All were recently completed or in the last throes of construction. As best he could tell the area had once comprised mainly two-storey terraced housing but these older buildings were slowly being torn down and replaced by multi-storey blocks of no particular architectural distinction. Some attempt had been made to landscape the surrounding area with artificial lakes and parks, but the stunted trees and grass had yet to take root in the parks and the lakes looked decidedly unhealthy.

Ying wound down the window and began chatting happily with a man about her own age who had approached the car and seemed to have some apartment-related role. Whether it was security, maintenance or some other supervisory position, Joe couldn't tell, but it was plain to see he was yet another of Ying's male fans. She may well have lost face in some circles at the time of her divorce but there was no doubt most people liked her now. And judging from the laughter that invariably erupted during every conversation, she must have great sense of humour.

When they got out of the car and walked past him, the guy regarded Joe with a mixture of curiosity and disapproval but managed a smile when Joe said G'day.

The building foyer was bare, unfinished and unimpressive and the newly installed elevator rattled on the way up. Yet from the look on Ying's face, you'd have thought they were about to dine at The Ritz.

The lift delivered them to a narrow, dark, wet corridor on the sixth floor. Assorted pieces of wood and plastic pails, some full, some empty, were scattered haphazardly along its length. The no-nonsense apartment doors spaced at regular intervals along the walls were dark and uninviting. Some were ajar.

Ying walked straight to the only door with a number affixed to it — 65.

She unlocked it and stood back to let Joe enter.

The brightness of the apartment was a pleasant contrast to the darkness of the corridor. The door opened into a living room alongside which was a kitchen that opened onto a narrow verandah behind glass sliding doors. Half-finished plumbing on the verandah seemed to indicate Ying planned to install a small laundry there. A picture window took up an entire side of the living room, filling the space with natural light and providing a panoramic view of the surrounding buildings, unfinished parklands and the dirty lake below. When the park began to flourish and the lake was cleaned up, it would most likely be a pleasant view. There were two bedrooms, one bigger than the other but each big enough to hold a double bed and some bedroom furniture. Closets and cupboards in the bedroom, kitchen and bathroom promised ample storage space for what was by any measure a compact apartment. Most of the walls were painted white although dabs of colour on the walls of the smaller bedroom suggested that room would eventually be painted another colour.

Ying beamed with pride.

She took him by the hand and led him across the living room to where a round recessed shape dominated one wall. It seemed a strange feature with no particular purpose.

A kitsch chandelier hung from the ceiling, which led him to scan the other lights in the apartment. None was to his taste. He wondered if she'd chosen them.

Ying was pointing at the recessed area. You paint, she said.

Me paint. What colour? he asked.

You paint, she repeated. Seeing that he misunderstood, she thumbed her phone. You artist. You paint on wall.

A mural ... you want me to paint a mural?

She frowned.

He thumbed his phone.

You want me to paint picture on wall?

Yes, she said. Please.

More translation device use ensued.

What do you want a picture of?

You choose.

What do you like?

I like red, black and white.

This was not exactly the best brief he had ever had.

I'll do some designs and you choose, OK?

OK.

I need art materials.

???

Coloured pencils and paper for me to do designs.
OK, I know. We go.

Within minutes they were back battling the Sunday motorist madness. Ying drove with purpose. That she would know where to buy art materials surprised him but she appeared to know exactly where she was going and he was more than happy to trust her. As it was, he'd spent most of every car journey with his eyes closed, that alone was an act of trust. It was also far better than subjecting her to the shrieks of terror he would have unleashed were he to keep his eyes open.

Thirty terrifying minutes later they arrived at an art college buried deep in the suburbs that was about the size of an average Australian high school. It must have catered for hundreds of students.

It soon became clear that Ying didn't have a specific art supply shop in mind, she'd just figured that the best place to find one would be near an art college and, from her years of driving taxis, she knew where one of those was. She was right, of course, there were a few art supply shops in the area. Not only selling art materials but reference books as well.

She beamed when Joe praised her initiative.

He soon had everything he needed.

Taking a little artistic licence he explained that he needed to be alone for the rest of the day and into the night in order to prepare a selection of designs for her to choose from. This puzzled her. She didn't understand what the hurry was. She didn't know that after he said what he had to say the next day, with Li Gan's help, he would be leaving Wuhan earlier than he'd originally planned. If he were going to paint a mural for her, it would have to be sooner than later. Assuming she'd still want him to paint one after tomorrow's thunderbolt. With this last thought in mind, he hadn't bought paint. He thought it better to wait to see if she liked any of his ideas and if, after hearing what he had to say, she would want him to proceed.

Somewhat reluctantly she agreed to his request for an afternoon of creative solitude, but only after he'd agreed to share a hotpot lunch with her beforehand.

Ying found a place to park in a crowded lane in front of what appeared to be a vast shopping plaza that had seen better days. Once again her ability to charm the parking watchdogs oiled the wheels. No money was exchanged during these amiable interactions, nothing so crude or obvious. Her power of persuasion involved smiling eyes and the right words in the right ears.

The multi-storeyed plaza was crowded and cacophonic. The chatter, though raucous to his ears, was patently cheerful. Especially in the vast restaurant on the top floor that Ying insisted was the best in town.

It certainly smelled good.

He had never in his life seen a restaurant of this size. It stretched further than the eye could see in a room fogged by the steam rising from the hotpots that occupied the centre of every table.

Even though it was only just past noon, the place was packed. Not just with diners but with seemingly hundreds of staff hurrying among the tables taking orders, giving orders and delivering orders in the form of huge plates of thinly sliced vegetables and meat. It was a veritable onslaught of sound and movement within which Ying seemed completely at ease and he most definitely was not.

On a more pleasant note he was happy to see the number of younger people dining there. There were, of course, the ubiquitous family groups you see in any Chinese restaurant — three of four generations watched over by a venerable grandmother with a disapproving visage — but here the majority of diners appeared to be groups of young couples in their late teens or twenties. Modern young adults complete with mobile phones, Western-style clothing and spiky hairdos.

Many looked up briefly at the older *gwai lo* lumbering past with an attractive mature Chinese woman leading the way, but quickly returned their attention to their meals and dining companions.

Their waiter, dressed like all the others in black slacks, red waistcoat and a white long-sleeved shirt, quickly found them a table and Ying set about ordering without consulting the menu. She was in her element and it showed. It also sounded like she was ordering enough for fourteen people.

Joe couldn't help noticing that all around them the young men and women interacted like equals. This wasn't what he'd expected. He'd expected Chinese women to, metaphorically, be walking two or three steps behind the men in every respect. To be retiring in nature and less inclined to talk than the men. Albeit that nothing he'd seen in Ying would indicate she was so inclined. Instead, what he observed, over and above the fact that the women contributed to the conversations at every table with enthusiasm and good humour, was that almost all of these younger women assumed much the same role he'd noted Ying assumed with him. In the same way she insisted on folding his clothes in the hotel and making cups of tea and peeling mandarins for him, the young women at every table took it upon themselves to take care of the young men in a subtle but emphatic way. They selected the bits and pieces to drop into the hotpot and constantly ensured the bowls of the young men were refilled with freshly cooked delicacies. There was nothing subservient in this. It seemed more a politeness, a kindness and, in some subtle way, respectful. Not a woman's respect for man but a respect for tradition. After all, it would be very easy for a young man to take offence at having his food selected for him — I'm quite capable of doing that myself, thank you! Instead the almost maternal actions of the young women were a seamless part of the dining ritual and reminded him of how his own mother would never begin her meal until she was sure all the rest of the family had been seen to first. To see this tacit arrangement being quietly enacted all around his was somehow reassuring, as politically incorrect as he knew it would be in some people's eyes.

Ying's eyes never left his face. After sending the waiter on his way she studied his reactions to everything around him. She knew he would find the size of the restaurant unsettling — his aversion to crowded places had been well-established during their months of email conversation — but she'd also told him crowds were part and parcel of life in Wuhan and he'd known that before coming. Nevertheless, she was determined to do her best to minimise his discomfort. When he looked at a waiter passing by with drinks, she assured him his beer was coming, beer being one English word she had full grasp of along with please and thank you.

When they'd arrived at the table, the metal hotpot divided into two separate semicircular sections was empty. Within minutes waiters arrived carrying broths sealed in plastic bags. One was milky in complexion, which Joe assumed would be a pork- or chicken-based broth. The other section was a fiery red liquid that he just knew must be based on chillies. Just the steam rising from this bubbling liquid as it was poured into the hotpot made his eyes water and the pungent aroma suggested more than chillies. He guessed it was Szechuan pepper, which he knew played a big part of the fiery cuisine in the region.

As if to confirm his suspicions, Ying pointed to the bubbling red liquid and said, Hot. And then to the pale liquid and said, Not.

They both enjoyed her wit. She'd made a little joke in English and this was not lost on either of them.

At that point more waiters arrived carrying two vast platters covered with thinly sliced meats and seafood as well as a healthy variety of greens. There were also some noodles and, unbelievably, another small plastic bag of what appeared to be extra chillies, like a liquid sambal, that Ying directed to be added to the hot side of the pot.

She must suspect what I plan to tell her tomorrow, Joe thought, and she's going to burn my tongue out to keep me silent.

Very hot, Ying said.

I bet, he replied cautiously.

Once the waiter had adjusted the gas flame to get the hotpot simmering in the correct manner, he departed and Ying began adroitly selecting meat, seafood and vegetables with her chopsticks to add to the white broth. Clearly she intended to start him slow and build up to the lava-like chilli cauldron. Each tidbit was added in an order that would ensure all would be perfectly cooked at the same time. The vegetables went in last.

In little more than a minute the food was cooked to

perfection and she filled Joe's bowl with a selection of steaming delights before attending to her own.

Despite her urging him to start, he waited until she, too, was ready.

Bon appétit, he said and immediately felt silly for saying it but she smiled nonetheless. She understood the sentiment if not the words.

They ate in silence. Well almost. Ying slurped her noodles. The sound was anathema to him, something he would never get used to — and another nail in her coffin.

Nonetheless, the food was delicious and he devoured it enthusiastically.

The ever-attentive Ying immediately refilled his bowl and when that, too, was eaten she looked at him mischievously and said, Now hot, OK?

OK, he said. Chilli held no fear for him.

(Once many years before he had made a similar misjudgment when tasting wasabi for the first time. On that occasion he had foolishly fobbed off the warning of a concerned friend that wasabi was 'hot' since, as he told his would-be protector, what was hot to your average European was usually only mild for him. Accordingly, he scoffed a teaspoonful of the innocuous green paste while his fellow diners looked in disbelief. For a few seconds he enjoyed their amazement and admiration. Then the heat hit him with all the subtlety of a hot poker being shoved up his nose. This was nothing like the tongue- and throat-searing heat of chilli that he knew. This was something else again: An internal fire that seared his sinuses and brain cells more than his taste buds. He remembered running outside in an attempt to seek relief by desperately inhaling the freezing night air and at one point even considered pouring ice-cold beer up his nose.)

The heat of the fiery red side of the Wuhan hotpot could be best described as chilli meets wasabi. So hot that it actually numbed his tongue. After just one mouthful he sought to douse the fire by swilling his beer and eventually called for a mug of ice that he could lap with his burning tongue.

The greater his discomfort, the funnier Ying found it. Those at neighbouring tables alerted by the loud JESUS CHRIST!!! that was triggered by his first mouthful were greatly amused as well. A young man with good English advised him to take it slowly and he would soon get used to it and even enjoy it.

Surveying the blurry faces thorough his watering eyes, Joe could not believe that so many people would voluntarily subject themselves to such a culinary ordeal. How could this be tasty? Surely it would be easier on your mouth and alimentary canal to sip on battery acid. Just the thought of this fiery fuel making its way through his system and having, eventually, to pass out of him caused alarm in his bowels.

Then slowly the fire eased. The numbness became almost pleasant. He avoided taking spoonfuls of the red broth and just ate the food cooked in it. The heat became bearable. He began to notice flavours other than chilli and pepper. He'd never describe it as a habit-forming dining experience but he could see how those raised with hotpots would come to enjoy them. Especially in the harsh winters when some form of internal combustion might be desirable. And good food shared with others, as a hotpot invariably is, is never a bad thing.

It was hard to tell what Ying was enjoying most, the taste of the fiery food or his reaction to it. All that was certain was that she was most definitely having a good time.

The best thing for Joe was the price. He'd anticipated a bill of a hundred dollars or more but it came to less than fifty, a cost Ying insisted had been blown out by his consumption of beer. To her, fifty dollars was an outrageous amount. She seemed apologetic that it had cost him so much. He could not find the right words to tell her that it was no problem to him whatsoever. Anything he could think to say would somehow seem critical of her sense of value. He chose just to reassure her that it was his pleasure to be able to buy her lunch.

As they walked back to the car, he couldn't help wondering how someone who had the healthy appetite she'd demonstrated during lunch could remain so slim. Not for the first time he was struck by the youthful sensuality of her body shape. He imagined her naked and it was not an unpleasant picture. His momentary shallowness surprised him. Such thoughts were tawdry in the light of what he was going to say the next day. It was not his finest hour.

Half-finished and discarded designs and assorted coloured pencils lay scattered on the desk in his hotel suite. He'd begun work soon after Ying had dropped him off but weariness and the digestion of the big lunch had caught up with him and he'd slept for the latter part of the afternoon. It was now eight in the evening. The park below was filled with people enjoying some kind of festive activity that involved the launching of candlelit paper lanterns that floated in the air like little hot-air balloons: scores of them glowing beautifully as they floated up and up and away into the still night air. A serene contrast to the gaudy, flickering neon of the buildings across the river. Faint music drifted up through the double-glazed windows. Not traditional Chinese music but Western-sounding pop tunes with Chinese lyrics. Melodic songs. More Cliff Richard than Guns N' Roses. A few couples danced randomly in the park. Old-time dancing where they held each other and moved in synch. It was nice to see.

Drawing the curtains, he returned to his designs.

He'd borrowed a plate from the restaurant and used it as a template for his circular designs. He found it a difficult shape to work within. Initially, he thought it demanded a geometric design — something symmetrical and balanced. He'd done a series of these in red, black and white but they all seemed too harsh. Dramatic in their way but hardly the kind of thing anyone would want on their wall.

He was sure Ying would prefer something peaceful— more illustrative, perhaps even impressionistic in style, which would allow him to incorporate her favourite colours in a natural way. With this in mind he explored a series of scenic designs. Landscapes as if glanced through a porthole. He felt sure that she'd like something along those lines. This certainty seemed to fuel his imagination and within two hours he'd completed six designs he thought would work well including one he hoped she'd choose ahead of all the others.

The work had been all consuming and for a precious few hours kept the thoughts of the next day's unavoidable conversation at bay. But as he tidied the desk, arranged the designs into a neat pile and returned the coloured pencils to their case, the dread of the morrow returned. He had no idea how he would begin the conversation and even less how it would finish. Somehow, sometime before midnight, he fell asleep.

Li Gan and Ying were due to meet Joe at 10 am. This would give them time for a long conversation before lunch. Ying was really looking forward to this. She wanted Joe to get to know her better: the real her. She could read the doubt that clouded his eyes whenever he looked at her. She thought she knew why: the need to use translation devices meant they'd had to limit their conversations to short simple sentences. They had conversed more like small children than mature adults. Despite their months of email exchanges, he must be increasingly thinking of her in these terms. He may even be thinking it had been Li Gan who was doing all the talking during their correspondence. Using his words, not hers. She smiled at that thought. She was delighted they would now finally have the chance to talk on a more meaningful level. They'd be able to exchange ideas, share dreams and explore possibilities with sensitivity, intelligence and wit.

She could hardly wait.

Li Gan was standing on the corner as arranged. He was wearing a tie. Apparently, he, too, was determined to make a good impression.

Joe heard the soft knocking on the door and reluctantly rose to his feet.

As he made his way across the room, his mind raced. Is there a kind way to say, I'm sorry but I will never love you in the way you want?

In any language it would be hard to hear.

He knew it wasn't going to be easy to say.

Ying looked beautiful. She was wearing a hint of make-up and red lipstick to match her red cashmere sweater. She surely did love the colour red. Her legs were sheathed in snow-white jeans that accentuated her youthful shape. A moment of uncertainty enveloped him.

Li Gan's youth took him by surprise. He looked little more than a boy. They looked more like mother and son than hopeful bride and interpreter.

He motioned them inside accepting a quick kiss from Ying as she brushed past him.

He shook Li Gan's hand as he closed the door. Pleasure to meet you, Li Gan.

The pleasure is all mine, Mr Wilson. Welcome to Wuhan. Although ... you have been here for a few days, right?

Call me Joe, please. Yes, I arrived on Thursday night.

I'm sorry I was unable to be here. I had to attend a family wedding in my hometown.

Yes, I heard.

Have you managed to talk? Li Gan asked, nodding towards Ying.

Only simply. With translation apps. She has no English at all.

Joe looked across at Ying, who had taken a seat by the window. The hint of a smile played on her lips. This only added to the illusion that she was a proud mother watching her son conversing in English. Apparently she liked Li Gan as much as he did her. This would make what he had to say even more difficult.

She is prepared to learn, Joe. She is a very clever lady.

I'm sure she is, but ...

Yes?

Li Gan, what I have to say is not going to be easy ...

Ying interrupted, speaking quickly to Li Gan and ending with a laugh.

Li Gan smiled. She says you look like a man about to face a firing squad.

I feel like one.

Li Gan passed this on to Ying.

She looked straight at Joe and said, Joe, be happy.

But Joe not happy, he said so quietly only Li Gan could hear.

Li Gan sensed immediately what was to come.

You don't love her, Joe?

No. Sorry. No.

Oh.

You have to find a way to tell her gently.

What can I say?

Just tell her I'm very sorry but I simply do not feel the magic I need to feel for her. I like her very much. I admire her. I think she is beautiful but the thing I need to feel, I do not feel.

Ying said something to Li Gan. There was an air of panic in her tone.

He replied slowly, quietly and, as far as Joe could tell, kindly.

Ying began to tremble. She looked askance at Joe for a few seconds then began to stare stoically at the floor. Her face flushed. She looked so very alone.

Joe felt sick. He wanted to hold her.

Li Gan watched and waited.

For a while the only sound was the muffled noise of the traffic below and the slam of a door out in the corridor.

After a few painfully long moments Ying seemed to collect herself. When she looked up she was actually smiling although the smile didn't reach her eyes. Instead there was a look of hurt and also ... incredibly ... kindness.

She began to speak directly to Joe, pausing occasionally to allow Li Gan to interpret.

It's okay, Joe. We always knew that this might happen. And I promised you that whatever the outcome we could remain friends. Are we still friends, Joe?

Yes, of course.

Do you think if I had been able to speak English we might have become more than friends? If I was more refined perhaps, like the young woman in the elevator.

Li Gan interjected. What woman was that, Joe? Did you meet someone?

No, Joe assured him and turned his attention back to Ying.

It's true that we do come from different worlds, Ying. Having had a glimpse of your world I am not at all sure you would be happy in mine. And I'm sure I would not be comfortable in yours. But that is not the reason. There is no real logic or rationale for my decision. I can only go on what I feel. This may be immature and I may be hoping for an ideal that does not exist or may even be unattainable at this stage of my life.

Ying listened patiently. Her eyes never left his face. The hint of a smile remained throughout. She seemed so much wiser than him. When he'd finished saying his piece, her smile grew even broader and she gave a small shrug.

There is no logic for love, Joe, she said. Life would be boring if we were expected to rationalise love.

She said that? Those were her words? Joe asked Li Gan.

Yes, that's exactly what she said.

Ying had remained seated throughout the conversation. Now she stood and came to him. Without looking up she put her arms around him and squeezed.

Joe tentatively hugged her back.

Then she leaned back and spoke to him gently with Li Gan translating in an equally soft and warm voice.

Will you still paint a mural in my apartment?

Of course, he said almost gratefully. I have some designs right here.

Not quite believing the conversation had so quickly changed course, he led her to the desk and spread the six designs on top of it.

Her face lit up. They are beautiful, Joe.

You did these? Li Gan said as he came to stand by them.

Yes, which one does she like the most?

This one, Ying said pointing emphatically to the very design he'd hoped she'd choose.

Good choice, he said, gently pulling her into his side.

Better choice than yours, she said and her eyes sparkled cheekily.

May Ling brought food she'd prepared herself: A mutton dish. It smelled delicious but Ying wasn't hungry. She sat looking out of the window at the buildings half hidden in the mist across the lake.

I wish spring would arrive. I'm tired of these cold, grey days.

May Ling handed her a cup of oolong tea. How are you feeling?

A little bruised. My heart hurts.

Did you drive him to the airport?

Yes.

And?

He was trying his best to be nice but I could tell he would rather I hadn't come. It was awkward ... hard ... pretending to be just good friends.

May Ling began to admire the mural on the wall. It was beautiful.

I tried to seduce him, you know, Ying said quietly.

May Ling whirled and raised her hand to mouth in feigned shock.

Mum! You didn't ... When? How?

The night before he left. I went to his hotel. I knew he had a sore back so I offered to massage him.

Subtle.

He was reluctant. But I had that muscle relaxant balm Yang gave me when I hurt my calf last year. I said it would help. He eventually agreed but he was so tense.

I can imagine.

It was almost funny. I made him strip to his underpants. He lay on his stomach like a wooden soldier. Not relaxed at all. Then as I began to massage him I deliberately let my hands wander.

Mum!

I just had to know that he found me sexy at least.

And?

He did ... but ...

But?

We didn't.

May Ling was still chuckling as she went again to admire the mural on the wall. Her mother's humour had seen them through many hard times. This latest disappointment was just another bump in the road. Soon it would be just another memory.

And one day, when the time was right, she would point out to her mother the true meaning of Joe's parting gift: On that tiny apartment wall he had painted the snowcapped mountains of New Zealand, the rustic hills of Tuscany and the lavender fields of France.

POSTMORTEM

I t would be fair to say that more than a few people, my wife included, were offended when I burst out laughing during the funeral for a dear departed friend. In my defence, I'd like to offer the following.

Terry sighed and rubbed his unshaven chin. 'I was never the perfect husband,' he said, and I wasn't about to disagree.

Given the circumstances it seemed inappropriate to point out that, far from being perfect, he'd been an unfaithful bastard whose marriage had survived despite his behavior, not because of it. Although, while it in no way excuses his waywardness, it would be fair to say that life as an international airline pilot had exposed him to more temptations than many a stronger man would have been able to resist. Irresistible opportunity notwithstanding, the immutable fact was that twenty-odd years of a 'what happens on tour stays on tour' lifestyle had morphed him into an ageing Lothario whose infidelity knew no borders.

Then Margaret fell terminally ill and it all changed. Her irreversible cancer brought him to heel with a suddenness and totality that surprised us all.

Within days he eschewed his high-flying vocation and wandering ways and dedicated himself to providing her with as much care and comfort as was possible while the agonising disease tortured her with unrelenting cruelty.

For sixteen terrible months they held the inevitable at bay aided by painkilling drugs and a battery of medical experts. But for the most part it was just the two off them fighting a losing battle against the devil.

Only the regular visits of a nurse and the mercy of Morpheus provided occasional respite and during these quiet times Terry was prone to sip whisky and rue the misdemeanours of his past with the kind of evangelistic fervour you most often hear from those who've given up smoking.

To relieve him of his self-flagellating introspection I'd find myself reminding him that there had been a great many happy times in his marriage. In fact, putting his infidelity aside, theirs had been a strong and supportive partnership. In most respects they were a well-matched and happy couple and admired by many for it. Were it not so, Margaret would never have stayed the course.

Underpinning their union was their shared love of many of life's finer things, not least their love of music. Ginny and I had often been entertained by them playing piano and violin late into the night at our small farm in the hills: Evenings of good food and laughter that forged the bonds of a friendship that held us together now in this darkest of times.

Three days ago, at 4 pm on a golden autumn afternoon, Terry finally agreed to let the doctors switch off Margaret's life support. She had not been with us in any real sense for over three weeks and known only agony in the weeks prior to that. Keeping her alive had been for him, not her.

They had no children and her parents were long gone so the decision was his alone — albeit with our support and the empathetic ministering of a South African doctor who had the physical presence of a front row forward but the compassionate countenance of an angel of mercy.

Personally, I found myself wishing that respite could have been provided weeks before when her suffering was at its worst and the outcome already known. There is no credible rationale for needless suffering. To subject anyone to agonising indignity at the end of his or her life is immoral in my view. No God would be so merciless, only misguided humans using God to justify their own point of view. I should have been distraught at Margaret's passing but found I was just angry.

However, as we sat at the kitchen table watching the ferry boats jockeying for position on the quay below, my anger was fading as the cold reality of our loss descended upon me. Terry needed my support, not my outrage. Now was not the time to discuss the rights and wrongs of euthanasia.

Ginny came in and placed a small pile of envelopes on the table. Terry had been staying with us since Margaret died and that morning Ginny had been to their apartment to check on things and clear the mail.

Terry looked at the mail without enthusiasm and murmured something that could have been a thank you. The size and shape of the envelopes seemed to indicate that the bulk of the mail would be cards of condolence. This proved to be the case. Terry scanned each one unseeingly before laying it on the table.

Ginny and I looked on in silence. I noticed she'd been crying.

Eventually all the cards were opened and Ginny began to gather up the empty envelopes.

'Wait!' Terry said with something approaching excitement in his voice.

He took one of the envelopes from her and a smile lit up his face. 'This stamp hasn't been postmarked. We can reuse it.'

Ginny looked at me as if to say, can you believe this guy? He's just lost his wife but he's excited over the thought of recycling a freaking stamp worth sixty cents. This might seem a great deal to convey in a single glance but if you knew Ginny you'd know it's possible.

'Really, mate? I can lend you a couple of bucks if you're that hard up,' I said.

Terry ignored my jibe. 'It's a sign,' he smiled as he began to pick at the stamp with a fingernail.

'I'll put the jug on,' Ginny said.

'I'd rather have a scotch,' I said.

'The steam will help lift the stamp,' Ginny explained, as if to a child.

'Yes, right, of course,' I mumbled.

Terry got to his feet with the envelope and followed her into the kitchen.

People came and went on the quay below. The sun sank slowly at the end of the working day and Terry returned holding the liberated stamp like a trophy.

'Good as new,' he beamed.

My incredulity was patent. This only amused Terry.

'Marg would have killed me if I'd missed it,' he offered by way of explanation.

'Missed what ... an unmarked stamp?'

'Yes. She has a drawer full of them she's collected over the years. You'd be amazed how often it happens. Although less so since people started using email.'

'Wouldn't they be outdated stamps?'

'Maybe. I don't know. I just know she wouldn't let an opportunity like that slip by,' he said admiring the pristine condition of the stamp. 'She was a Scot by birth and by nature.'

'That's a bit clichéd, mate. And wrong. Marg was one of the most generous people I ever met.'

'True, but she would never spend a penny when she could save one. She prided herself on that.' He paused as if remembering something, then brightened with the thought of it. 'Which reminds me, she wanted a no-frills funeral. She was adamant about this. No fancy coffin. Just a cardboard box for her cremation.'

'You can't do that,' Ginny protested as she walked back into the room.

'It's what she wanted,' Terry insisted quietly. 'And I promised.'

Theodore Silverman was born to be a funeral director. Literally. For three generations his family had buried the people of Hillsdale. Terry's parents had been among the many who'd been dispatched to the afterlife by Silverman and Sons. Empathy was their profession.

Though naturally quiet of voice, which one assumes is paramount in the profession, Theodore did not have the foreboding, bony-shouldered, Dracula-like presence one imagines with funeral directors. He was large and broad in stature and avuncular in nature. In another life, he could have been an amiable doorman.

He towered over Terry. 'A cardboard coffin?'

'Yes. Is that possible?'

'There's not much call for them.'

'But you can do it?'

'Of course, but ...'

'But what?'

'Sir, the coffin will be visible to everyone during the ceremony. And ... cardboard looks so ... you know.'

'She's being cremated. It's all just fire fodder in the end.'

'Well ... yes.'

'It's what she wanted. She insisted. It's not my choice, it's hers.'

Faced by such intransigence, Silverman had no choice but to relent.

'Would you like to see what a cardboard coffin looks like?'

'I think we should,' I said, hoping that confronting the reality of sending his beloved into eternity in a shipping carton would shock Terry back to his senses.

Needless to say, there were no cardboard coffins in the showroom; the best Silverman could do was to show us a selection online. There was a surprising array of them. From those that made some attempt to look like a real coffin to those that looked more like large mail order packages.

Terry chose one of the latter. A design so basic I felt I should object.

'Mate, that's too tacky. It's just a packing case.'

'It's what she wanted,' Terry insisted. 'Let's say it's by unpopular request,' he added trying to make light of it.

'Jesus.' I walked away to disassociate myself from this

madness. As I made my way out of the office I heard him say to Silverman: 'However, I do have one requirement of my own ...'

I'm never comfortable in a church on any occasion and far less so at funerals. Margaret's ceremony took place in a small chapel that was part of the crematorium and the usual superstitious mumbo jumbo that ensued only served to aggravate me as always and this only added to Ginny's misery, which was due in part to the passing of a beloved friend but equally by the presence of the cardboard coffin. And, as if the choice of a no-frills send-off was not enough of an insult in itself, Terry's personal touch had been the final straw.

What he'd asked Silverman to do was now plain for all to see. The entire coffin was plastered with stamps. The very stamps Margaret had collected over a lifetime would now accompany her in death. Her coffin now looked more like a large mail order delivery than even I'd imagined possible.

Everyone was mortified except Terry. He seemed mightily amused.

'Margaret would have loved it,' he assured us. 'She'd see the funny side.'

I was less convinced.

The ceremony was the usual balance of sermonising

and eulogies. Some people spoke by request and others because they couldn't help themselves.

Terry's words were inspired, heartfelt and heartbreaking. He had us all in tears until he asked us to come up and sign our names on the coffin. Most found this distasteful and refused to comply.

Undaunted, he picked up a large permanent marker and wrote on the box himself. When he'd finished he looked at me for support. Despite my discomfort I relented. I got to my feet and took the pen from him.

As I bent to add my name to the gaudily stamp-covered coffin, I saw what Terry had written on it: RETURN TO SENDER.

About the Author

Born in Kuala Lumpur, Malaya, to a Chinese mother and a New Zealander father of Swedish/Irish/Scottish extraction, John Hanlon was Eurasian way before it was fashionable.

He was raised variously in a peaceful seaside village in New Zealand, the spice-scented bustle of post-war Singapore, the transported Englishness of a West Australian boarding school and the adventure-filled environs of an iron mine deep in the jungles of Malaya.

Reaching adulthood in Auckland, New Zealand, he trained as a graphic artist and began to earn a living briefly as a cartoonist but mostly as an Art Director in Advertising.

In the early 70's, just as he was morphing into an advertising copywriter, he accidentally became a Pop Star.

A few hit songs and a significant number of awards followed in his brief, four years career as a singer-songwriter before he chose to walk away from the limelight and seek a quieter more private life.

He then spent three decades as a Creative Director in Australia, before returning to live in New Zealand and explore less certain creative pursuits like writing fiction, songwriting and painting.

For more about John and his work, visit johnhanlon.co.nz

Photograph: Andrew Pettengell